Sunrise on the Battery

**Center Point
Large Print**

Also by Beth Webb Hart and available from Center Point Large Print:

Grace at Low Tide
Adelaide Piper
The Wedding Machine
Love, Charleston

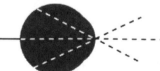

**This Large Print Book carries the
Seal of Approval of N.A.V.H.**

Sunrise on the Battery

BETH WEBB HART

CENTER POINT LARGE PRINT
THORNDIKE, MAINE

This Center Point Large Print edition is published
in the year 2012 by arrangement with
Thomas Nelson Publishers.

The text of this Large Print edition is unabridged.
In other aspects, this book may
vary from the original edition.
Printed in the United States of America.
Set in 16-point Times New Roman type.

ISBN: 978-1-61173-275-7

Library of Congress Cataloging-in-Publication Data

Hart, Beth Webb, 1971–
Sunrise on the battery / Beth Webb Hart.
p. cm.
ISBN 978-1-61173-275-7 (library binding : alk. paper)
1. South Carolina—Fiction. 2. Large type books. I. Title.
PS3608.A78395S86 2012
813′.6—dc23

2011035874

For Frances and Edward

So don't sit around on your hands! No more dragging your feet! Clear the path for the long-distance runners so no one will trip and fall, so no one will step in the hole and sprain an ankle. Help each other out. And run for it!

HEBREWS

Chapter 1

MARY LYNN SCOVILLE

December 24, 2009

It was the morning before Christmas, and Mary Lynn was preparing for her sunrise jog around the tip of the Charleston Peninsula. She stretched her thighs and calves in the gray light of her piazza, then bounded out of her South Battery home, traveling west toward the coast guard station like she did every morning as part of her effort to "finally get back in shape" since her fortieth birthday, six short months ago.

By the time she reached Tradd Street, the gray had turned to a soft, creamy light, and she hung a left and rounded the corner onto Murray Boulevard where she traced the west tip of the peninsula as buoys bobbed in the churning water of the harbor and pelicans—beak first, wings pulled tight against their large prehistoric bodies—dove for breakfast in a thrilling kind of free fall.

At her husband Jackson's strong suggestion, she stayed clear of the darkened cars parked along the edge of the waterway leading up to White Point Gardens. Unseemly characters gathered along the water's edge at night and often fell asleep there, not to mention the handful of homeless folks who made their berths on park benches. There had been a murder in one of the cars last year as well as a rape, but the light was too high in the sky for any of that now. As her friend from her bluegrass days, Scottie Truluck, boldly proclaimed the day after someone broke into her house and took off with her laptop and her sterling silver tea set, you couldn't let fear get in the way of your city life.

Mary Lynn hit her stride, as usual, at the High Battery as a lone sailboat with little blinking white Christmas lights encircling its mast pushed through the choppy water. She felt her heart rate rising and she became conscious of her breathing, so she attempted to take her mind off of her workout and the pounding of the pavement on her knees by going through her to-do list for the day as she passed the Carolina Yacht Club where Jackson had been offered a membership after his second time through the application process. Hot dog! An invitation to join this exclusive, tight-knit club was a kind of proof that they had been officially accepted by Charleston society. Not an easy feat in this historic southern city that, after two brutal wars and a depression that stretched on for half a century, had good reason to be wary of outsiders. Of course, they both knew they had Mark Waters—an older friend with hometown ties—to thank for this and many of the doors that had been opened to them.

Still, Mark didn't run the entire city (especially not the old-Charleston set) no matter how deep his pockets, and the yacht club membership meant that they had finally passed some sort of insider's test after their move to the city ten years ago. And that, along with the invitation Mary Lynn received last year to join the Charlestowne Garden Club and another to serve as chairman of the board of the old and prestigious Peninsula Day School, made her feel like this truly was their home. Their real home. She smiled even as she panted. She and Jackson, two country bumpkins from Meggett, South Carolina, were somehow making their way into Charleston society. Who'd have ever thunk it?

But that wasn't even the primary goal for Jackson, who was the sharpest, most focused man Mary Lynn had ever known. The real goal for him (and he had written it down and asked her to put it in her jewelry box in an envelope marked "family mission statement") was to give their three girls the life he and Mary Lynn never had. This meant a top-rate education, exposure and immersion in the fine arts, and frequent opportunities to see the big wide world beyond the Carolina lowcountry or the United States for that matter.

"Not just education, baby—*cultivation*," he would say as they lay side by side in their four-poster antique bed purchased on King Street for a pretty penny, Jackson resting some classic novel he should have read in high school on his chest. Then Mary Lynn would look up from the *Post and Courier* or *Southern Living* or lately, the little black leather Bible Scottie had given her after the birthday luncheon meltdown, and smile.

Every time Mary Lynn and Jackson discussed their children, she had an image of her husband tilling the soil of their daughters' minds and dropping down the little seeds like he did every spring growing up on his daddy's farm. "Just like the tomaters, darlin'," he'd say in his exaggerated country accent. "Only now it is little intellects that will one day be big as cantaloupes!"

A pretty lofty mission. But a worthy one, Mary Lynn supposed. Though sometimes she grew nervous that he rode the girls too hard with their school work and over scheduled them with extracurricular activities—strings lessons, writing workshops, ballet, and foreign language. They sure didn't have much time to lollygag or linger or strike out on an adventure as she had as a child roaming the cornfields on her uncle's farm, climbing trees, building forts, or spending the night in a sleeping bag beneath a blanket of stars. Despite her mama's missteps and mean old Mrs. Gustafson, who made sure the whole town knew every little detail about them, Mary Lynn had a sanctuary on her uncle's farm. Much of her childhood she was ignorantly blissful of all the trouble and the gossip that surrounded her family as she played hide-and-seek in the corn husks with her mama, running fast through the papery leaves that gently slapped her face. Then crouching down as she heard the sweet voice of her only parent call, "Ready or not, here I come!"

But Mary Lynn had to acknowledge the fruit of Jackson's labors. Thanks to his staying after them, the girls were well on their way to mastering a stringed instrument and they could carry on a conversation (and for their oldest, read a novel) in French and Spanish. Imagine!

Who would have guessed the upward turn their lives would take after Jackson's daddy's death revealed the little real estate gems up and down the South Carolina coast he had inherited from a great uncle? The timing was right and Jackson had been shrewd. He turned to Mark Waters, who showed him just how to go about it. This was in the early '90s, well before the economic downturn, and Jackson sold each piece of property for five and even ten times what his great uncle had paid for it. Then he bought more land, bought several low-end housing projects Mark introduced him to, invested in some of Mark's big commercial and condo development ventures, and did the same year-in and year-out for more than a decade as the market soared.

"Boy, you picked wisely," Mama had said the

first time she came to visit them at their new home on South Battery. She narrowed her eyes and looked up at Mary Lynn. " 'Course I thought Mark was going to gnash his teeth when he got a gander at the skinny farm boy you had fallen for."

"Mama, Mark was married by that point."

"Not that nuptials ever meant much to the Waters clan." She winked, then shook her head. Mary Lynn guessed her mama was thinking of her own engagement to Mark's father, who had proposed after she ran his office for years. They never did make it to the altar. "But you saw something in Jackson no one else took the time to see, smart girl." Then she walked carefully over to the portrait of some eighteenth-century British gentleman that their decorator had insisted they purchase for the foyer, rubbed the corner of its gilded frame, and shook her head in disbelief before turning back. "You saw the man in the boy, didn't you?"

Mary Lynn had smiled. Then she walked over and kissed her mama's made-up cheek. It felt cool like putty.

"I was just lucky, Mama." And that was the truth. Jackson was the only boy in town she ever dated, though Mark Waters had told her more than once he'd wait for her to grow up. Of course, she wasn't surprised that he didn't.

Her mama had nodded her head as she walked into the foyer and rested her hand on the grand staircase's large pineapple finial. Then she gazed up the three flights of intricately trimmed hardwood stairs, clucked her tongue, and said, "Everybody gets lucky sometimes, I reckon."

Now if Jackson stuck with Mark and played it right, he might not have to work for the rest of his life, and he and Mary Lynn would leave a pretty penny to their girls someday. With financial security and intellects as big as cantaloupes, what more could their daughters need?

But back to the to-do list. Mary Lynn still had a few presents to wrap, and she needed to polish the silver serving pieces for the "show and tell" tea party they had hosted every Christmas afternoon for the last eight years. Jackson, who had taken up the cello a few years ago, was trying to get their three daughters to perform a movement from a Haydn string quartet (Opus 20, no. 4 in D major, second movement to be exact), and he had played the slow and somber piece on the CD player so many times over the last month that Mary Lynn found that she was waking up from her sleep with the notes resounding in her head.

She'd never really known of Haydn; she never knew a lick about classical music until they moved to Charleston and started going to the symphony and the Spoleto Festival events. Eventually they became supporters of the symphony and the College of Charleston's music department, and now she found she could recognize a few pieces by ear, though in all honesty, she always daydreamed when she went to a concert. Sometimes it would be over, the audience would be standing for their ovation, and she'd be lost in thought about shelling butter beans on the back porch with Aunt Josey or sitting by Uncle Dale in the rocking chairs as he tuned his mandolin before they started in on "Man of Constant Sorrow" or "O Brother, Where Art Thou?" with him singing low and Mary Lynn singing the dissonant high lonesome sound while she twirled and twirled around. Uncle Dale said she had a voice that was pure sugar and more moves than a croker sack full of eels. And once when Mark Waters and his daddy, Cecil, were over, Cecil teared up over the singing and the twirling and then insisted on underwriting voice and guitar lessons from a famous country music writer who had settled in Charleston. Mary Lynn and her mother drove the fifty minutes into town for the next seven years until she graduated with two offers: one from her guitar instructor to join his newly formed bluegrass band as the lead singer, and an academic scholarship to USC-Beaufort. Since she was smart enough even then to know that an eighteen-year-old girl didn't need to be traveling in a band, and since Jackson had proposed on bended knee, she did what felt right to her heart: she chose the scholarship and married her sweetheart.

But on those mornings when she dropped the kids off at school and had to run a few errands, she turned back to the radio station she grew up listening to, an old blend of rock 'n' roll and country and bluegrass, and tapped along to Elvis Presley or Johnny Cash or the Stanley Brothers as she drove through the historic streets with her windows rolled up as if she were in her own secret time capsule, transporting herself back to when she was thirteen, dancing and twirling with her mama to "Return to Sender" on the screened porch as Aunt Josey and Uncle Dale clapped and laughed.

Catherine and Lilla, Mary Lynn's oldest girls, both played violin, and Casey, the baby by five years, played the viola. Their family quartet sounded all right, except for the cello, which made an occasional alley cat screech when Jackson came at it a little off angle. She imagined they'd be practicing all day to get it right for tomorrow's performance.

The sun was beginning to warm Mary Lynn's back when she turned from East Bay Street onto Broad where she planned to sprint all-out to Meeting Street, then stop and walk briskly home the rest of the way, her hands raised and clasped behind her head, her heart pounding, then slowing moment by moment as the brisk air chilled her sweaty body to the bone. What a way to wake up! She loved it. And she had shed twelve of the fifteen pounds she had been trying to get rid of since her big birthday.

But this morning, just after she bounded at full speed across Church Street and back onto the uneven sidewalk of Broad Street, the front tip of her left running shoe caught for a split second in a crooked old grate so that when she slammed her right foot down and lunged at a sharp angle to keep herself from somersaulting, she heard a tear just below the back of her knee and a pain blasted through her calf as though she had been shot at close range.

"Agh!" she screamed, falling hard on her side and grasping the back of her right leg.

She knew what had happened, and she wasn't sure if it was her knowledge or the pain that was causing the intense wave of nausea. She spit and attempted to will her stomach to settle down as her aching muscle throbbed.

The injury, she was sure, was tennis leg, a rupture of the calf muscle on the inside of the leg. She had suffered the same kind of tear in the same place two other times before. Once when Scottie had taken her to a Joni Mitchell concert in Atlanta and she had danced a little too hard to "California," and just two years ago, when she was standing on the top of her living room sofa, hanging a new set of silk drapes hours before hosting a Parents Guild luncheon.

Mary Lynn put her forehead on her knee and

16

ground her teeth. The stones from the old sidewalk were cool beneath her legs, and a chill worked its way up her spine. At best, she would spend the next ten days on crutches icing down her leg every few hours. And then another six weeks in physical therapy. Or worse, she would have to undergo surgery—something Dr. Powell had warned her about after her last rupture. "Surgery means no bearing weight for four months," he had said, looking over his tortoise shell bifocals at her. "So be cautious, Mary Lynn."

The street was quiet on this early Thursday morning. No one was around to gawk or help her up, and she started to weep—more from the frustration, from the time she would lose in the days and weeks to come, and from the stupid grate that no one in the city had bothered to right in maybe one hundred years than from the pain that seemed to compound itself with every new beat of her heart.

She put her clammy palms on the sidewalk and rotated her body over to her left side toward the entry way of the Spencer Art Gallery, and then she slowly felt her way up the side of the stone building until she was upright. She would have to walk on her tippy toes until she flagged someone down or found an open store where she could use the phone to call Jackson.

Mary Lynn swung her head back and forth in an effort to shake off the stars she was seeing. She walked a good block, carefully, on the balls of her feet to the corner of Meeting and Broad singing "Walk a Mile in My Shoes" by Elvis just to keep herself going. When she rounded the corner where St. Michael's Episcopal Church stood, she spotted Roy Summerall, the rector, chatting animatedly to a familiar-looking man who leaned against a parked taxi cab, steam rising from his coffee mug.

She recognized the man as soon as he glanced in her direction. It was Craig MacPherson, Alyssa's father. (Alyssa was one of Catherine's best friends.) He had lost his job as a real estate appraiser during the recent economic crisis, and he was forced to pull Alyssa out of the Peninsula Day School, the private school Mary Lynn's daughters attended. Now she could see that the rumor she heard was true. He was driving a cab to make ends meet.

Then just as she relaxed the balls of her feet after her favorite line in the chorus—"Yeah, before you abuse, criticize and accuse . . ."—in her relief over finding some folks she knew could help her, the pain shot through her leg, worse than before, and she leaned forward and vomited all over the base of the large white church column closest to Broad Street.

The men must have heard her retching. By the time she looked back up again, wincing and straining to get upright and back on her tip toes, they were by her side, gently placing her arms around their shoulders.

"You all right, Mary Lynn?" Reverend Summerall asked. She had been attending his church with Scottie every now and then, and she had met him once briefly at a Downtown Neighborhood Association gathering awhile back, but she was sort of surprised that he remembered her name.

She pulled her arm back around, wiped her mouth with the back of her fleece jacket, then placed it on his shoulder again. "Tennis leg." She shook her head in disbelief. "I tore a muscle in my calf. It's happened to me before."

The men made a quick plan to carry her to the cab.

"On three," Craig MacPherson said, and after he called out the numbers, she felt them lift her up and carefully scurry her down the sidewalk before setting her gently in the backseat of Craig's taxi.

"Let's get you home," Craig said.

"Wait." Roy put his hand on her shoulder and uttered a quick prayer. She couldn't make out the words, but that didn't matter. She had no problem with prayers. In fact, she was starting to like them. She'd been going with Scottie to a women's prayer group at the church every Wednesday afternoon for almost two years now, and she had become downright used to listening to folks pray out loud for one another's needs, though she'd never had the nerve to join in.

"Thank you." She looked up and swiveled her head back and forth to meet both sets of sympathetic eyes. "I'll be okay." And then to Roy, "Sorry to leave a mess on your portico."

The priest smiled. "Don't worry about that. Just take care of yourself. I'll check in on you later."

Mary Lynn nodded, and Craig gently closed the cab door and walked around to the driver's side. She was surprised by how clean the car was. It smelled like soap and maybe gardenias? Some sort of flower, anyway. And when she looked up to see Craig's picture and license displayed on the visor, she noticed a drawing that Alyssa must have made for him. It was of the steeple of St. Michael's with the sun shining through the second tier balcony. The one with the handsome arches. Then she saw the girl's name inscribed in the far right corner.

Sitting down felt much better, and Mary Lynn was astonished by how much the pain receded when she took weight off of her leg. She needed to get ice on her calf as soon as she got home, and she would have to elevate her leg (up higher than her heart as she recalled) to stop the ache. That was how she would spend the whole afternoon— her leg in a pillow with a rope tied to the ceiling beam. That and calling all of the guests to cancel tomorrow's tea.

But she felt so much better at this moment.

Whew. Sitting down in the back of the clean cab with the bright sunlight shooting through the windows, she felt relief. As if, for a moment anyway, it had never happened.

As they turned off of Meeting Street onto South Battery, she could see her historic white clapboard home in the distance, particularly grand in its Christmas décor—fresh garland around the doorway and piazza rail, two magnolia-leaf wreaths with large gold bows on each piazza door, and even a little red berry wreath around the head of the statue in the center of the fountain in the side garden. That had been Casey's idea, and it added a little whimsy to the decorations, Mary Lynn thought. To her it made the house wink to the passersby as if to say, *There are children who live here! It's not just a photo from* Architectural Digest. *See?* Every time Mary Lynn saw it, she grinned.

As Craig went around to help her out of the car, she turned to face him and still did not feel the pain. He took out his cell phone. "Should I call Jackson to meet us down here?"

"No," she said. "He's probably on his morning walk and I'm sure the girls are still asleep." She reached out her hand. "If you help me out, I can make it in on the balls of my feet."

Like Mary Lynn, Jackson had a morning ritual—walking their black Labrador, Mac, up King Street to Caviar & Bananas, munching on a

21

scone and an espresso, reading the *New York Times*, preparing for a meeting with Mark or mapping out the day, the week, or the month—depending on how exuberant he was—and walking briskly home. Sometimes she ran into him a block from their house on her way home from her morning run. He usually brought something back to her—a muffin or a strawberry dipped in chocolate, which she discreetly gave to Anarosa, the housekeeper, to take home to her little boys. And now that the girls were out of school for the holiday, he brought something for them as well. Casey always enjoyed her treat, but the older girls were watching their weight and they, too, gave their treat to Anarosa.

When Craig leaned forward, she put her arm around his shoulder and let him hoist her up on her tippy toes. Then she took a step forward on the balls of her feet, still leaning on him, and she didn't feel any pain. She took another step. Nothing. Her calf felt normal. She almost put her heels down, but she was afraid to.

When a horn from a driver stuck behind the recycling truck blasted just yards ahead, she was so startled, she leaned back and was forced to put her heel on the sidewalk.

The pain behind the back of her knee was not there.

She looked up at Craig. Her eyebrows furrowed. She rubbed the back of her leg. No tenderness. Nothing. What in the world?

"Hurt bad?" he said. He shook his head in an effort to commiserate. Then he stepped back and leaned forward with his hands on his knees to give her a little space. Maybe he thought she might get sick again.

She looked up at him. Had she dreamed the whole thing? No. She had heard her muscle rip. She had felt the shot of pain. It had happened to her two other times in her life, and she knew precisely what it was.

She decided not to answer Craig. It was just so strange. After a few seconds he lifted out his hand and she leaned into it expecting the pain to kick in, but it didn't. Once she was on the piazza, she thanked him and he headed back to his cab. Then she unlocked the door, walked in the house with her heels firmly planted on the hardwood floor.

Was she fine?

She shook her right leg out. She walked. She did a few lunges, then jumped up and down several times, which caused Mac to bark and run into the foyer where he stopped, stared, and tilted his head as if he were as confused as she was.

Had Reverend Summerall's prayer been answered?

"How was your run?" Jackson handed her a chocolate croissant in a waxy little bag. He was back sooner than she expected.

How many calories in a chocolate croissant?

Way too many for a gal beating back a middle-age paunch in the midst of the holiday season. And how was her run? Well, she wanted to tell him the whole story, but something held her back. He had made it clear since she started going to church with Scottie that he had no interest in religion. He wasn't going to stop her. It didn't bother him that she went. He just didn't want her to expect him to follow along with all of that. He had a mission, after all, and he was focused.

He cocked his head. "Your jog all right, baby?"

She looked into his bright green eyes. They blinked slowly. It was the first time they had made eye contact today.

"Amazing," she finally said. She smiled and lovingly squeezed his shoulder. Then she gently accepted the little waxy bag and headed to the pantry where Anarosa kept her purse.

Chapter 2

CATHERINE

It was eight a.m. and Catherine's mind was still racing. Her hands were clammy and her head felt as though it weighed seventy-five pounds in and of itself. It was the morning before Christmas and the three Tylenol PM pills she had taken around two a.m. had not done much for her this time. Her sleep was fitful, and by the time her parents were up a few hours later, their firm steps causing the floorboards of the antique Charleston house to creak, she couldn't manage to drift off at all.

Now she could hear her sister, Lilla, snoring lightly from the bedroom across the hall. Lilla was younger by a year but she seemed, in some way that was hard to pin down, older to Catherine. Just last night Lilla had taken the Dickens novels they were both supposed to read for their post-Christmas trip to England, as well as Catherine's SAT vocabulary flash cards, and shoved them under the bed. "We're on break. Give it a rest."

Lilla had nodded to the window above the second-floor piazza in Catherine's room. It was the one Lilla crawled out of every now and then before shimmying down the roof and onto one piazza after the next and then out to the sidewalk to meet a group of neighborhood friends late at night. "Go out with us tonight." She licked her thin red lips. "Departure time is one a.m."

Catherine had rolled her eyes. They both knew she couldn't stomach sneaking out of the house. She'd tried it once and had a miserable time, always wondering what would happen if their little sister, Casey, or one of their parents made their way up to the third floor to look in on them.

A misstep like that and she'd never get back on the cross country or the track team. And she might never get another good night's sleep. Without those two goals to strive for, she couldn't imagine mustering the strength to raise her SAT score another two hundred points as her father insisted she do.

Now Catherine shook her head slightly at Lilla sprawled out on top of her bed in her jeans and fleece jacket, sleeping soundly with her cell phone still in her hand and the second book in the Twilight series open to the last chapter. It was her third time reading it through. Her late-night trip had been canceled at the last minute after one of the other girls' parents seemed suspicious, but she didn't even bother changing into her pajamas. She was a fast talker and could surely convince Mama that she had just fallen asleep in her clothes if pressed on the matter.

The Scoville house rule was to leave the cell phones on the charger downstairs every night at nine, but somehow Lilla managed to sneak hers up every now and then. Her friends texted one another all night, and Lilla seemed to have no problem waking up, texting back, then falling right back into a deep sleep.

Lilla had scored a 2090 on the SAT last summer, so their father wasn't breathing down her neck. Catherine's highest score was an 1810, putting her in the 81st percentile. The consequence? An indefinite leave from the cross country and track teams (despite the coaches' pleadings) and impromptu SAT questions any time of day or night from her father, who was constantly studying his own practice test booklet. At their quartet practice yesterday, he had taped a question on her music stand:

Hoping to _____ the dispute, negotiators proposed a compromise that they felt would be _____ to both labor and management. (A.) enforce . . . useful (B.) end . . . divisive (C.) overcome . . . unattractive (D.) extend . . . satisfactory (E.) resolve . . . acceptable.

At dinner last night, another was taped to her napkin ring:

If p is an odd integer, which of the following is an even integer? (A.) $p - 2$ (B.) $p2$ (C.) $p2 - 2$ (D.) $(p - 2)2$ (E.) $p2 - p$

She tried to hold in the sighs, she tried not to roll her eyes, but when she couldn't help herself he would lean forward and say, "Do you want to go to an above-average college?"
You know I really don't care, Dad. What I'd settle for is a chance to run again and get a decent night's sleep. But she bit her lips to keep her thoughts from coming out.

Now Catherine walked back into her bedroom. It was illuminated by the morning light that poured in both the windows facing west. By all appearances her room looked like one belonging to a very happy girl. There were the framed pictures above her bed of Catherine and her sisters on Sullivan's Island laughing barefoot in the dunes, their white sundresses billowing out. There were strips taped to her vanity mirror of fun park photos of her and Alyssa, her best friend, making funny faces. There was even the corsage from her good-looking neighbor, Tres King, pinned to her bulletin board. He had invited her to the home-coming dance, only to consume too much vodka from his hidden flask before passing out in the boys' bathroom. The track coach's son, Bryan Christiansen, had driven her home. Thankfully her parents never found out.

One of her bookshelves had been set aside for her cross country and track certificates, trophies, and number tags. Last year Peninsula Day had won the cross country conference and was second runner up in the state championship. Both times she had scored number two on the girls' team behind Martha Marion, who was a senior and had the longest, strongest legs Catherine had ever seen. Her coach, Ms. Christiansen, told Catherine she ran the five kilometer like a gazelle and predicted she'd get a number one spot this year. With Martha gone, the team had needed Catherine and Bryan, one heck of a finisher, to bring home the state trophy last fall. But they didn't have

Catherine and they didn't win state. Now Bryan seemed to scowl at her every time she passed him in the hall. And once last October when her mother and father were strolling around campus with the Head of School and the representatives of the architectural firm to go over the plans for the expansion, she saw him set his jaw and turn the other way so as to avoid the sight of them.

Now Catherine's hand tremored slightly as she pulled the study books and flash cards out from under her bed. She opened the case to the *R* section and started flipping through: *regale, regurgitate, rehash, repel, repentant, retroactive, revive, revoke* as she heard the light, quick footsteps of her baby sister, Casey, bounding up the stairs.

Suddenly the girl was on the threshold of her door. She was growing up too, Catherine realized, as she gave her a good hard look for the first time in a long while. Casey had just turned ten and her Christmas pajamas from last year with the candy cane print were already well above her knobby ankles.

"Hey," Casey said. She walked over to Catherine and sat down beside her on the bed.

Catherine stroked the little girl's long dark hair. "What's up?"

The girl rubbed her bright blue eyes. "I think Dad wants us to practice soon. I heard him going over today's schedule with Mama."

Just then her mother alighted at the door. "Morning, loves," she said. She had a glint in her eye that made Catherine feel suddenly at ease. She grinned at them before glancing at her wrist watch. "Dad wants you all ready to practice the quartet in an hour. Why don't you come on down and get some breakfast?"

Catherine nodded.

"Yes, ma'am," Casey said. Then, "Who is going to wake up Lilla?"

They all looked at one another. "Why don't you, Case?" Mama said. They all knew what a bear Lilla could be in the morning, but like everyone in the family, she had a soft spot for Casey. It must be nice to be the baby.

Casey bit her lip and patted her index finger on the side of her full cheek. "Well, since it's Christmas Eve and since Santa Claus is watching . . ." She turned back to Catherine. "You know I'm back to believing in him, don't you?"

Catherine chuckled. "Yeah, I heard that."

Casey had asked Lilla the truth about Kris Kringle last year and without hesitating she spilled the beans, and she let her know where their parents often stored the gifts, in the closet beneath the stairs in the carriage house. It took Casey about a day to let it sink in. She refused to check out the booty in the carriage house when Lilla invited her and moped around until evening looking like a balloon someone had popped with a pin just for sport. Then she perked up all of a sudden at dinner the following night and proclaimed, "I'm just going to pretend I never had that conversation with Lilla."

"Good," they all said, even Lilla. They much preferred the perky Casey to the one with all of the sighing and frowning.

Now Casey stood up and headed toward Lilla's room. "Wish me luck," she said without looking back.

"Good luck," their mama said.

As Casey walked across the hall, Mama looked at Catherine and narrowed her eyes. "You look tired, Cat. You feeling okay?"

The fingers on Catherine's left hand were trembling a little and she tucked them behind her back. She nodded.

Her mama looked around at the study books and the index cards and the Dickens novel.

"Why don't you take a break? It's Christmas. I think your dad will stop drilling you at least for the week until we're home from England."

She inhaled deeply. The next SAT test was the first Saturday in March. Could she afford to take a week off?

Her mama reached out and rubbed her shoulder. "Come on, honey." She shook her slightly until her tense arms seemed to give way. "Relax."

"Will you ask Dad to let up?"

Her mama nodded and then looked toward the

window as if she were preparing just what she would say. Catherine knew by now that her mother didn't have full sway with her father, but if she came on strong enough there was a fifty percent chance she could convince him. Her mother nodded and looked her in the eye. She touched her chin. "I'll have a talk with him this morning."

Catherine mustered a smile as her mama leaned forward and kissed her forehead. "You won't always have this test hanging over your head."

Catherine made her hand into a fist to stop the tremors. Mama had a way of leavening the heaviest of situations.

She almost wished she could tell her everything. The tremors in the hand. The trouble sleeping, the nightmares. How her stomach had been winding itself tight like a spring ever since she received the test scores in late August. Or how when she went on that college tour trip to the northeast with her class in October, her roommate, Reeves, had given her some dex and for the first time in a long time she had felt light and free like she did when she was running. How even now there was a little orange Adderall pill Tres King had given her in the bottom of her jewelry box, and she was thinking of taking it tomorrow to help her get through the quartet and the tea and the rest of *A Tale of Two Cities* before their trip.

But it was Christmas Eve. Her mother had a lot

to do today to get ready for tomorrow's festivities, and then the day after that they were all heading to England. It would pass. It would all pass sooner or later.

"I know, Mama." She mustered a smile. Her mama smiled back and squeezed her daughter's trembling hand before she corrected her posture, gently slapped her knees, and said, "Oh, don't forget to give me your passport tomorrow, sweetheart. I want to keep them all together in my carry-on bag."

Then her mother stood and headed to the door before calling over her shoulder, "Now come on down and eat something."

Catherine rubbed her left hand with her right. "Yes, ma'am."

Chapter 3

MARY LYNN

Mary Lynn stood in front of her vanity mirror pointing and flexing her right leg to the tune of "Stone Walls and Steel Bars" in her head as Jackson snapped the sapphire-encrusted clasp of her double strand pearls. Every year they attended a Christmas Eve party hosted by their neighbors, the Kings, complete with a champagne toast and all of the most wonderful treats of the season—

beef tenderloin, poached salmon, assorted caviars, cheeses and fruits, truffles, and candied pecans. Mary Lynn wanted to skip out on the party earlier than usual to attend the evening church service at St. Michael's, but she didn't want to disappoint Jackson, who loved this kind of annual event; she had not worked up the gumption to speak to him about it. When had she stopped telling him what was on her mind?

Now she felt Jackson put his large hand on her waist and she met his eyes in the mirror. He was a tall, broad-shouldered man who had gained some needed weight and was aging well—a little gray on the sides of his black hair and lines on his fore-head that made him look wise and rugged, not old or frail. He looked more dashing and at home in a tuxedo than ever before. So polished compared to the tall, lanky farm boy in his blue jean cut-offs who tugged on her ponytail at the Meggett Fourth of July parade the summer she turned sixteen. And, yes, even more handsome.

"You're a beauty." He gently patted her side.

Mary Lynn was starting to feel her age. Her hair was still a rich and shiny mahogany, and she did have an unusually pretty face like her mama's with ivory skin, small, well-proportioned features, and big brown eyes that Jackson said were as heart-stopping as a doe caught in a flashlight beam. But now there were crow's feet on the outer edges (she had sworn not to go the Botox route after seeing what it did to Cecil Waters's third wife after she had a stroke). And despite her decent height and the good posture she'd honed through the years, there was that small but undeniable bulge just below her belly button that after eight months of working out (and dropping pounds) did not seem to want to go away. Thanks to a pair of Spanx and the black silk shutter-pleat cocktail dress with the tasteful v-neckline Bev King helped her pick out at Saks, she felt as though she could hold her own in a room full of her contemporaries. In fact, she was aging better than most. Though she was aging, nonetheless.

When Mary Lynn met Jackson's eyes in the mirror, she knew that he meant what he said. That to him, she was still a beauty, and she blushed just a little before she broke into a smile.

The thought crossed her mind, as it had many times over their nineteen years of marriage, that they were probably going to go the distance. That their union would last. Sure, it was not without its ups and downs or even dry spells, but they got along better than most couples she knew. And they lived in a constant state of awe with the one thought they shared like a trophy among a winning team. *Can you believe how far we've come?*

And far was the truth. Her mama used to love to drive up from Meggett with Aunt Josey. They'd sit in the living room drinking iced tea and munching

35

on Aunt Josey's homemade fudge before her mama would say, "Well, let's go see the stuff!" And by stuff she meant the antiques, the silver, the china, all of which Mary Lynn and Jackson had acquired over the years through the meticulous eye of Seabrook Childress, a famous Charleston decorator and antique dealer who happened to be a good friend of Sammy Smoak, a boy with Meggett ties who'd been as mistreated in the place as Mary Lynn was.

"We're going to fix you up right, Mary Lynn," Sammy had said to her when she moved to Charleston and looked him up. "All those awful girls back in Meggett. They're going to be gnashing their teeth when they see your home featured in *Coastal Living!*" He took a drag of his cigarette, shook his head, and said to Seabrook, "Oh, they were awful to her. All those ugly lassies with their thin foreheads and their big horse-shaped teeth. They used to put white gloves with mud on each fingertip in her locker on cotillion days." He exhaled through his nose and looked over to Mary Lynn, who blushed a little at the thought of those hurtful afternoons when she'd open her locker, swing open the metal door, and find the dirt-encrusted fingertips as the girls walked by in their fancy cotillion dresses. She hadn't been invited to take part in cotillion even though her aunt had submitted her name. "I guess they were just jealous. Was that it?"

36

Mary Lynn tucked a strand of hair behind her ear. She felt a sting in her eyes but blinked back the tears. The wound from those days was always with her, but she hadn't pictured those gloves in a long, long time. "I think it had more to do with Mama than anything."

"Ah," Sammy said. "Your mama was a looker too. But what did she do wrong other than look pretty and turn a few heads?" He winked at Seabrook. "Including the big fish, Cecil Waters, who she worked for."

Mary Lynn took a deep breath and raised her dark eyebrows as she pictured her mama. "She was never married." Her illegitimacy was not something she pondered much or spoke of out loud after she married Jackson and started her new life outside of Meggett.

"Ahhh," Seabrook said. "That'll certainly ruffle some old biddies' feathers."

Mary Lynn nodded her head. "That, and the fact that my father was engaged to someone from a good family." She patted Sammy on the arm. "He was engaged to Dr. Gustafson's daughter."

Sammy crossed his legs. "Now this is interesting. I had no idea. No wonder those Gustafson girls . . ." He turned to Seabrook. "They ruled the social scene of Meggett." He chuckled. "The pitiful social scene of Cool Whip and gelatin salads and tea so sweet your tongue would curl!"

They all laughed. "Horse bones and food coloring! That's what those awful gals thought was a fancy time!" Sammy said.

Mary Lynn nodded. "Yes, well, my father left town in a hurry at eighteen, and I suppose the Gustafsons blamed Mama. Of course Mama said he was dodging the draft and planning to come for her after he made a little money in the music scene in Toronto. He had a guitar and a nice look about him, and I guess he thought he could be the next Elvis or something." She looked down at her hand, at the tasteful solitaire Jackson had flown to Tiffany's in New York to buy for her after the money came in. He bought a pair of ruby earrings for her mama that time. Just because he knew she'd always wanted some. And she was so thrilled she danced all day the day she received them. "Though Mama was just a kid. Seventeen when she had me. How bad of an influence could she have been?"

Sammy ashed his cigarette in a gaudy faux crystal ashtray Mary Lynn's mama had given her one Christmas.

"What happened to your daddy?"

Mary Lynn bit her lip. "He was killed in a car accident before I was born. Hitching a ride somewhere outside of Portland, Maine. A truck driver who picked him up fell asleep riding over an overpass."

"I'm sorry, Mary Lynn."

She shrugged her shoulders and waved it away. "Another life ago." They all chuckled, then Sammy scrunched up his nose, lifted up the tray, and said to Seabrook, "This is so hideous it's almost fabulous!"

They laughed and Sammy said to Seabrook, "Let's remake it all for Mary Lynn, all right? Give her the life a gal like her deserves." He patted her knee. "She gets to start over in the most cultured, most beautiful town in the south, with a handsome man, three darling daughters, and a big, fat bank account!"

Sammy lifted the ashtray up to the sunlight as the prisms cast their rainbow chips all over his pressed linen pants. "It does my heart good, Mary Lynn. I can tell you that! There's nothing like starting over!"

He put down the ashtray and patted her on the knee as he stared into her eyes. "And you've got that kind of natural grace. You and Jackson both. Plus you've got Mark Waters to guide you. You two can pull this off. I know it."

Yes, Mary Lynn and Jackson had journeyed their upward slope hand in hand. And they had loved each other well before their financial and social success, which gave them a unique kind of trust and reliance on one another. Now they were focused on their next goal, their mission statement. To give their children the best life possible, and this mission was another fetter that bound them to one another.

Of course, they lacked romance from time to time and even emotional intimacy as they packed their days with so many activities that it was rare to find more than a few minutes to connect, much less take enough time to share their deep-seated thoughts or hopes or fears. That would come back again, Mary Lynn imagined, once the girls flew the nest. And she looked forward to that time. What they had for now was little moments—like this one in front of the mirror—where their love for one another surfaced for a moment and was quite clear. And because of the sum of the years and the accomplishments, surely it was deeper than ever.

Now Jackson spun Mary Lynn around and kissed her sweetly. "I love this time of year!" he beamed.

"I know you do." He had such a wide grin that she knew he was up to something—probably concealing some unexpected gift he could hardly wait to bestow. He was worse than the girls when it came to Christmas. Not so much about the gifts he would receive, but more about the ones he had to give. He approached gift giving like everything he did, with a determination and energy that was unstoppable, and he could hardly rest until he found the ideal present for every member of the family that he would wrap, as best he could, and hide deep beneath the Christmas tree.

The best part about his gifts was that he created hints before he presented them. He had a little wood-working garage behind the carriage house in the back of their property (one of the benefits of a high school spent taking shop class). And he would always make some sort of wooden clue about his gift and place it in the very bottom of everyone's stocking. He'd been working on those clues since late September. Mary Lynn had heard the buzz of the saw in the late morning just after summer break and smiled knowing he was already up to Christmas.

Mary Lynn had not even wrapped the last of her presents. Instead, she'd thought all day about what had happened on her morning jog. When the kids and Jackson practiced the string quartet after lunch, she called her friend Scottie.

"You experienced a *miracle,* Mary Lynn," Scottie had said. "What a gift! What a thing to be the recipient of! If you don't write a song about it, I will."

A lump had formed in Mary Lynn's throat. A miracle? She deserved no such thing. What skin would it have been off of her back, really, to be laid up for a few weeks? Even to undergo surgery? In the great scheme of things, none. The Christmas tea, England, the Charlestowne Garden Club luncheon that she'd been planning since last year's. They all could wait.

"Why me?" she had said.

"Why not?" Scottie replied. "He makes all things new. And that's not just in the afterlife, but in the here and now."

Mary Lynn paused. Then she heard Scottie's youngest whining loudly in the background before something made a crashing sound.

"Gotta go," her friend said. "Hope to see you at church tonight!"

Mary Lynn couldn't get over Scottie's faith. Scottie *expected* miracles to happen. How fortunate Mary Lynn had been to meet this fascinating gal in Paul Allen's songwriting class. That was over a decade ago—back when they lived outside of Beaufort on a big plot of land Jackson had bought. Mary Lynn still wrote songs and played her guitar. She sang to Jackson and Catherine and Lilla, who were little then and loved to dance and sing. She would drive to Charleston once a week for the class at the college where she learned that the lyrics of any successful country song almost always had to have either the word *mama* or *Texas* in them. She had written a song called "Barefoot Mama" about the wife of a tomato farmer and she had set it to music, but she hadn't thought about it, much less picked up her guitar and played it (or anything), in several years.

Scottie was from old Charleston stock, but she had more or less bucked the family by marrying a songwriter from Tennessee whom she met in music school at Vanderbilt. Her parents had no interest in "show people," but it was hard not to warm to Scottie's husband, Gil. He made a good living writing songs, and after quite a religious conversion, he became the head of a Christian music company that she persuaded him to locate in Charleston, because despite the family's ruffled feathers, she missed wetting a fishing line and the sound of the ocean and the sun setting behind the city on her evening walk around Fort Moultrie at the tip of Sullivan's Island.

While Gil had an endless supply of inspiration for the music, he leaned on Scottie, who had a gift with words, and she was trying to understand the arc of a song so she could keep turning them out and secure a life for the family she hoped to one day expand in Charleston. Professor Allen had paired Mary Lynn and Scottie up together to write a song about pluff mud using the words *Daddy* and *Carolina,* and they had instantly hit it off creating a fun little tune titled "Between My Toes." Professor Allen liked it so much that he continued to pair them up for the rest of the semester.

Scottie made the effort to keep up even after they both started their families—even though it was challenging—and Scottie was the only one outside of the immediate family except for Mark Waters who bothered to attend Mary Lynn's mother's funeral in Meggett a few years ago. She would never forget looking up from her umbrella that rainy April day as they buried her mama right next to her Aunt Josey and Uncle Dale on the farm to see Scottie standing there respectfully with a homemade carrot cake in a Tupperware carrier in her hands.

The next week the two shared a cup of tea on the piazza where Mary Lynn reminisced, in truth, about her mother—her youthfulness, her zany ways, her ill-fated romances with Mary Lynn's young daddy and much later in life Cecil (who died shortly after he proposed to her)—until tears pricked her eyes. She even told Scottie how her mother had confronted the teachers and the principal in middle school to complain about how the other girls had bullied Mary Lynn, and how she never told her mother that this had only made it worse. (The next week she opened her locker to find white gloves with muddy finger-tips plus strands and strands of fake pearls coated in dirt and a pair of smudged white stockings.) Scottie had wept when she heard that story and she hugged Mary Lynn real hard for whole minutes before she left.

Scottie was a good friend who genuinely cared for Mary Lynn (probably the only real one she had in Charleston, if she was honest with herself) so of course she accepted her invitation to the women's prayer group when she sent it the following fall, though neither

44

she nor Jackson had set foot in a church in years.

Now, just as Jackson helped Mary Lynn into her long, black fur coat, the phone rang and he turned to get it.

"Hello?" There was a long pause.

"Hi there, Reverend." He looked to Mary Lynn, the lines above his forehead deepening. "Feeling all right? Why wouldn't she be?"

It must be Roy Summerall. Jackson knew him from the Downtown Neighborhood Association. They had sat on the playground committee together. Goodness, what would she say now?

Jackson turned to examine Mary Lynn's feet in their black silk five-inch heels. "Don't know a thing about that. She seems fine to me. In fact she's dressed to the nines and ready to head over next door to a party."

He paused. He laughed. "Merry Christmas to you too." Then he put the phone gently in its cradle.

"That was Father Summerall from St. Michael's."

"Oh." She felt a pinprick of guilt for not telling Jackson about what had happened.

"He says he was calling to check on you. Did you hurt yourself on your jog this morning?"

Mary Lynn blushed. She swatted at the air. She didn't like to keep things from Jackson, but he was a skeptic, and she needed to believe in this miracle. She wanted it to be so, and she was

45

afraid he would rationalize it or shoot the whole notion down altogether. He could be that way.

"I stumbled, but I'm fine." She spun around in her heels. "See?"

Chapter 4

MARY LYNN

After a good bit of calling up to the third floor, they finally gathered the girls in the downstairs foyer so they could walk to the party together. They were a handsome crew, the girls in their green velvet tea-length dresses and their matching gray wool full-length coats with dark fur-lined hoods. Catherine, the oldest, was their preppy, sporty All American one. She had straight golden brown hair, olive skin, and a perfectly round face with Jackson's bright green eyes. She did wear makeup, but it was hardly noticeable, and she had purchased her first heels this year, which she now wobbled back and forth on before catching her balance on the uneven South Battery sidewalk. She was miserable not running for the cross country and track team, but as soon as she pulled up her SAT scores she'd be back. And she'd be thankful she took the time to focus on the test. At least, Mary Lynn hoped so.

Lilla was fifteen months younger, but she was

nearly as tall as Catherine and twice as lanky. She appeared delicate like a willow tree, but she had a fire in her belly, a quick wit, a vintage style that was all her own, and just the faintest streak of rebellion that worried Mary Lynn from time to time, though she usually chalked it up to a "strong will." Her lipstick was deeper, her eye makeup darker, and her thick brown curls were lovely against her pale face that was nearly consumed by her large, dark hazel eyes.

Casey, the tomboy, had straight black hair, rosy cheeks, and bright blue eyes that were hers and hers alone, and they would stop you in your tracks when she looked up and smiled. She relished her role as the baby, and she still liked to hold parental hands in public and even sit in a lap from time to time.

Mac, their black Labrador, barked from the side garden just after they locked the piazza door, and Casey ran to the wrought iron gate to give him one more kiss. At ten, she didn't mind having to wipe dog slobber off her cheek like the other two who had fussed over their makeup and hair for at least an hour, no matter how subtle it looked. Casey grinned at her mama, the dog slobber glistening on her pink cheek. Mary Lynn came over and wiped it with the cuff of her fur coat and they headed down South Battery.

"Shall we practice the quartet once more after the party?" Jackson asked them.

Catherine wrung her hands and looked to Lilla, who rolled her eyes, flipped the waves out of her face, and said, "Ughhhhh."

"I think we're good, Daddy." Casey reached up high and grabbed him by the elbow. "Plus, we've got to get good and asleep so Santa will come." (That was Casey. A kid's kid.)

"Oh, let's perform once for your mama, pumpkin," Jackson said. "I bet she wants to hear us again, right, honey?"

The door of the King home opened and the sounds of the party poured into the street— guffaws, the clink of glasses, the scrape of a chair, and loud booming voices. Through the door the girls could see some of the boys in front of the dining room table throwing green olives toward the ceiling and catching them with their mouths. Then the girls picked up their hems and charged ahead and into the roar of the large, crowded house.

Mary Lynn stopped on the bottom step of the piazza. She thought again about going to church tonight—the eleven p.m. service after the party. For the first time in years, it didn't seem right to partake in all of the peripheral festivities without a visit to God's house. It seemed as silly as doing a Maypole dance without the pole. She pictured herself holding an unfettered streamer, moving this way and that across the garden until the streamer looped back on itself so many times it became a knotted, tangled heap.

She planted her right foot firmly on the ground, still amazed that there was no pain in her calf, before gently tugging on Jackson's elbow.

"I'd like to go to church tonight. After the party."

He stopped and turned to her before inhaling deeply. He scrunched up his nose as though he'd just come across a small pile of one of Mac's outdoor surprises. "Really?"

"Why don't you come too?" She took a deep, hopeful breath, then nodded toward the girls whom she spotted through the window. They were laughing with their school friends, and Catherine and Lilla were already throwing olives toward two boys from cotillion class who were opening their mouths wide. "We could all go."

"Nah." He blew the air out through his lips in a quick stream. "I'll stay home and tuck the girls in. Maybe we'll have one more practice and record it for you to critique when you get home."

Mary Lynn rolled her eyes. "They'll *love* that." Instantly, a part of her regretted the sarcasm in her tone. She hadn't realized how much she wanted them to go to church as a family, and she was disappointed.

"They'll thank me later, Mary Lynn," he said firmly. He stopped and pressed his hand into the small of her back before whispering, "Think of all the things we wish our parents would have made us learn."

She didn't roll her eyes again, but she wanted to. How many times had he asked her this question when she felt he was pushing them too hard? Jackson wanted to right the wrongs of his childhood, of his unreached potential. His daddy let him know his IQ score was in the 98th percentile—but only the year *after* he had convinced him not to pursue a four-year college degree once he finished his time at Trident Tech. Jack Sr. was ill and needed him to take over the farm.

After his mother's death when he was nine, his father never encouraged him when it came to school. He wanted him to farm, work with his hands, and earn a simple living. He insisted Meggett High remove him from the foreign language courses, arts, and upper-level academic classes where he was originally placed and made sure he took two sections of shop and tech courses each year. If it weren't for a full ride to Tech to study horticulture, Jack Sr. would never have let Jackson go to college. It never occurred to the man that there was another path for his son—and that it was up to him to help his son find it. This enraged Jackson, even now. He felt he had been woefully shortchanged.

Now the hostess, Bev King, stood in the doorway. She wore a red silk cocktail dress that was a little too short and a little too tight. It gripped her hips and made a wide, horizontal pleat across her waist. *Should have gone for the larger size, Bev,* Mary Lynn whispered to herself. It was tough for middle-age folks to admit they'd gone up a size. (It was tough for middle-age folks to admit they were, in fact, middle age.)

"Come in, you two." She motioned to them excitedly. "Almost time for the toast!"

Jackson held out his arm and Mary Lynn took it gently, and they walked sure-footedly up the stairs and across the garland-draped threshold. He helped her off with her coat just as Hollis King handed them each a flute of champagne.

" 'Tis the season, Scovilles!" Hollis said.

"Yes, indeed!" Jackson clinked glasses with the host before turning and reaching his tilted glass toward Mary Lynn's.

After several toasts and conversations with neighbors that ranged from the fear of the cruise line industry wreaking havoc on downtown to the unknowns about this new president who was either a near savior or the devil-incarnate (depending on which side of the political aisle you fell), Hollis asked everyone to follow him up to the second floor where they had converted an old ballroom into a kind of performance space / learning center for their children, complete with a small theater in the round, chop blocks and professional easels for art stations, and off to the side two soundproof rooms for their myriad of instruments.

Like the Scovilles, Hollis and Bev King were "come-yas" as opposed to "been-yas" (your ancestors had to have landed on the peninsula before 1850 to officially be considered a "been-ya"). But the Kings were come-yas from Connecticut with old family money and impressive northeastern pedigrees. Hollis made sure you knew that he graduated from Yale within the first ten minutes of any introduction, and Bev often reminisced about the childhood summers she spent on Nantucket in an old family cottage she had finally inherited after her mother's passing a few years ago.

Nonetheless, Hollis was drawn to Jackson. He seemed to study his every move, though aside from their desire to raise bright and cultivated children, they couldn't be more different. Jackson had means, but he was still a man's man. He worked with his hands. He had been fishing and hunting since he was a young boy, and he knew and understood the creeks and backwoods of the lowcountry like no one else Mary Lynn had ever known. Hollis always wanted to tag along when he saw Jackson dressed in camouflage or hauling his fishing rods into his truck. (Yes, he still drove a pickup, even though Mark Waters shook his head from his silvery Mercedes and said, "Mary Lynn, talk him into getting something nice.")

After Jackson would take Hollis to sit in a deer stand in Meggett, Hollis would invite Jackson on some grandiose hunting or fishing trip to Montana or North Dakota and even once to Africa. Jackson had been on a couple of these trips with his neighbor and somehow Hollis usually became sick or wounded early on in the journey, and he never actually did much hunting or fishing. Jackson suspected he much preferred to be laid up in the lodge or the chandeliered tents eating croissants and reading the *New York Times* on his Kindle.

Hollis was a man who enjoyed the creature comforts. He was well-dressed and manicured. Like a lot of the South of Broad come-yas, he had all of the money he could ever want. His hope was on his children too. He had two sons and a daughter, each within a year or two of the Scoville girls.

Now Hollis stood and nodded his head toward Dr. Leslie Owens, the new composer-in-residence at the College of Charleston. Mary Lynn and Jackson were big supporters at the college where Jackson had gone back and obtained—at long last—a college degree with a double major in literature and history. He had graduated with highest honors, and he was planning to go back for a second double major in music and French while maintaining his position on the board of Waters Ventures, LLC. He would start this new course of study this coming semester.

"We commissioned Dr. Owens to write a piece

for the kids to play tonight." Hollis squeezed Mary Lynn's elbow. "Can't let your lesser half one-up me."

Then he stepped away and gathered all the guests together.

Mary Lynn cleared her throat and leaned in. "How did he know about tomorrow's string quartet?"

Jackson rolled his eyes. "He heard us practicing last month when he dropped by with an early Christmas present."

"Ahh." She nodded her head.

Jackson raised his eyebrows and turned to Mary Lynn. "I bet he has no idea what he's in for."

She smirked. They had listened to some of Dr. Owens's music. It had a hypnotic style, sort of Morton Feldman, with a lot more monotony and plunk-plunkiness.

Hollis was an extreme delegator, Mary Lynn had begun to realize. He usually had an idea, made a call, threw a little money around, and didn't show back up until the thing was done, so he probably had no idea what to expect.

The piece was for piano, xylophone, and drums, and as it started with its non-melody and its repetition of the same four notes, the faces of the onlookers began to twist.

Mary Lynn looked around noticing that a couple of the younger children were actually holding their ears.

After an excruciating fifteen minutes of clangs and clamors that ended as abruptly as it started, everyone clapped; the composer stood and took a bow and motioned to the King children, who received more applause.

Hollis shook the composer's hand and then he and Bev kissed their three children, the oldest, Hollis III (nicknamed "Tres"), rolling his eyes with each parental peck.

Mary Lynn couldn't tell if Hollis and Bev were embarrassed or delighted with the thorny, post-modern piece. Hollis didn't give much away, though Mary Lynn detected the slightest strain on Bev's face as she thanked the composer.

"That was horrendous." Mary Lynn felt the warm breath on her neck, then she turned around to see Mark Waters—as tall as Jackson, though a bit broader through the midsection and with a particularly tanned face—in a tux with a little Band-Aid on his neck and a very young looking redhead in a blue sequined dress on his arm.

Jackson stuck out his hand. "Hi there, partner." Though they had probably seen each other just yesterday, Mark squeezed back tight, shook off his young date's hold on his arm, and embraced Jackson first, then Mary Lynn.

"Merry Christmas, Mary Lynn," he whispered to her, then he drew back, holding her shoulders for a moment in a kind of tender appraisal before turning to the redhead. "Let me introduce y'all to my friend, Jenna Gower."

Mary Lynn held out her hand. The girl shook it loosely. Her hands were warm compared to Mary Lynn's, and the woman quickly turned to Jackson and offered him the same hand.

Mark bent Jackson's ear long enough for Mary Lynn to find out that Jenna was a yoga instructor at Holy Cow and had met Mark through his second wife, who had felt he needed to get back in shape and stretch. Their marriage hadn't lasted long—three years at the most, as Mary Lynn recalled—but he had enjoyed yoga, and just as the ink was dry on the divorce papers last month, he had asked Jenna out.

Now Jackson steered Mary Lynn over to his favorite place, the caviar station, just as Hollis sauntered over and grabbed Jackson's elbow. "Have you heard our big news?"

"No."

"Next year we're taking the kids out of school and heading to Greece for a semester. We want them to learn Greek. To study the classics in their original form."

"Well, that sounds exciting." Mary Lynn smiled. She loved to travel from time to time, but she hoped Jackson didn't want to one-up Hollis now and set up temporary digs in France or Italy.

Hollis turned to accept the compliments of another guest and Jackson put his arm around her. He smelled like shaving cream and the sap of the second Christmas tree she had convinced him that they needed in the den for tomorrow's tea. "You all right?" she asked.

"Yeah. You?" She looked up at her husband. He stopped to look her in the eyes. No, she was not all right. She wanted to go to church and she wanted him to go with her. And their kids. A lump formed in her throat.

"Don't you ever feel like we're part of some 'look how brilliant our offspring are' circus?"

He narrowed his eyes. "What do you mean?"

"I don't know, sometimes it just seems like our kids have to perform like trained animals."

"Mary Lynn." He rolled his eyes. "You're being a little dramatic. I know it was a bad performance, but it is important for our children to—"

Someone tapped Jackson on the elbow. She nodded her head and he turned and put his arm out to shake hands with Kyle Pritchard, the vice-chairman of the board for the Charleston Symphony Orchestra. Jackson always enjoyed talking music with Kyle. They were often discussing the demands of the players' union and their fear that the development director was not raising the kind of funds they needed to sustain the orchestra through these troubled times.

Mary Lynn scanned the room. She saw Catherine and Lilla chatting with two other teenagers from the neighborhood. Around the corner she could see Tres King discreetly pulling a bottle of gin from the wet bar and pouring it in a glass. He walked over to Catherine, lifted it up for her to smell. She made a face and stepped away and then he took a hearty sip.

Mary Lynn's mind reeled with questions she'd been just beginning to grapple with. What about this upper class, education-obsessed society? They had worked hard to make their way into this kind of a world. Now that they were here, was it what was best?

Mary Lynn had lived a simple life until their move to Charleston, and as her children grew older, these were the concerns that continually surfaced: Was a life of meager means in the backwoods of Meggett so bad? Or was she viewing it now with an unrealistic nostalgia from her own comfortable—if not stifling—perch?

Bev waddled over with a stiff smile. "Having a nice time?"

Mary Lynn turned to face her. "Yes, of course. But I hope you don't mind me suggesting that you check the contents in Tres's drink." She leaned in. "It may look clear, but I don't think it's tap water." Bev's eyes widened, her face whitened, and her red lips frowned. She looked a little bit like the joker in the latest Batman film.

Bev squared her shoulders and bit her lip. She put down her glass of champagne, waddled over to where her eldest son stood, licking his lips and talking to a group of boys. She whispered something in his ear and then grabbed the drink from his hands. His face turned red and he excused himself. Was her outrage over her son drinking or from another mother catching him in the act? Probably both, Mary Lynn thought.

"Mama!" Casey called from the dining room. "Watch this!" Mary Lynn turned and watched her little girl throw a black olive several feet up in the air. Then she bent her knees, wobbling back and forth with a wide-open mouth. She moved a little to the left and caught it, before chewing it up and smiling with her hands on her hips and her black velvet bow now dangling a little off center on the top of her head.

Mary Lynn clapped and smiled.

Chapter 5

MARY LYNN

St. Michael's Episcopal Church was a remarkable place. The sanctuary was handsome with a rich and dramatic two hundred and fifty-seven year history. But more importantly, the priest and many of the parishioners had genuinely kind and loving hearts.

As a child, Mary Lynn felt this same sense of peace in the simple Bible church one town over in Adams Run where her Uncle Dale served as a deacon. What she remembered from those rare visits in that small clapboard chapel was the short, scrawny preacher with sweat dripping down his flat, pink face as he gesticulated and called out with a hoarse and weary voice about God's love for the world while she peered out of the window at the morning light making its way through the rows and rows of thin pine trees. Uncle Dale, with the cane he'd needed for his twisted right leg (since he battled polio at age six), would lean toward her as he followed her eyes into the woods. He'd point to the beams of light and the tooth-picked forest. "Now that's God's glory," he said more than once, and she had nodded because something in her spirit said, "Yes."

She had always wondered why Uncle Dale didn't attend the Canaan Baptist Church less than a mile down the road from the farm or why Aunt Josey and Mama seemed to squirm in the seat of their pickup every time they drove by it.

It wasn't until one hot September morning in fourth grade that Claire Gustafson made sure Mary Lynn knew the secrets of her past as well as her place. She was whispering loudly to Penny Mills one row over in the cafeteria as she slurped from a little sweaty carton of chocolate milk.

"Mary Lynn and her mama aren't allowed to go to Canaan Baptist." Claire shrugged her shoulders and smiled as if she had just swallowed a canary whole.

Mary Lynn shook her head. She didn't know the word *absurd* at the time, but she remembered thinking, *That's the silliest thing I've ever heard. Who wouldn't be allowed in church?* Then she turned her head just slightly to the side to hear more.

Claire licked her pale lips as Penny took a bite of her mushy tomato and Velveeta sandwich. "How do you know that?"

"Because my mama told me." Claire spoke a little louder and turned to the side to make sure she had Mary Lynn's concealed attention.

"What did she say?" Penny sucked the soggy bread off of her braces and pushed up the glasses on her freckled nose.

"She said that girls who have babies out of marriage aren't allowed in church. They're not clean."

"What baby?"

"Mary Lynn, stupid!" Claire pinched Penny's forearm. "Mary Lynn's got no daddy. Didn't you know that?"

Penny raised her eyebrows as if this was a turn of events that was morbidly fascinating to observe. Like looking at stitches on a busted chin or the leftovers of a car wreck after the passengers had been carried away so that all was left were the scrunched up cars and the shattered glass like bright green ice on the asphalt.

"Un-unh," Penny said.

"Yep." Claire tilted the milk carton nearly upside down and poured the last stream into her mouth.

"You can't go to church if you start life like that. And you can't go to cotillion either. And I bet there are a lot of other things you aren't allowed to do."

Mary Lynn's heart had nearly beat out of her chest that day in the cafeteria. She knew her daddy had died traveling north, and she knew he had been young because she loved to look at the little picture of him leaning against a pale blue Chevrolet convertible. The photo was in an envelope that was kept tucked in the very bottom of her mama's jewelry box. But Mary Lynn didn't know that he and her mama were never married. Or that his family, her relatives, might be right there in Meggett. By recess she was getting sick in the bathroom and the nurse sent her home.

It took two days for Mama and Aunt Josey to pry it out of her. Once they did, Uncle Dale hit the side of the wall in the kitchen so hard it left a dent as he shouted, "That Gustafson girl is the devil incarnate!"

"No." Mama pulled back the fist of her older brother. "If anybody's the devil, it's her mama."

"You're right about that," he said. "What a case. She never would accept the fact that Mickey wasn't going to marry her." Then he limped into Mary Lynn's room and hugged her so tight she couldn't breathe for a few minutes. "You're the most precious girl that ever was," he said. "Do you know that?"

Mary Lynn remembered pulling back, the tears filling her eyes. "What about Mama and Aunt Josey?"

He bit his lip and she couldn't tell if he was going to laugh or weep. Then he pulled her close, not so tight, but strong enough to feel secure. "They're a close second, I reckon."

He breathed in and out several times before he lifted her chin. "Don't you listen to those girls. They're mean and they don't know squat about squat, you hear me?"

Mary Lynn nodded her head. Her uncle was a man of few words, and he didn't usually give many hugs, so she took him seriously.

"Okay," she had said as she nodded. She wiped her cheeks with the heel of her hands. "Okay, Uncle Dale."

A year or so later she had asked Mama about her daddy's family, and Mama just shook her head and said, "They don't live here anymore, Mary Lynn. It was just his mama, and she left when you were just a baby. I don't know if we'll ever hear from her again."

And her mama was right. They never did.

But back to St. Michael's. Mary Lynn didn't know if it was the aesthetics or the history or just

63

a kind of warm spirit that infused the place, but St. Michael's, in its own way, reminded her of the Cottageville Bible Church. The greeters and the ushers and the priests and the people in the pews seemed genuinely glad to see visitors, like her, who darkened the door this time of year.

Mary Lynn took a place toward the back in a small side pew on the north side. While she attended the women's prayer group quite regularly, she had only come to church a handful of times, and she was nervous about finding all the right places in the prayer book and hymnal. After she scanned the bulletin and marked her place in both books with pens and little pieces of the news-letter she discreetly tore during the trumpeter's pre-service solo, she looked up to take in the beauty of the place all dressed up for the great birthday party. The dark wood columns were lined with fresh green garland and so was the balcony, with large wide arcs decorated with a red berry wreath where one arc ended and another began. The candles on the lush advent wreath by the pulpit were lit, the gilded altar was covered in garland and bright red poinsettias, and there were fresh green wreaths in every window made out of large, waxy magnolia leaves. The chandeliers were turned down low and the whole place seemed to twinkle with splendor. *What must it have been like on that very night of His birth?* she wondered for the first time in her life.

When the crucifer carried the large brass cross down the center aisle as the grand organ piped out the first stanza of "O Come, O Come, Emmanuel," Mary Lynn noticed as she had before that many people leaned their head forward as if to bow and she found herself doing the same thing.

By the time they were singing "O Little Town of Bethlehem" just before the sermon, she felt a burning in her chest, like she had fallen asleep facedown on a heating pad. It wasn't uncomfortable, but it felt full of energy, and she sensed that God's love for her, something wholly undeserved, was working its way into her very bones. It was the best feeling she'd ever known. She did not want the burning to end.

The service continued smoothly. The sermon was about a gift—a pair of all-weather gloves a child worked hard and saved for and gave to his father, who disregarded the present and threw the gloves in the back of a flatbed truck shortly after he received them. It ended with a question, *Who is the pair of gloves? What have we done with our gift?*

Mary Lynn wondered, *If you never really knew you had the pair of gloves, could you be held accountable for not appreciating them?*

During the announcements Mary Lynn waved to Scottie, who was sitting with Gil and their crew of four kids on the opposite side of the church.

Then she watched Roy Summerall and his wife, Anne, stand and take their place in the pew marked "prayer ministry," and she thought how nice it was that people prayed for others in need, though she couldn't imagine working up the nerve to walk up there in the middle of a service.

Next was Holy Communion, and by the time she walked up to the altar and back down to her seat, she noticed that the door to the prayer ministry pew was open. Before she knew it, she was walking back down the aisle toward the open pew. She couldn't believe she was doing this, and in earnest, she had no idea what she might say. She hadn't a clue what she wanted or needed prayer for. As she neared the pew, she thought of something she could utter. *I experienced a healing, Reverend Summerall, when you prayed for me this morning. God is trying to get my attention. What do I do next?*

But when she sat down in front of them and Roy and his wife smiled and leaned forward and took her hands, something very different came out of Mary Lynn's mouth. She met both of their warm eyes and what had not yet been put into words, what had been eating her for months though only now did she realize it, came out in words that were as hard and beautiful as little clear crystals. "I want my husband to know God."

They smiled lovingly and made a side glance at one another. Then they put their warm, solid hands on hers and bowed their heads. As they prayed she heard the word "glory" throbbing over and over in her chest as the lights went down and the organ softly played "Silent Night."

She came home to a quiet house. Jackson was asleep in the den with his cello leaning on his knee. She studied him—his wide shoulders, the soft layers of skin on his long neck, his tall chest lifting and falling with each breath, his large, capable hands that were tanned even in December. He didn't look any different. In fact, he looked a little older and even a bit weary as if he had aged ten years and gone almost completely gray over the last two hours. And his face, the skin of his jowls were sagging the way his father's used to. She supposed that even handsome Jackson couldn't beat back age and gravity, especially when his guard was down.

She massaged the back of his neck until he woke up, and she took his hand and led him up to bed.

"Merry Christmas," she said.

He kissed her sweetly. "You too, baby."

Chapter 6

MARY LYNN

Christmas morning seemed to go too quickly. The afternoon tea was in the back of all of their minds, and it felt to Mary Lynn as though they were rushing through the gift giving. They only had a couple of hours before they needed to brew the tea, set out the silver and crystal, get showered and dressed, and practice the string quartet at least one time through.

Casey came over to Mary Lynn and curled up in her lap. She was shaped like a string bean, and she still liked to be held. She would fold herself up like an accordion, lean back into Mary Lynn's chest, and nuzzle. Mary Lynn loved this. She could never get tired of holding a child in her lap. It was one of the best feelings in the world.

Casey looked up and sighed. "Why do we have to have a party on Christmas Day?"

Mary Lynn took a deep breath. "I'm beginning to wonder that too." She pulled the girl close. "Maybe we can scratch that next year."

"Yeah." Casey buried her forehead in the nape of Mary Lynn's neck. "I just want to spend the day in my pajamas."

"Same here." Mary Lynn pulled her closer.

Mac came over and licked Casey's fingers. "Oh, I almost forgot!" The little girl unfolded herself and stood up. "I got you a present, Mac!"

She ran upstairs and came back down with a big bone that she must have purchased at Burbage's grocery down the street with her allowance. She took off the plastic wrap as he stood stone still in expectation. Then she handed it to him, and he trotted over to his bed in the den to savor it. Mac had a good life.

"That was sweet of you." Mary Lynn reached out her arms and the girl shrugged her shoulders and curled up in them again.

Now everyone had received their wooden clue from Jackson except for Catherine. Lilla had a musical note and a chess piece, which meant the iPod touch she'd been talking about for months and a hard-bound copy of the third Twilight series book, *Eclipse*, which she could read after the trip to England. For now she needed to catch up with Catherine and finish *A Tale of Two Cities* by Dickens in order, as Jackson had said as he gave them the books over Thanksgiving, to fully appreciate her first trip to London.

Casey's wooden clue was a little sea turtle, which meant she could take the after-school class at the sea turtle hospital at the aquarium that she'd been begging to enroll in after she watched a rehabilitated turtle released at Folly Beach last summer. (The turtle had a GPS glued to his back and Casey had followed him on the computer for months. He made it all the way to the waters off the coast of Japan before the signal was lost.)

Mary Lynn's wooden clue had been a lounge chair, which meant she could refurbish the furniture around the swimming pool. The taupe-colored cushions had become worn and mildewed over the last couple of years. She'd go with something darker this time. Maybe a burgundy or a hunter green. Seabrook and Sammy would advise.

Catherine was the last to receive her clue. Mary Lynn noticed that she seemed nervous as she reached in her stocking. It was as though her whole body was shuddering ever so slightly. And Mary Lynn noticed ash-colored circles deepening around her eyes. They all watched as she pulled out a wooden key, looked around the room as though she'd been shot with adrenaline, those big green eyes of her daddy's suddenly alive again despite the circles. Then she started to bounce up and down. Mary Lynn's heart raced. Catherine had received her driver's license just a week after her sixteenth birthday in October, but the child had been told that she wouldn't be getting any transportation of her own until she went off to college. Mary Lynn and Jackson had agreed to that. *Oh, Jackson, did you jump the gun?* Catherine handed Mary Lynn the wooden key. She licked her chapped lips and looked eagerly back and forth between Mary Lynn and Jackson. Her left hand was trembling from the excitement. Mary Lynn watched as Catherine kneaded her left hand with her right as if she was massaging a muscle cramp. No one else seemed to notice.

"C'mon." Jackson motioned toward the back door. "It's just a little set of used wheels." He turned and they all followed him out to the drive-way where a white mini Volvo station wagon was waiting with a big red velvet bow on the top. At least it was something safe.

"Daddy!" Catherine squealed. She hugged Jackson and Lilla joined in too. She would be sixteen next year, and she hoped this was a fore-taste of what was to come her way.

"Now there are plenty of rules that are going to go along with this." Jackson smiled but tried to hold his finger up like a stern headmaster. "I want you to take your sisters to school every morning and get them there *on time*."

Catherine squealed and continued to rub her trembling hand, and he started to wag his finger. "I want you to keep up with your strings and foreign language lessons."

She covered her mouth and jumped up and down.

"You need to keep your grades up and always let us know when you go out and where you are going."

"Yes, sir! Yes, sir!" She bobbed on the balls of

her feet as her eyes seemed to dart back and forth from the car and back to Jackson. "No problem!"

"And if you get a traffic ticket?"

She nodded as seriously as she could as she jumped up and down. He put his large hands on her shoulders to settle her down. "If you get a ticket for some driving offense, it's going back to the dealership, understand?"

"Yes, sir! I get it!"

Then he reached in his pocket and pulled out the big black key that he'd attached to a Vineyard Vines key chain with rows of little pink whales swimming across a pale blue canvas.

Catherine and Lilla jumped and screamed together. Casey squeezed in between them and started jumping and squealing too just for the fun of it, Mary Lynn supposed. Joy was contagious.

Mary Lynn didn't quite know what to feel. She was happy for Catherine. Catherine was growing up, and she was exceedingly responsible and had proven herself trustworthy time and time again through babysitting Casey, taking care of Mac, practicing the violin regularly, keeping up her grades, and working every spare moment to prepare for her next SAT test.

It would be nice, she supposed, not to have to drive the girls to school every morning, but this was a job Mary Lynn had been doing for ten years, and she wasn't sure she was ready to hand that responsibility over. And what about Jackson jumping the gun? Why hadn't she been included on this decision?

Jackson walked over to Mary Lynn and put his arm around her as the three girls jumped in the car and Catherine started the engine.

"This is a surprise." She looked up at him. She could not hide the frustration in her tone.

He met her eyes and bit his bottom lip until it whitened. "I know. I hope you're okay with it, Mary Lynn." He squeezed her shoulder. "I spotted it on the lot last week when I was on my way out to the deer stand, and I just thought, why not? She's worked real hard, and I do feel a pang of guilt from time to time about the whole cross country thing."

By now the girls had found their favorite radio station and some awful Lady Gaga song was blaring from the stereo.

Jackson pointed at the car and shook his head. "Not that junk."

Within less than a second, Catherine navigated to NPR and Jackson clapped as Handel's *Messiah* filled the driveway with its masterful sound.

"I knew it was coming." Mary Lynn reached over and pulled him closer. "I would like to have been in on the decision."

He raised his eyebrows and exhaled. "I'm sorry, Mary Lynn. You're right." He pulled back and looked her in the eye. "I should have talked to you first."

Then he hung his head and reminded her of a balloon that had just been deflated. She took his hand. "It's okay. I know it's probably time. But don't you feel like it's going too fast?"

He squeezed her, then pulled her back and looked down to her with a very serious stare. "Yeah, it is." He kissed her forehead. "They'll be gone before we know it." He whispered in her ear, "I hope we're getting it right, baby. That's what I want more than anything."

Mary Lynn took a deep breath. She savored this moment of connection, and she wished she could tell him all that was on her mind: her healing yesterday, the heat she felt in the church, the prayer she prayed for him. But even in this moment of intimacy, she didn't feel that she could open all the way up and reveal her heart.

She turned back, following his eyes to the girls who were opening the electronic gate and heading out into the street in the bright, white little station wagon.

Casey looked back from the backseat and waved to them.

"Me too," she said and stood there quietly beside him until the rumble of the new motor could no longer be heard on the quiet, pristine street.

Chapter 7

MARY LYNN

The Christmas Day party had become a bigger deal over the last couple of years as the Scovilles made strides up the social ladder. This year, both the commodore of the Carolina Yacht Club and the president of the Charlestowne Garden Club had responded positively, and it was the first time either of these been-yas had ever dawned the door of the Scoville home. Plus, it was rumored that the Debutante Society of South Carolina was considering inviting Mary Lynn to join, and the president of the society, Weezie Pruitt, had also accepted the invitation.

But most thrilling of all—yes, she must admit it—was that Sammy Smoak (whose mother was a neighbor of Claire Gustafson Greeley, the awful girl from Mary Lynn's childhood) had persuaded Claire to attend the party. He knew the Greeleys had family in Mount Pleasant who they dined with every Christmas Day, and on his last visit to Meggett, he had stopped in to say hi to Claire and said, "Oh, just pop in and see your old buddy Mary Lynn downtown on your way home on Christmas Day. She hosts one of the loveliest Charleston teas of the year, you know."

"No, I did not know," Claire had said as her twin boys circled around Sammy before bounding off of the porch and into the front yard to wrestle. "But if she sent me an invitation, I would attend."

"I'll let her know," Sammy had said. And then he called Mary Lynn on his drive home. "If you don't send that terror an invitation, I'll never speak to you again."

She had smiled. "Sammy, I don't know if this is a good idea."

"Now, I know you've been dipping your toe in the church thing and all, Mary Lynn, but you just can't deprive me or yourself of this one little indulgence, you hear me, girl?"

Revenge was sweet, and Mary Lynn knew that Sammy wanted her to taste of it. She looked out into the garden where Catherine was seated on the rim of the fountain, speaking French with a teacher from the College of Charleston.

"She said she *wanted* an invitation?" Mary Lynn asked. She imagined the forty-year-old version of Claire Gustafson—a round pink face, thin brown hair, and unflinching gray eyes.

"Yes. She said she would attend if you invited her." He cleared his throat and honked his horn before squealing, "Look out little rabbit," under his breath. Then he was back with his full and persuasive voice. "Now, Mary Lynn, don't make me beg you."

She chuckled. "All right. I'll send her one."

76

・・・

It was a half hour before the guests were to arrive when the doorbell rang unexpectedly.

Through the peep hole Mary Lynn spotted Jackson's first cousin, Ticky, a short round fellow with tattooed forearms who showed up every few months in hopes of getting a loan or, more accurately, a handout.

Mary Lynn waved to Jackson, who was tuning his cello as Anarosa set a silver tray of strawberries dipped in chocolate behind him, and pointed to the door. "It's Ticky."

"Perfect timing." Jackson shook his head. "Let me deal with him."

"Shouldn't we invite him to the party?"

Ticky was family, though he didn't have an address or a phone at the moment so she couldn't send him an invitation. He was not the most stable or mannerly fellow, but it was Christmas after all. And wasn't there a scripture about inviting people to a banquet—especially ones who can't return the favor? She'd have to ask Scottie.

Jackson strode toward the foyer, opened the door, and walked out on the piazza closing the door tightly behind him. Ticky's eyes were darting back and forth through the living room window where a silver tea service and a three-tiered tray of fruit tarts and cream puffs had already been set up.

"Mommy, will you tie my sash?" Mary Lynn

turned to find Casey in the powder blue silk dress she'd bought for her at Strasburg in Atlanta. She tied a nice square bow and spread out the sash as she tried to make out the muffled conversation on the piazza.

"Who's Daddy talking to?" Casey attempted to jump and peer over Mary Lynn's shoulder.

"Uncle Ticky." Casey loved Ticky. He did all sorts of silly tricks for her like making half his thumb disappear and come back, and he always called her sweetness.

"Let's go say hi!" The girl took her mother's hand and pulled.

Mary Lynn followed Casey out onto the piazza, but she could already hear the motorcycle taking off down the street.

"Where's Uncle Ticky, Dad?"

"He had to go."

Mary Lynn turned to Jackson. She could feel the worry lines forming on her forehead. "Didn't you invite him?"

"Mary Lynn." He shook his head at her.

Casey ran out to the sidewalk to catch a glimpse of him.

Mary Lynn whispered, "Well, it's Christmas. I wonder how in the world he's spending his?"

Jackson pulled her close and put his lips to her ear. "If his breath is any indication, I have a strong hunch it's in some dark, crusty watering hole." He stepped away and glanced toward the street. "He's not a good influence on these kids."

Mary Lynn looked down at the freshly painted piazza and supposed her prayers for Jackson and his faith either had not been answered or were not going to be answered anytime soon.

"I wrote him a check," he said as Casey came back in and closed the piazza door. "We'll probably see him in a couple of weeks when he's blown through that, and we can have him over then."

Casey scurried back and cocked her head. "Did he ask about me?"

Jackson kissed her on her forehead. "Yes. He said, 'Tell sweetness Merry Christmas.' Oh, and he wanted you to have this."

He handed her a little pack of Juicy Fruit gum, and her eyes lit up so bright you would have thought it was the best gift she'd received all day.

"That was nice of him," she said.

Jackson nodded his head. Then he stepped back. "Wow, you look beautiful, Case."

She twirled around in her dress and then unwrapped a piece of gum.

"Thanks, Daddy."

"You're welcome," he said. Then he watched her fold up the putty-colored rectangle and pop it in her little red mouth.

He patted her shoulder. "Be sure and spit that out before the guests arrive, all right?"

"Yes, sir."

Then Mary Lynn was off to put the final touches on for the party. Anarosa and her two sisters had come for the afternoon to help serve. They were receiving double pay, but even so, Mary Lynn hated the thought that they were away from their families. Oh, but she needed them to pull this off.

And she needed Seabrook and Sammy too. Sammy had worked with Tiger Lily on the flower arrangements, and Seabrook had brought some of the most beautiful silver tea services from his antique store so they could offer tea in three different rooms: the dining room, the living room, and the den.

It was a true English high tea with scones, clotted cream, homemade preserves, watercress and smoked salmon and shrimp finger sandwiches, fruit pastries, chocolates, a variety of teas, and champagne.

All of the usual folks were there, Bev and Hollis King, Mark Waters and his two college-age children from his first marriage, the board members and Head of School from Peninsula Day and some of the favorite teachers and coaches, the officers of the Downtown Neighborhood Association, Francis LaRoche, the conductor of the local symphony orchestra, Nick Mumford, the director of the Spoleto Festival, and a variety of music, literature, and art professors from the College of Charleston.

A string quartet comprised of some of the symphony's top players performed in the formal living room just to the left of the fireplace. They were playing one of Mary Lynn's favorites, Mozart's string quartet in C major. The sweet sounds of the bows on the strings made Mary Lynn's shoulders relax for a moment as she stopped in the foyer to hear, *Dum, dum, dum, dum, dunta-dunta-dum.* For a moment she was transported back to Uncle Dale's farm one Christmas morning. It was the year Mama had saved up and bought her a real Cabbage Patch Doll with adoption papers and all, and Aunt Josey smocked several day gowns for it, and Uncle Dale had made a little wooden cradle. All the gifts were laid out under the Christmas tree and she held the baby, Sarah Louise, tight for days, putting her down only to change her into another lace-trimmed gown.

When she looked up, the large front door opened, and there on Sammy Smoak's arm was Claire Gustafson, a good eighty pounds heavier than when Mary Lynn last laid eyes on her at their high school graduation. She was sporting a green and navy plaid wool jumper and a white frumpy blouse with puffy sleeves and ruffled edges, a style that had made a brief comeback among the preppy set in the nineties. Mary Lynn couldn't help the thought that crossed her mind: Claire looks like a Catholic schoolgirl on steroids.

The weight gain made her eyes look like two thin slits, and she smiled knowingly as she spotted Mary Lynn by the antique clock at the bottom of the staircase in her black Armani wide-legged pants, a tailored ivory silk blouse by Akris Punto, and a long strand of pearls tucked neatly beneath the shirt collar.

This was a terrible idea, thought Mary Lynn as she pressed her cinnamon painted lips together. Nothing good will come of it. She knew Sammy was well-intended, but the whole thing just felt miserable and mean-spirited, and she had no idea what she would say.

"Hello, Claire." Mary Lynn stepped forward and extended her arm.

Claire batted the arm away, leaned in abruptly, and embraced Mary Lynn tight for several whole seconds as Sammy smirked from behind and a little man, presumably Claire's husband, cleared his throat and looked around the room. The little man darted straight for a sandwich tray and selected an open-faced smoked salmon one before turning back.

"So good to see you." Claire pulled back and squeezed Mary Lynn's arm. Then she glanced into the dining room and into the parlor where the quartet was playing.

"Well, it's all true, I can see. You have a beautiful life." She inhaled deeply. "And why not?" she said. "Why the *heck* can't someone from

Meggett take a step up every now and then?"

Mary Lynn felt herself blush as Jackson came up and stood beside her. He put his hand on the small of her back. "Why, hello there, Claire." He nodded, dapper as ever these days in his navy blue suit and burgundy-and-green-striped bow tie. "So nice to see you."

She stepped back and onto her husband's toes. He let out a muffled squeak of protest.

"Jackson Scoville. Well, I sure did overlook you in high school, didn't I? Where were you back then?"

"I was older, for one." Jackson nodded good humoredly. He turned to Mary Lynn and smiled, a gleam in his eyes. "And I was mostly in shop class."

Claire spread out her fleshy hands as the guests clapped at the end of the final movement of the Mozart piece. "You must have learned more than just how to saw a two-by-four. That's for sure."

Sammy chuckled with delight, put his hand on Claire's husband's shoulder, and proceeded to introduce him to Mary Lynn and Jackson just as Lilla and Catherine came running over with their violin cases. "Dad, it's time," Catherine said. Her eyes looked jittery and Mary Lynn knew she was nervous.

"A pleasure to meet you, Bo." Jackson gave him a firm handshake, which he seemed to appreciate. "If you all will excuse me, I have to get my cello." He nodded toward the foyer. "I hope you'll come on in the living room for our little family concert."

"Concert?" Claire looked back at Mary Lynn. She rolled her eyes. "My!"

Sammy piped up. "Yes, Jackson and the girls are performing a string quartet. They've been practicing for months now."

Claire pumped her arm and elbowed her husband. "A string quartet, Bo. Can you believe it?"

Bo nodded. "It's Charleston, Claire. Everyone around here"—he glanced at Sammy—"is into arts and such."

"Yes, indeed," Sammy said. "Now why don't y'all find a place in the parlor, and I'll get you a cup of tea or champagne?"

"Champagne," Claire said. "That sounds nice." Bo nodded. "One for me too, Sammy. Thank ya."

Claire pointed to Mark Waters who was chatting with the yacht club commodore. "Well, if it isn't the man who runs Charleston." She nudged Bo, who followed her gaze.

"Sure is. I feel like I'm reading about his projects every week in the paper. He must be a gazillionaire by now."

Claire cocked her head. "And still handsome too. What marriage is he on now?"

"Just been married twice," Mary Lynn said.

"Oh," Claire said. "But the real question is how many affairs has he had?"

Oh goodness, Mary Lynn thought. This was

surreal. The girl who mistreated her much of her life now in her new home, in her new life, sipping champagne from her new crystal flutes talking about Mark Waters and his love life. She spotted Casey coming down the stairs with her viola and made a way for her to get through the crowd and into the parlor.

The Scoville quartet took its place, tuned for a few minutes as the guests gathered round, and then with a firm nod of Jackson's head started in on the Haydn.

Dum dum data dum . . . dum dum da dum.

It was not half bad. Not at all. The strings sounded as elegant as the girls looked in their pale blue silk dresses, and Jackson's bow was steady and sure as he stared at the music on the stand in front of him.

Lilla was playing first violin, leading beautifully, but about halfway through, Mary Lynn noticed that Catherine was nearly a half beat behind Jackson and Casey. She could see Jackson's wrinkled eyebrows as he looked over toward his oldest, nodding for her to catch up. Then Mary Lynn looked up and noticed young Tres King eyeing Catherine's every move. The girl had noticed it too, and she was blushing and trying to catch up with everyone else. Her left hand, the one steadying the violin, trembled.

Tres had gotten a car this morning too, a black Land Rover with a Yale sticker already placed squarely on the back. (They must have a drawer full of them somewhere!) He'd come over shortly after Ticky left to take Catherine for a ride.

"She's getting ready for the party," Mary Lynn had told him. "Maybe another time."

She hoped he would have his eye on some other girl by the time they returned from London.

Jackson furrowed his brow and eyed Catherine steadily. She remained a half step off, her eyes shaking as she followed the notes on the music stand. Her face was red, and Mary Lynn noticed a little vein protruding from the center of her forehead as her hands worked quickly pushing the bow up and back along the strings. She was flustered, but she managed to skip a note or two to catch up. It would be hard for anyone other than Mary Lynn or the symphony players to notice.

Thankfully, Lilla was flawless and Casey was as steady as the rain. Jackson was holding his own too, though Mary Lynn noticed a drop of perspiration roll down his cheek.

When they finished, the room exploded with applause. Bo and Claire Greeley were right in the middle of it all, Sammy holding their champagne flutes so they could clap and hoot.

"Nice," a rich, familiar voice behind her whispered. "But I'd still choose a Stanley Brothers tune with you and your uncle any day." He patted her shoulders firmly with his large, strong hands. "Hope you still sing sometimes."

She turned ever so slightly toward Mark and nodded. "Sometimes," she said. "Usually in the shower."

He raised his eyebrows and chuckled. She hadn't meant to make a risqué remark and started to blush.

"You have a beautiful family, Mary Lynn," he said, his eyes gazing down on her with that familiar glint she had known for years. "Don't let Jackson take away the soul, though."

She turned back to watch her crew get up and take a quick bow. Hollis looked at Bev, and Mary Lynn thought she could detect the slightest roll of his eyes. Tres walked over to congratulate Catherine. She stood, nodded slightly, blushed again. Mary Lynn could see the perspiration above her lip. Then Jackson tapped Catherine's shoulder and whispered something in her ear that Mary Lynn hoped wasn't too strong of a reprimand. She watched the child's head hang down as if she was suddenly in need of studying the pattern of the Oriental rug beneath her.

Next the Scoville quartet moved out of the way so the symphony players could resume their places. They started with an early Beethoven quartet.

The party did have a celebratory feel to it. The commodore of the yacht club was laughing heartily by the blazing fire in the den and Weezie

Pruitt was chatting animatedly to the head of the Peninsula Day School and some of the other neighbors by the watercress sandwiches. Oh, Mary Lynn couldn't help but hope for an invitation into that club. After what she had been through opening her locker every Tuesday afternoon at age eleven, and twelve and thirteen, well, that might all seem like a distant dream if her daughters could make their debut among the elite of the state! Abundant recompense or some such thing. That was what Wordsworth called it, right? You didn't have to be a nineteenth-century poet to get it. Well, Mary Lynn wouldn't say no to it. And in that way, she was a lot like Jackson.

Last night after church, Mary Lynn had invited Roy Summerall and his lovely wife, Anne, and their daughter, Rose, to attend the party, and she was delighted to see them out on the piazza pointing to the statue with the red berry wreath. Mary Lynn walked out to say hello. She noticed Anne holding Rose's hand and she wondered if they were planning on extending their family.

"Have you had a good Christmas?" Mary Lynn bent down to ask the little girl.

"Yes, ma'am," she said. She took a deep breath and smiled. "I didn't get my first wish, but I got all my others." She started to name them on her fingers: an Easy Bake Oven with two chocolate cake mixes, an American Girl doll—Molly from

World War II—and the rest of the Boxcar Children collection.

"How wonderful," Mary Lynn said.

"Yeah," said Casey, who was sitting on the joggling board on the porch. She took a step closer to Rose. "I have the Emily doll from the same time period. Wanna come to my room and see?"

Rose's eyes grew wide. "Really?" She looked to Anne, who nodded reassuringly, then back to Casey. "Yeah!"

Casey grabbed her hand and the girls ran through the foyer and up the stairs.

Roy, Anne, and Mary Lynn chuckled and turned as Jackson came through the door grinning with the commodore, who was stepping outside for a cigar. Though Jackson wasn't a smoker, he always carried a silver lighter in his pocket for occasions like this, and she watched him pull it out deftly and light the commodore's Cuban.

"Is your leg all right?" Anne asked Mary Lynn.

"Yes, she's fine." Scottie Truluck, who had come over from the garden with her husband, Gil, leaned into the conversation. She was dressed in blue jeans and cowboy boots and Gil was in a black t-shirt, a tattoo of a cross showing beneath the dark hair of his arms. Mary Lynn wondered what Scottie's mother, who was also somewhere at the tea, was thinking. "It was a miracle, you know? After Roy prayed for her."

Anne smiled and casually twisted her long red hair and let it rest on the left side of her shoulder. She took a deep breath. "I love it when that happens."

"Don't you?" Scottie grabbed Mary Lynn's and Anne's hands and squeezed. "It's like the natural order, the way things were meant to be breaks through for a moment and we catch a glimpse of what we have to look forward to."

Gil shook Roy's hand and started bending his ear about how Clemson might fair against Kentucky at tomorrow's Music City Bowl.

"God is good." Scottie winked at Mary Lynn.

"Yes, he is," Anne said.

Mary Lynn smiled. It was a relief to talk to these women. She didn't have to make sure her shoulders were upright or that she impressed them with her vocabulary or her knowledge of art, culture, or social etiquette. She didn't feel as though she was being scrutinized, though (by God's grace) she had somehow stood up to the scrutiny thus far.

Then Bev King pulled her over to the corner of the piazza. "I heard Weezie say something about the annual debutante meeting and wouldn't your garden be the ideal spot for it next year."

Mary Lynn took a deep breath and attempted to hold in her stomach. "Really?"

"Yes. I just know you're going to get an invitation."

Mary Lynn squared her shoulders and smiled at

Weezie, who was heading through the door with a glass of champagne.

"Put in a good word for me, won't you?" Bev said as she stepped away. She had not yet been invited to join the debutante club despite her northeastern pedigree, and this was driving her a little crazy, though it would be several years before her daughter would be of age.

"*If* we are invited I will, Bev."

"Such a lovely home," Weezie said. "You've done such a nice job with it, Mary Lynn."

Mary Lynn adjusted her posture and took another deep breath. "Thank you, Weezie."

"And your daughters. Well, they couldn't be lovelier."

Mary Lynn smiled and exhaled. Life was so full of surprises. Mama never would have believed this. Claire Gustafson never would have believed it, except that she was here now, watching this beautiful gathering.

"Let's get together after your trip." Weezie nodded. "Do lunch in January. Sound good?"

"Sounds great," Mary Lynn said.

Weezie leaned in and kissed her cheek. "Thank you for having me. And have a fabulous time in England!"

"Thank you, Weezie," Mary Lynn said. As soon as the woman walked away, Bev came over. "This is so exciting, Mary Lynn! I just know she's going to ask you."

"We'll see, Bev."

Bev smiled but she seemed anxious. Her eyes darted back and forth.

"I feel sure you'll get in," Mary Lynn said. "If I do first, I'll do whatever I can to further that along."

Bev squeezed her elbow. "Thank you, Mary Lynn. You're a good friend."

At the end of the party, everyone received a hand-carved Christmas ornament that Jackson had been crafting in the tool shed over the last month. It was the profile of an angel blowing a trumpet. Casey had helped him paint the ornaments. She made their dresses a pearly white, their hair every shade of brown, yellow, or black, and each pair of wings were a wonderful tarnished silver that gave the appearance of pewter thanks to the acrylic paint they had found at the art supply store on Calhoun Street. Jackson had carved the words "Christmas 2009" and his and Casey's initials on the backside of the ornament.

"Well," Bev said as she received the parting gift. "No one can one-up the Scovilles when it comes to throwing a party. That's for sure." Hollis cleared his throat. "Let's go," she thought she heard him say and she couldn't help but chuckle.

As the guests started to say their farewells, Scottie came over and handed Mary Lynn a gift. "Oh wait," Mary Lynn said. She ran to the closet and pulled out the pre-wrapped gift she had for anyone who brought something by. Assorted Godiva Chocolates. What a rotten friend she was!

Scottie smiled. "Thank you," she said. Her eldest son, in his own black t-shirt, his hair spiked with gel, grabbed them out of her hands. "Awesome!"

"Call me when you get back from your trip."

"I will."

That night Mary Lynn walked up to the third floor to kiss the girls good night. Catherine was looking out of the window at her new car—or was it at Tres's room across the garden? Mary Lynn hoped it was the former. Casey was explaining to the fish in her aquarium that Anarosa would feed them in her absence, and Lilla was actually reading *A Tale of Two Cities*. She looked pretty into it. Well, good for her.

Mary Lynn inspected their bags. This was their second international trip, and they seemed to know what they needed: a couple of dresses, a rain coat, boots, plenty of underwear, a couple of pair of jeans, and one heavy coat. She had their passports in her carry-on along with the tickets. They would be headed to London late tomorrow. What a life these kids had. Had she known them during her own childhood she would have envied them and yet she could never regret the love of her mama and the simple pleasures of growing up on her uncle's farm, feeding the chickens, milking the cows, rolling out the biscuits with Aunt Josey, and chasing Mama through the cornfields.

She found Jackson in the bed rereading Chaucer's *Canterbury Tales*. "The party was a success, don't you think?"

She smiled at him. "Yes. It gets better every year."

A motorcycle rumbled down the street and she thought of Ticky. He probably spent the rest of his day at Wet Willie's or Big John's Tavern. What were those places like on Christmas Day?

Something wasn't right, but Mary Lynn couldn't put her finger on it. She supposed this was the onset of the letdown. She always had one at the end of Christmas Day, and she should have known to brace herself for it. It was a kind of bleakness that seemed exacerbated by the beauty of their home and their life.

She walked to the window and felt a chill move its way up her spine. The letdown would be worse tonight than usual. All the work, all of the excitement, and suddenly it was over. She was tired. And in her heart of hearts, she just wanted to crawl under the covers and sleep for three days without talking with anyone. *Why did this come over me?* she wondered as she looked out and into the darkness of the harbor where the water endlessly churned.

The burning in her chest last night was the opposite of the hollowness she felt now. The longing in her heart was deep and cold, and if she thought about it for too long, it was almost unbearable. She felt lonely and empty and weary . . . very, very weary. How could someone in her privileged shoes feel so down?

She walked over to her bedside table and opened her gift from Scottie. It was a book called *The Message* by Eugene Peterson and was some sort of New Testament translation in contemporary language.

She crawled into bed with the book. Jackson reached over and patted her knee from atop the covers.

"You all right?"

She breathed deeply. She longed to weep in front of her husband, to tell him how blue she felt and what was really on her mind. But she was too tired or too wary of his response. Whatever the reason, she had become a woman who bit her tongue. "Yeah," she said. "I'm all right."

Then she read a few pages before her heavy eyelids won out. She tucked the book in the carry-on bag for tomorrow's flight.

Chapter 8

CATHERINE

Catherine was packing her suitcase when Lilla crept into her room, cell phone in hand. She handed it to her older sister who read, "Tell C to look out window—T."

Catherine furrowed her brow, handed the phone back to Lilla, and slowly walked to the window where she bent down and could see Tres beneath the street lamp, motioning ever so slightly with his head for her to join him.

He pulled out his phone and started texting again. In seconds Lilla's phone buzzed, and she handed it back to Catherine. "Need to see u bf u go. Pls."

Catherine bit her lip and turned back to Lilla, who shrugged her thin shoulders before grinning ever so slightly. "Want me to tell you how to get down?"

Catherine looked out the window to Tres who was rocking forward and backward with his hands in his pockets. When he saw her he cocked his head to the side and put his hands together as if in prayer before looking up and mouthing, "Please!"

Catherine put on her jeans, her running shoes, and her fleece as Lilla whispered instructions. "Be sure to hold on to the sill until you can feel the gutter. Then inch your way down until you can reach the outside column of the piazza. Then reach your foot down to the railing."

Catherine nodded and Lilla broke into a smile. She squeezed her sister's shoulders. "Will you just have some fun for once in your life?"

"I guess." Catherine groaned. Then she slowly raised the window and put one long leg out and then the next.

Lilla patted her sister's hands, which were white-knuckled and tightly gripping the sill.

"Hold on until you can feel the gutter with your feet."

Catherine bit her lip as she felt her way down to the gutter with her right foot. "Got it," she whispered, then she slid down and grabbed hold of the second-floor piazza column.

She felt for the railing on floor two and then moved down to the first-floor railing before jumping a little too loudly onto the downstairs piazza. The thought to scurry back up to her room crossed her mind, but Tres was opening the privacy door now and reaching out his hand.

She took it and he quickly pulled her out before gently closing the door back. Once Catherine was on the sidewalk, she looked up to the window where Lilla was giving her a thumbs-up before returning to her phone and answering some other text.

Tres swung his arm around her. "Let's head to the park." He nodded toward White Point Gardens. It wasn't exactly the worst place to be in the middle of the night, although sometimes homeless men slept on the benches and there were creeps who parked along the battery in the dark hours, according to her parents. But it was Christmas and Catherine suspected that even the homeless people as well as the creeps had something better to do on this one night of the year. Then again, she didn't.

"I had to see you before you took off." He pulled her close. He smelled like mints and cigarette smoke.

Cat and Tres had only been on one official date—the homecoming dance where he became too sauced to drive her home. They hadn't ever kissed, and while she cared about Tres on some level, she knew, at this point anyway, that the feelings were wrought more out of sympathy than attraction. Not that he wasn't hot. He was, in that sort of way that preppy guys who were well-shaved and wore nice clothes were hot. And he could be kind too. He had picked up her backpack one rainy morning in the quadrangle and carried it into the school building for her, and she had seen him look out for his own little sister before, carrying her over a puddle on a day she didn't wear her rain boots. But even though Catherine had lived what many would call a life of privilege, she didn't have that kind of "I deserve it" mind-set that seemed to be the strongest part of who Tres King was. That attribute was not very hot.

White Point Gardens looked dark and quiet as they reached it, and they sat beneath one of the giant live oak trees where they watched the mist on the water and noticed a few bats swooping in and out of the eaves of the stately High Battery homes that had been built by the wealthy rice and cotton planters who needed a house in the city for the social season during the antebellum era.

Once their eyes adjusted, they could make out the statues and the monuments and the historic cannons and mortars placed around the edges of the park to commemorate the Revolutionary War and the Civil War. Both the park and the harbor had seriously dramatic roles to play in US history. Not to mention the fact that the "gentleman" pirate, Stede Bonnet, and fifty others like him were hung here at one time in the 1720s as the townspeople filled the gallows area and jeered. The place was steeped in history and lore.

They were quiet for a few minutes as they breathed in the cold, moist harbor air. It felt good to Catherine, and she was thankful to be away from her room and the packing and the SAT flash cards.

After a few deep breaths, Tres dug into the pocket of his fleece and pulled out a Ziploc bag. He licked his lips and she thought she could see him grin as he held the translucent bag up. "Been pharming in my parents' medicine cabinet."

She rolled her eyes. "That sounds safe."

He chuckled. "Yeah. Between my mom's anxiety and my dad's back pain, they've got some serious meds." Then he wiped his nose with the top of his wrist. "It's awesome when you don't have to deal with a dealer."

Now he opened the bag and offered it to her. She shook her head no and turned slightly away from him, wondering why she had come out here in the first place. She needed to be packing. She needed to be looking over her words. What if her dad decided to drill her during the downtime on their trip? She wouldn't be surprised if he did. She could picture him in the airport or in line to see a museum saying, "The following sentence contains a single error or no error at all . . ." Ugh. Her head pounded at the thought of it. Or maybe the pounding was from the Adderall she had swallowed just before tea.

Next Tres dug in his jeans pocket and pulled out some Robitussin cough drops. "How about just a little dex, then? Reeves told me you're into this."

She looked at the little green pills in their plastic casings and then to his eyes, which seemed to glisten with the distant reflection of the street lamp. She remembered how the pills had made her feel the night of the college tour trip, light as if she were floating. And she had slept well, very well, after she'd taken them.

It was cough medicine. Over the counter stuff. That wasn't a big deal. She nodded and tore open a couple. He nudged her playfully with his shoulder as he pulled out a bottle of water from the other pocket in his fleece. Boys were good at stashing things, she thought.

He swallowed a few of the pills from his baggie and she swallowed two of the Robitussin. He reached out for her hand and she gave it to him, not so much because she wanted to, but because it was nice that someone wanted to hold it. Nice that someone, some male, just wanted to sit still and relax with her.

"Have a good Christmas?" He squeezed her hand gently.

"Yeah," she said. "I can't believe my dad gave me a car."

"Why not?" He squeezed her hand again and started to rub it with his thumb.

She shrugged. "It just doesn't seem like him." She cleared her throat. "Of course it's going back if I make one screw up."

He chuckled. "Yeah, I got that lecture too." He rubbed his head against hers. "But can you really imagine them taking it away? I mean, it makes their life easier not to have to cart us around or give up their wheels when we need to borrow them."

"Tres." She turned to him and swallowed hard. "You know my dad."

"Yeah." He rubbed his forehead and met her eyes. "You're right. He'll take it away if you screw up."

She leaned back and took deep breaths. The counselor at school said deep breaths did wonders to release stress. She wasn't so sure. Now she thought of Bryan Christiansen, thought of him running cross country at the state finals and how much she would love to have been there too. Not just to run but to cheer on the team, especially Bryan. He was relentless in trying to beat his time each race. She had seen him running along Lockwood Boulevard more than once this fall, breaking into a full out fly. He was unbelievably fast.

Bryan's mother (her track coach), Ms. Christiansen, had dropped by the tea this afternoon, but he hadn't showed, which disappointed her. She knew he hated her parents. They had lost the overall state competition in late October by just a few points. He blamed them.

"How's the studying going?" Ms. Christiansen had asked her as the crowd of well-coiffed people circled around them with their laughter and their chatter.

"Fine, I guess," she had said. "Maybe I can join the track team after I take the test."

"That would be wonderful," Ms. Christiansen had said. She looked a little out of place at the tea in her corduroy pants and blue jean jacket. (She was most at home in shorts or sweatpants.)

Catherine smiled at her coach as Ms. Christiansen rested her hand lightly on the girl's shoulder. She wasn't one to show much affection, so Catherine tried to soak it in. The teacher leaned forward and whispered, "But don't put too much pressure on yourself, Catherine. Just try your best."

"Yes, ma'am," Catherine had said. She looked back to see her dad talking with Mark Waters and some other man who was probably an investor in their real estate ventures. Ms. Christiansen was watching him too. She turned back to Catherine. "I know your parents want the best for you, sweetheart."

Catherine nodded and exhaled. "Just give it your all and let it go after that. That's all anyone can do, right?" said Ms. Christiansen.

"Yes," Catherine had said. "Thanks for coming, Ms. Christiansen. Tell Bryan Merry Christmas for me."

Ms. Christiansen broke into a grin. "I will do that as soon as I get home."

Then just as the coach stepped away she turned quickly back and pulled a little wrapped package out of her pocket. "Almost forgot." She handed Catherine the present. "For your trip."

Catherine opened it right on the spot. Beneath the wrapping was a little blue velvet box, and when she opened it she saw a silver necklace with the St. Christopher medallion hanging from it. Bryan had one just like it, and he wore it every time he ran.

Catherine tried to contain her grin. "Thank you, Coach!" she beamed. Then she gave the woman a big embrace. "I'll wear it the whole time."

"Good," the coach said. "It's just a symbol, but it's a good reminder that you aren't alone."

Catherine swallowed hard and nodded. "Yes, ma'am," she said. "That is good to know."

"You know what I can't wait for?" Tres released her hands and sat up with a sudden jerk. She came out of her dreamy state and watched his back tense up as he turned quickly to her.

"What?" she said. She knew he was getting ready to go into some sort of monologue so she settled back into the tree. She was starting to float. It was just on the very edges of her fingers and toes but it was coming. Relief.

He turned around to face her. "I can't wait to be out from under their roof. Once I'm off to college I'm never stepping foot in the state of South Carolina." His eyes were beginning to dart around a little and then he settled back on her. "Except maybe to see you."

"Why wouldn't you come back?" Her limbs were starting to feel light but her stomach ached a little. Maybe the Adderall was still wearing off and the dex didn't mix well with it. She took another sip of the water and breathed through her mouth.

"Because they're pathetic." He gestured with his hands open, then he curled them into tight fists. "All they think about is how to get into this or that society or club. How to impress this or that old Charlestonian." He turned to spit and looked back at her. "As if it really matters. As if this isn't some washed-up town whose glory days are centuries behind it. As if this is a place where *anything* interesting, where anything *new* goes on."

She closed her eyes to savor the floating. Honestly, she didn't really care about the places where new and interesting things went on. What she cared about was peace and relief from the pressure. If she could find that, just a little bit of that, she would have what she wanted.

Through her closed eyes she could feel him start to shiver. Whatever mixture from his parents' medicine cabinet he had consumed was working its way through his veins now.

"So where do you want to be?" she said through her closed eyes. "Where do new things happen?"

He drummed on his knees with his thumbs and spit in the grass again. "I don't know. New York, Hong Kong, maybe somewhere in Europe? I'm certainly not going to move to South Cackelacky and spend the rest of my life trying to kiss everyone's old Southern butt just so I can eat a sub-par meal at the yacht club or go to some dance with a bunch of crusty old people in their hand-me-down jewels, I can tell you that."

She opened her eyes. She was almost floating now. "So why did your parents move here anyway?"

He shook his head. "No clue, Catherine." He wrinkled his brow. "Something about a good place to raise kids . . ." He wiped his nose. "But you know what I think?"

She took a deep breath. She was feeling a little nauseous. She wasn't sure if she'd spoken or not so she said it again. "What?"

He breathed deeply. "I think they were bored with Greenwich." He shook his head back and forth in disgust. "And they just wanted to come down here to see if they could do it . . . see if they could make it in Charleston where they had no connections or old family name. Like a challenge, you know?"

"Yeah," she said. The breeze lifted her hair and she felt the faintest tingling work its way across her scalp. "I know what you mean."

Whole minutes passed between them before he reached out, squeezed her knee, and asked, "Why did your parents move here?"

She breathed through her mouth. The air was refreshing and cool. She thought it was staving off the nausea. She mulled the question over as the tingling worked its way from the back of her head to the tip of her toes.

"They wanted to give us a better life," she said. "And this was the closest place where they thought they could do it."

Tres seemed anxious now. He picked up a stick and started digging in the dirt.

"Is it?" he asked, poking her ankle with the stick. "Is it a good life for you, Catherine Scoville?"

She felt the tingling move to her ankle. She pushed the stick away and started to rub it.

"I think I better go home," she said. "I don't feel too good."

He breathed deeply, then grabbed his own belly. She watched as he scurried over to another tree and vomited.

"You okay?" She stood and walked toward him. She hung back a few feet. Her head was pounding now. Maybe Adderall and dex didn't mix. Her limbs still felt like they were floating.

"Ack." He stood back up and wiped his mouth with the sleeve of his fleece. "Sorry about that. It happens sometimes."

"Tres." She put her hand on his back. It felt warm in the cool night.

"Don't do this pharming thing. You're going to hurt yourself."

He sniffed and then turned to spit.

He looked back at her. She felt sympathy for him and rubbed his arm. "You're going to hurt yourself and then you're not going to be able to go anywhere."

His eyes glistened as he looked over to her and nodded.

"Let me walk you home," he said. "Next time I'll just stick to booze."

They turned and headed toward South Battery. "Or maybe coffee?" she said.

He didn't take her hand or put his arm around her this time, which somehow made her breathe easier. Instead he stuffed his hands in his pockets like a little boy.

"Maybe," he said.

When they reached her house, he helped her up onto the first railing. "Wait," he said, steadying her legs. He pulled the rest of the Robitussin capsules out of his pocket and handed them to her. "Have a good trip." He patted her foot as she put them in her pocket.

"Thanks. And stay away from your parents' stuff," she whispered as she started to climb.

He cleared his throat quietly. "We'll see."

Chapter 9

MARY LYNN

The next afternoon Anarosa's husband, Carlos, drove the Scovilles to the Charleston Airport. They were headed to London Heathrow by way of Dulles, and they were going to spend three nights in London, two in Stratford-Upon-Avon, and three more in Hampshire at a Four Seasons Resort in an old English manor.

Mary Lynn watched Jackson pack his carry-on bag that morning. He'd stuffed it with his soft-bound editions of Chaucer's *Canterbury Tales*, Defoe's *Moll Flanders*, and Shakespeare's sonnets.

"Got to bone up on my pre-nineteenth-century British lit." He'd winked at her.

"I don't think even *you* could read three books that thick on an international flight."

"Why not try?" he'd said, and later that day when they were seated on their connecting flight from Charleston to Dulles, she watched him put the books in a little stack beneath his seat. He started with Chaucer.

Mary Lynn had read Chaucer the spring of her senior year in the AP English class at Meggett High School. Although Jane Gustafson, the head of the PTA (and nearly every other influential and social organization in town), tried to keep Mary Lynn out of the upper-level classes, her mama won that battle. Mary Lynn was bright. All the test scores had shown that, and Mama and Aunt Josey knew she had real potential. So Cecil Waters (who was head-over-heels with his secretary, Mary Lynn's mama, by this point) hightailed it from Charleston over to Meggett High just before her freshman year and had a word behind closed doors with Principal Dewberry.

Mary Lynn would never know what happened at that meeting (and she really didn't want to find out), but she did notice Principal Dewberry had traded in his Oldsmobile sedan for a red convertible Mustang the next week, and she was smart enough, even then, to assume that Cecil had done what he and Mark seemed to do best—grease palms. Bribes or not, Mary Lynn was grateful for the chance to be challenged academically and to study with the best teachers in the school. College was actually a prospect. None of the adults in her family had attended college, and Uncle Dale made it clear he would support her if she was accepted.

By her senior year in high school, Mark Waters was married to his first wife, the winner of the Miss South Carolina pageant, and Mary Lynn and Jackson were serious. They had started dating the summer before, after he had read a poem she had written about harvesting corn for a contest in the local paper. It had been selected. He was already out of high school and working with his daddy on the tomato farm while studying nights at Trident Tech.

By December she had been accepted to the Beaufort branch of the University of South Carolina and her family had a plan. She'd live at home and commute. They would take care of the tuition and books. At least that *was* the plan until

110

Jackson picked her up one Friday night for a date and drove her to Charleston where he'd made a reservation at Robert's, the fanciest restaurant in all of the lowcountry, where Robert, the proprietor, sang opera arias to the diners.

He'd told her to wear something pretty, and she had put on the pale yellow dress her mama had bought her for her college interviews. It had a tasteful scalloped neck, a wide yellow belt, and a full skirt that stopped at the knee. She made herself up real nice, and Aunt Josey lent her the imitation pearls Uncle Dale had given her for their twentieth wedding anniversary.

Mary Lynn and Jackson had dinner that night and listened to Robert sing. It was like nothing she had ever heard before. The man had a deep, moving voice, which moved Jackson to tears when he sang the aria, *Che gelida manina* from *La Bohéme.*

Mary Lynn had looked over to the tall, thin man beside her as he patted his eye with the pressed dinner napkin.

She reached across the table and squeezed his large hand.

"I don't know anything about opera, do you?" he asked.

"No. Not a thing," she said.

"There's so much I want to know about, Mary Lynn." He took a sip of his ice water and his eyes glistened. "There's so much to this world, so many layers. And I want to know it all. Don't you?"

She smiled at the handsome young man with his big dreams. He was an anomaly—a farm boy by day, bush-hogging or picking tomatoes, and by night, a student of literature, history, and music. She'd seen the stack of books in his den when he had her over one afternoon.

"I love to read, don't you? Right now I'm reading the nineteenth-century poets—Lord Byron and Shelley and Keats. They were a wild bunch, I tell you."

Mary Lynn supposed that Jackson admired her smarts, the AP classes she aced, and her acceptance into college. He was proud of her. Almost as proud as Uncle Dale, who took the whole family out for steak at Ryan's in Cottageville the day she received her acceptance letter.

That night, after a lovely dinner at Robert's that included delicacies of which neither one of them had ever partaken—foie gras, veal, and crème brulee—they strode slowly along the battery looking at the beautiful historic homes that over-looked the harbor. They were the city homes of the plantation owners back in the 1800s, and each one was painted a pastel color with huge double and triple piazzas and stunning views of the harbor.

Jackson stopped in front of a pale pink house. Inside the large silk-draped windows, you could see a grand piano and two couples sitting in an ornate living room sipping from sherry glasses.

"We might live like that someday, Mary Lynn."

She smiled as she thought about their respective farm houses, both in need of some serious repairs and a fresh coat of paint. She had always imagined life in a little ranch house with central heating and air and maybe a little patch of a backyard with a few trees for children to climb.

"Maybe," she said.

Jackson was a country boy, but there was something about him that made her imagine life beyond Meggett. There was a lot to him, and he had gumption. She was already convinced of that. He wanted to take a big bite out of life, and she thought he just might be able to do it.

As she looked back through the window at the elegant living room with a portrait of some historic figure hanging over the fireplace, he got down on his right knee and opened up a little blue velvet box with a solitaire diamond so small it barely caught the light.

But the light was in him. And she looked at the little ring and then back at him. His eyes twinkled like the chips of water catching the moon's glow on the harbor. Like big chips of stone.

"Marry me, Mary Lynn," he said. "I promise I'll take good care of you. We'll move to Beaufort, you'll go to college, and we'll start all over. Both of us. On a much higher plane this time."

Engaged before high school graduation. Even

by Meggett standards that was young. That was exactly what her mama had hoped to be, engaged her senior year instead of carrying a swollen load in her belly without a man by her side. Her daddy was long gone by then.

Mary Lynn looked down at this lanky mother-less boy, Jackson Scoville, on bended knee. He was in a coat and a tie he'd bought at the Belk's in Walterboro. It must have cost him two weeks' pay. And though he was skinny, his shoulders were broad and he was one of the most handsome boys she had ever laid eyes on. He would fill out well, she knew.

He lived life in Meggett under the radar just like her. He didn't play football because his father needed him on the farm, but he was built and he had something more than that, a mental strength, a will to succeed that was wholly attractive. Any girl from Meggett would have been fortunate to marry him. And she suspected, any girl from any-where would have felt the same.

"Yes," she said before she even knew what she would say. "I'll marry you, Jackson."

He stood, picked her up, and spun her around, and he smelled so good, like Ivory soap and like the earth, like the dark soil in the tilled fields after harvest season, and she kissed him long and hard on the High Battery as the wind gently lifted her long, dark hair and the folds of her yellow dress swayed.

It wasn't until they boarded the international flight at Dulles that she watched him reach in his carry-on bag and then give her a look that was a startling blend of confusion and despair.

He snapped his fingers, then pounded the armrest with a tight fist. "I left the books on the other flight."

She patted his forearm. "I'm sorry, honey. Maybe you could sleep?"

He furrowed his brow and a little puff of air escaped from his full lips.

All it took was a glass of pinot noir with a warm dinner to put Mary Lynn out on an international flight, but she doubted it would work for him. Too many ants in his pants.

And if there was one thing Jackson couldn't stand, it was idle time. Five and a half whole hours of sitting still without educating himself in some form or fashion might send him over the edge.

He motioned to the flight attendant as she walked by.

"Got a copy of the *Times* or the *Wall Street Journal*?" (He had already read both papers that morning, Mary Lynn knew, but a second go round couldn't hurt.)

"I always learn a new word when I read the *New York Times*," he had said back when they lived in Beaufort with barely two pennies to rub together. (He had to justify why he needed to spend a dollar on that Yankee paper every day.)

The flight attendant brought the papers over, and he'd all but devoured them by the time the dinner arrived, beef bourguignon, with a side of asparagus and mashed parsnips. Mary Lynn ate her meal slowly as she sipped her wine. It was not half bad. She kind of liked airplane food. And she kind of liked being forced to sit still.

Just as she was dozing off, he blazed through the papers a second time and started tapping his fingertips on the armrest. Then he unbuckled his seat and peered over to the third row behind them where the girls were seated already draped in blankets, each with their nose in a book and their ears plugged with their little white iPod buds.

Mary Lynn looked back to survey his options. Catherine was reading Proust's *Swann's Way* in French. (She was glad her child had finally put down the SAT cards for a little while.) Jackson planned to major in French next semester, but right now that wouldn't do him any good. He just wasn't that far along. Casey was reading a Nancy Drew mystery, which probably wasn't his cup of tea, but then there was Lilla reading *A Tale of Two Cities*, looking downright engrossed.

He turned to Mary Lynn. "Maybe Lilla will lend me her Dickens for my sanity."

She nodded. "I'm sure she'd be delighted to start her vampire tale."

He nodded, unbuckled, and walked back.

It wasn't until Mary Lynn heard the angry whimpers from Lilla that she turned back. He held up the outer case of *A Tale of Two Cities* and showed Mary Lynn that their middle child had cut out the Dickens novel and replaced it with the pages of *Eclipse*.

Mary Lynn nodded her head in disappointment, though inside she was chuckling a little. How awful could it be to want to read a book so badly?

She could hear about every third word of his reprimand as the air burst from the knob above his seat. Something like "Education . . . appreciate . . . make the most of . . . travel." Then she heard him say, "Well, do you at least have the innards of the Dickens novel somewhere?"

She turned around and watched Lilla rustling through her backpack. In a few moments, she pulled out not the innards of the novel but a thin, bright yellow booklet—CliffsNotes of *A Tale of Two Cities*.

She watched him shake his head and heard just the word "shortcut" in the middle of his hushed but livid rumblings.

His sigh was slow and deep when he crossed Mary Lynn and plunked down next to her again. "After the trip, there will be a consequence."

Mary Lynn nodded. "Well, at least she's reading something."

He looked at her with concern. She knew there

were times when he was disappointed in her; she did not always champion their mission with the same fervor as he did.

Oh well. She was tired. And she just wished he would relax for five minutes.

After the flight attendant dimmed the lights, Mary Lynn went back to kiss the girls good night. She shushed Lilla, who said, "Mama, he's so unbelievably uptight."

"I know." She squeezed her daughter's hand, noticing for the first time the black polish on her nubby nails. She must have painted them sometime between the tea and the flight. "It will be OK." Mary Lynn kissed her daughter's hand and then held her nails up to the light. "Well, you'll fit right in in London."

Lilla cracked a smile. "Pretty punkish, right?"

Her second daughter loved to try on different styles. "Yeah," Mary Lynn said.

After Mary Lynn rubbed Lilla's back for a little while, playing her usual role as good cop, she turned to Catherine and gently pulled a plug out of her ear. "I saw the cough medicine in your bag. Are you feeling all right?"

Catherine cleared her throat and looked up at her mother for quite some time as if she were just remembering where she was. She blinked. "Those were in my bag from the last trip, Mama."

"Oh," she said. "Good. Because I hadn't

remembered giving you any, and you don't seem like you have a cold."

Catherine turned back to her book. She rubbed the smooth surface of the page and then cracked the spine. "I'm fine, but it's nice to have them if someone gets sick."

Mary Lynn bit her lip and studied her eldest daughter, who had already put her earbuds back in and was flipping to the next page in her thick French novel. Then she kissed both of her children on the forehead, leaned back to the next row and kissed Casey too.

When she settled back in her seat, she realized Jackson was fiddling with his fingers. He pulled each of his knuckles until they popped and then he started tap, tap, tapping on the armrest beside her. He would be a nightmare to sit next to for the entire journey, and even the glass of wine from dinner wouldn't lull her to sleep with that tapping. The man needed something to read.

She glanced into her carry-on bag. She had the last two issues of *Southern Living* and *The Message New Testament* from Scottie. She reached in, grabbed the paperback firmly, and without thinking too hard placed it on his knee.

He eyed it suspiciously as if it were something foreign that could possibly pose a threat. He was wary of religion, she knew. More than once he had called God sadistic, and she knew that the wound from losing his mama was still raw after all these years. But as far as she could tell, his theology was a bit off.

After a few moments of eyeing the Bible on his knee, Jackson shrugged his shoulders, slid it out from beneath her hand, and started right in with the introduction. Within a half hour Mary Lynn was dozing off. The last time she looked up he was cranking his way through the gospel of Mark.

She woke up four hours later and he was still reading. He was on his second go round, midway through the book of Acts.

He eyed her. "Have you read this whole thing?"

She yawned and stretched her arms. She felt coated in a kind of thick travel glaze. "I've read the New Testament, but not this translation."

Mary Lynn glanced back to find Casey moving down the aisle toward her. She pulled the girl into her lap for a moment and gave her a tight squeeze. "Look, Mama." Casey pointed to the little airplane icon on the television screen above them. They were just miles away from the Heathrow airport.

Jackson reached over and patted her back gently. "Better go sit back down, sweetheart."

"Daddy?" Casey cocked her head. "Are you reading a Bible?"

He turned to her, his eyes bloodshot but quite alert.

"Why, yes I am, love bug."

She shrugged her shoulders. "Oh."

He lifted his eyebrows. "Have you ever read the Bible?"

"No," she said. "But Mama tells me some of the stories sometimes. Like the boy who ran away and spent his dad's money or the man who was beat up on the side of the road." The child nodded her head. "Those are pretty good."

"Yeah." Jackson turned to Mary Lynn and cocked his head. Then back to Casey. "They are."

The girl nodded and went back to her seat just as the pilot announced that they had started their descent. Mary Lynn pulled her seat up and prepared for a landing as Jackson, eyebrows furrowed, a little drip of perspiration rolling down his cheek, flipped the page before turning back to her. "Since when did you start telling her Bible stories?"

She shrugged. "The last year or so. Since I went to that women's group with Scottie. She likes them. They are good."

He bit his lip and examined a little brown spot on the back of the chair in front of him, maybe a little drip from his coffee or his wine. "I guess." Then he rubbed his chin and turned to her. "We have to be careful about this stuff with our kids. We need to have a united front."

She took his hand. "Jackson, we both grew up going to church, at least every now and then. It did a lot more good than harm, don't you think?"

His eyes moved back and forth as though he were reading from an invisible book right in front of her. Then he looked at her dead on. "Speak for yourself," he said.

Chapter 10

MARY LYNN

As soon as they were settled in their hotel, the Ritz London on Picadilly, Jackson went to the table on his usual side of the bed and opened a drawer.

"No Bible. Humph."

"Guess the Gideons don't go overseas," Mary Lynn said as she started to hang up her dresses. She perked up her ears as he dialed the concierge and asked where the nearest bookstore was.

Then he turned to her and said, "I'll be right back."

"Now wait a minute, honey." What in the world was he up to now?

The girls were taking a nap in the adjoining room. Their first day in London was a jam-packed one. They were scheduled to have tea at the Brown Hotel at four p.m. and then go on to the Barbican where they had tickets to Rachmaninoff's *Piano Concerto No. 3* at seven p.m. Then they had a reservation for after-concert snacks back at the

Ritz. (Jackson was of the mind that the best way to overcome jet lag was to take a little nap and then push on through the first day.)

"You're never going to make it without some sleep." She crawled into bed. "I slept four hours and I'm still exhausted."

He looked at her beneath the silky sheets of the plush bed and then collapsed beside her. He put his arms around her and squeezed. "I've got to read the whole thing start to finish, Mary Lynn. Old Testament and all."

She wondered what his motives were. He seemed more antsy than usual and that was saying something. Was he starting to get into the Bible? Or was he just going to read it all the way through so he could say, "I've read it, and I don't buy it"?

She decided to bite her tongue for now. "All right," she said. "You've got a nice long vacation ahead of you. There's plenty of time."

He nudged his head in the direction of the little paperback *Message* whose cover was already cracked around the corners. Jackson was hard on books. "I mean, I don't believe it. I just need to read it all so I can say I did."

Ah, there it was. He wanted to read it and put it behind him for good. She exhaled deeply. She was tired, and she wished he would open his mind or soften his heart or *something*.

"Do you actually buy this whole thing, Mary Lynn?"

She stared into his large green eyes and thought of her healed calf and the burning in her chest at the Christmas Eve service just a few days before. She nodded slowly. "I think I do, Jackson."

He tucked a stray strand of her mahogany hair behind her ears. He squinted his eyes as if she were a mystery. As if there were much more to her than met the eye. As if he hadn't spent nearly every day of his life with her since he was seventeen years old.

She loved him, but she wished he wasn't so hard in so many places. She kissed his forehead. "Get some sleep." He fell back into the pillow on his side of the bed and within minutes he was, at last, snoring.

The next day after breakfast they trekked seven long city blocks to a church bookstore where he bought a paperback *New King James Version* of the Bible. He put it in his backpack and they made their way over to the Tate Museum.

After a slow tour of the Tate galleries, lunch at Harrods, and then an afternoon at the Tower of London, they collapsed and ordered room service. The girls were giddy and exhausted, fighting over which part of the city they should shop in tomorrow. (Jackson had promised them a little afternoon spree after they toured Westminster Abbey and Big Ben.) Then the shopping debate somehow morphed into a pillow fight where

Catherine's reading glasses were knocked off the bed and crunched by Casey, who dismounted quickly as Lilla came after her with a big silk sham.

Catherine started to cry, her left hand trembling like a leaf. "Oh no!" She plunked down on the floor and buried her head in her hands. Big tear drops were falling down her cheeks and the sight made Casey cry. "I'm sorry, Cat. I'm really sorry."

Jackson and Mary Lynn looked at one another and back to Catherine. Clearly she was over-reacting. Lilla furrowed her brow and bent down toward her older sister. "Get a grip. Get a grip!"

"It's okay," Jackson said as he strode over and took her trembling hand in his. Mary Lynn came behind Catherine and rubbed her back while Lilla consoled Casey in the only way she knew how, by rubbing the top of her head and saying, "It's not a big deal."

Mary Lynn watched Jackson as he gently rubbed their eldest daughter's hands. She had been under too much stress. Something made Mary Lynn's stomach churn. Was Catherine all right? Had they been too hard on her? Why would she fall apart over this small thing—didn't she know it could be solved in a matter of hours?

"Cat," Jackson said gently. He looked up to Mary Lynn and back to their daughter. Mary Lynn was hoping that he was thinking what she was thinking. When the girl finally caught her breath and opened her eyes, he rubbed her tear-streaked cheek and said, "I bet they have a store somewhere in London where we can get glasses."

Catherine wiped her face with the heels of her trembling hands and Mary Lynn handed her a Kleenex. She blew hard and then looked back and forth between her parents. "Really?"

"Sure," he said. "We'll get your prescription and get you a new pair tomorrow."

She breathed through her nose and nodded. "Okay. Thanks."

"Of course," he said. "No need to get so upset, baby. You know we'll take care of you."

Catherine nodded and Jackson released her hand and went over to check on Casey. Mary Lynn just held Catherine tight from behind and rocked her back and forth. "It's all right, sweetie. It's no big deal. Be at peace."

Catherine turned to her and her green eyes filled with tears again. "Yes, ma'am," she said. "I'll try."

Mary Lynn held her tight until she finally settled down.

Once the tears were dry, Jackson stood up and said, "C'mon, girls! We're on vacation. Let's have some fun!" Then he ordered popcorn, candy bars, ginger ale, and a movie, *Because of Winn-Dixie*— it had to be something Casey would like and she had recently finished the book and was missing

Mac already. They all settled on the bed and watched it together. Catherine's shoulders finally seemed to relax as she lay there on the bed, cuddled between her two sisters. Mary Lynn hoped that their oldest child would find a way to relax.

When Mary Lynn tucked the girls into their adjoining room, she came back to find Jackson at the desk by the window reading Genesis. She wanted to talk to him about Catherine, but she didn't want him to break stride. What Catherine needed, what they all needed, was the message that book had to offer.

Penetrate his heart and mind, she prayed. She curled up with her *Southern Living* and fell asleep.

The day after that they hopped in a limousine bound for Stratford-Upon-Avon as Jackson read Isaiah. By this point he had read more of the Bible in three days than she had in the two years she'd been going to the women's group with Scottie.

They took a tour of Shakespeare's home town and went to see an evening performance of *Much Ado About Nothing* and then the next day, an afternoon performance of *Romeo and Juliet* with a fairly graphic stab scene that upset Casey so much that Jackson walked her out of the theater before the end.

He was consoling her across the cobblestone

street at a coffee house when Mary Lynn and the other two girls found them after the performance.

"That was scary." Casey looked up at Mary Lynn. "I mean, what was it even rated?"

They all chuckled. Casey was sensitive, and she did not like to be scared. Even high culture could be frightening.

"I'm sorry," Jackson said. He rubbed his little girl's back. "It's my fault. I was just so excited for you to see it. I forgot how brutal it was."

They took a train to Hampshire the next morning where a limousine from the Four Seasons Hotel picked them up at the station. The hotel was actually an old English manor on a rocky coastline with ten guest rooms, and they had a whole wing of the house to themselves overlooking a snowy hillside and a blue-green lake. There was an award-winning spa, twenty acres of stunning English gardens, and at night you dressed for dinner in formal clothing and sat at a long table with other guests for a delectable five-course meal.

Jackson kept reading his Bible. He often clenched his right fist when he read, which didn't seem like a very good sign to Mary Lynn. They had passed many a bookstore by now, but he didn't bother picking up another copy of Chaucer or Defoe or Shakespeare. He'd gotten through the Old Testament once and was heading back into the

New. He wanted to read it all in order. From Adam and Eve to the book of Revelation.

The second morning in Hampshire, the girls took off for a riding lesson and Mary Lynn and Jackson made their way down to the spa for a morning of treatments.

After Mary Lynn's facial and her hot stone massage, she sat down by the hearth lounge area with a glass of Perrier and *The Message* Jackson had given back to her now that he was onto his *New King James*. It was kind of chilly in the spa, which was a part of the original castle, so she pulled her robe tight and put a heavy blanket over her legs. She was reading the book of John, the opening where it said, "In the beginning was the word and the word was God and the word was with God" when it occurred to her. The Word, the Bible, was God. She held the soft book in her hands. It was bigger than Jackson and his hardened heart. She knew she should just keep quiet and trust.

She was fanning herself when Jackson burst into the lounge in one of the spa's white bathrobes and disposable flip-flops, waving the heavy Bible with his large hands. His eyes were bloodshot and grave. "This can't be true, Mary Lynn. It can't be." He put the book on the table between them. "The people are crazy in this book and God is all over the place! One century He's wiping wicked people off the face of the earth and the next

He's bringing the dead back to life and canceling the record of their wrongs. Who can go for all of this?"

He stood and paced back and forth as one of the attendants peeked in and asked if he'd like a Perrier.

"No, thank you," he said gruffly.

He was angst-ridden as though he was fighting something. As though a monster was in the cage of his chest, and he didn't know how to release it.

He pulled his BlackBerry from his pocket, looked up the St. Michael's website, and e-mailed Roy Summerall a note tagged as high importance. When he didn't hear back from him in the next twenty minutes, he scrolled through his Downtown Neighborhood Association contacts, found Roy's home number, and called it.

"It's four thirty in the morning in Charleston." Mary Lynn made a swipe at the phone, but he was too quick for her. "Call him this afternoon," she pleaded.

Someone must have picked up the phone because Jackson leaned forward and said, "Hi, Reverend. This is Jackson Scoville. Sorry to call so early. I'm in England, but I get home day after tomorrow. I've been reading this Bible and I can't stand it. When can you meet with me?"

There was a pause.

"I get home Sunday at five p.m."

Another pause. Jackson cleared his throat and

then picked at a loose string on his spa robe for a moment.

"Okay. Thank you. Sorry to wake you."

He clicked his phone off and looked up at Mary Lynn. "I have a meeting with him first thing Monday morning."

That was his first day back at the College of Charleston, and he had two morning classes. "What about school?"

"I'll skip it."

"Okay." Trust and wait, she said to herself. That was all she could do. She lifted her glass again, but remembered it was empty.

As if on cue, the attendant poked her head back in to check on them. Mary Lynn showed her the empty glass. "I'd love another."

Chapter 11

CATHERINE

Catherine and her sisters nearly collapsed into Carlos's van at the airport. They had been delayed in Dulles three extra hours because of a snowstorm, and everyone (with the exception of her father, who kept writing fast and furiously on his yellow legal pad) was exhausted. It was the fourth of January, but it was an unseasonably temperate Charleston evening in the midsixties, and the soft, thick air she took in from her brief walk from the airport to the van reminded her of Meggett and the farm where her mama grew up. It was as comforting as a well-worn blanket.

The family trip had beat expectations. She studied some, but she didn't stress too badly, and she loved the plays at Stratford, especially *Romeo and Juliet*, and the horseback riding in Hampshire. She had even gone for a long run two days in a row around the castle resort, her legs pounding on the green mossy trails that led her down to the rocky coastline. Her favorite part about running was feeling her heart pumping. It resounded in her ears. It was pure, and if there was a God out there, she felt closest to Him when her heart pumped hard, when the fresh air filled her nostrils, when her arms and legs pumped and pumped as she reached a destination much faster than she anticipated, flying beyond it over the next curve in the road and continuing on. She had slept soundly all three nights in Hampshire, which was a good thing because she was out of the dex by then.

But now it was back to reality, she thought as she felt for the St. Christopher around her neck. She hadn't taken it off during the whole trip, and she sensed somehow that maybe the baby on the man's shoulder, the Christ, had protected her not only on her travels but from the anxiety that often overtook her mind. He was heavy with the weight of the world, why not let Him take hers too? The SAT was just two short months away and her dad would be grilling her good between now and then. Plus there was a violin recital in a few weeks, and she still had a major Mozart sonata to learn.

Now Casey rested her little dark head on Catherine's shoulder and sighed. Catherine knew just how she felt—weary—and she rubbed the crown of her sister's head gently as the van pulled out of the airport and headed toward the peninsula.

Catherine woke from her doze when Carlos pounded on the brakes by Colonial Lake near their home. Someone was racing across the intersection in the dark, pumping their arms and legs briskly as if it were the end of a race, and Catherine recognized him immediately: Bryan Christiansen. He'd probably spent all holiday running, preparing for the spring track season. He was a senior and had already received a cross country scholarship to the University of North Carolina, but he was never satisfied with his performance in cross country or track.

Catherine felt the medallion around her neck. "Can you pull over, Carlos?" she asked. Then she rolled down the window and called out, "Bryan! Wait up." He slowed down on the other side of the road and looked back.

"I'm going to go say hi to him, okay?"

Her dad was busy looking at his notes. He

looked up at Bryan and back to Catherine. "I don't know . . ."

Catherine's mom squeezed her dad's forearm. "It's her friend, honey. We're two blocks from home."

"Catherine has *several* friends," Lilla said, opening her eyes long enough to roll them good before shutting them again.

"Okay," her dad said. "Have him walk you home, all right, Cat?"

"All right." She bolted out of the car realizing she was icky to the core and in serious need of a shower, but she just had to say hi.

He waited for a moment and she came running over toward him. Out of the corner of her eye, she watched Carlos drive on.

"Hey," he said. "What's up?"

"Just got back from our trip." She nodded toward the van as it crossed slowly over Broad Street.

"How was England?" She detected the slightest sarcasm in his voice.

"Nice," she said, staring him down until he had to look at her. "I had one of the best runs ever in this place called Hampshire. It's really green and has this rocky coastline."

He was catching his breath. His nostrils flared. He softened as he met her gaze and smiled. She noticed his St. Christopher medallion resting in the center of his neck, catching the light from the street lamp.

"You would love it," she said.

He put his hands behind his head. "Let's walk, Scoville."

"Okay," she said as they headed around Colonial Lake. Bryan was lanky and a good foot taller than Catherine, but even though he was thin and tall, he was also strong. The muscles in his legs were more defined than any she'd ever seen and she remembered what Alyssa said one day as they watched him racing across Calhoun Street. "No one has better legs than Bryan Christiansen."

She looked up at him as they walked. He had a look of concentration on his face as he inhaled and exhaled. "So . . . getting ready for the season?"

"Trying to," he said. Then he turned away to spit in the opposite direction before turning back and looking down at her. "Not that we'll win."

Ouch. She bit her lip.

"Any change from your old man?" he asked.

"No." She shook her head. She made one of those vows kids make when they know their parents have made a poor choice. "I'll never keep my kid from their sport."

He reached over and squeezed her shoulder for just a moment, then returned it to behind his head. "I know you won't."

They walked around and around the lake, then over toward the High Battery. At the coast guard station she looked down at her jeans and her running shoes and back at him. "Wanna race to White Point Gardens?"

He turned to her, the light from the moon now catching his dark eyes. He stretched his shoulders and grinned. "Yeah."

She did a few quick calf stretches, patted his back, and said, "Go!" She zoomed past him along the sidewalk that traced the water's edge.

"Hey," he called and caught up within seconds. "Nice," then he whizzed past, slowing after a few blocks so that they both touched the edge of the park at the same time.

"Not bad," he said as he squeezed her shoulder and walked her over toward the water fountain with the sculpture of the little angel girl. They both took a sip, and as Catherine looked around the park at a homeless man settling into a bench she remembered being there with Tres the night before she left for England.

As they climbed up on an old cannon, taking in the water and a few sailboats bobbing beneath the moonlight, he turned to her. "Listen," he said. "The junior/senior is coming up."

She looked up at him and smiled. With Christmas and preparing for the SAT test, she had completely forgotten about the Peninsula Day School prom. Well, almost forgotten.

He blinked back the sweat dripping down his eyelid and looked her in the eye. "I'd really like to take you."

She thought of Tres King just a block away. They weren't dating officially or anything. He would probably be angry, but then again there was a line of girls who would want to go with him. And he had left her alone at homecoming fending for herself.

"Yes," she said. "I'd really like for you to take me." She took his hand for a minute. It was warm and she could almost feel the pulse. She had only really kissed one guy in her life and that was Otto Finley, who had taken her to the prom in ninth grade before he moved to Atlanta. She had never done anything so forward—taking a guy's hand in her own—ever. Maybe it was *Romeo and Juliet* getting to her or maybe it was the high from the run or the familiarity of the soft, warm night. She held his hand tight, and he seemed to appreciate it as he smiled and squeezed back hard before leaning over and kissing her tenderly on the cheek.

"Are you going to be able to stand seeing my dad when you pick me up?"

He put his other hand on top of hers in a way that was both tender and reassuring. "For a date with you, Catherine, I'd endure a lot more than that."

She smiled and could feel her cheeks redden. He looked out at the water for a minute and then back to her. His face was serious but a good kind of serious. There was a lot to Bryan Christiansen, and she respected him more than any other kid at school. He was his own man, really—a runner, a

137

health nut, a focused student, someone who had no interest in drinking or pharming and now that she remembered, he was someone with a faith. She had heard about him being a counselor at Camp St. Christopher, the Episcopal camp on Seabrook Island, and once Alyssa had told her she'd heard that he gave his testimony to a group of kids there and that he had a real story—a kind of shocking story—that had brought him to God. She wondered as she looked at him. She wondered what his story was.

"Speaking of your dad." He squeezed her hand again. "I better walk you home."

They climbed down from the cannon, and this time he reached out to take her hand in his as they crossed through the park and over King Street toward her home on South Battery.

"See you at the school house in a few days," he said as they stood on the threshold of the piazza privacy door. He squeezed her hand tight and then gently released it.

"Okay," she said, trying to hold back a full grin as he turned and walked down the sidewalk back toward Colonial Lake where he must have parked his car.

She didn't tell anyone about her invitation to the prom that night. Her dad was busy writing on his yellow pad and her mama was helping every-one unpack the essentials so they could take showers and hit the hay. Once the house was bedded down, Lilla came tiptoeing into her room with two texts from Tres, but Catherine decided not to answer them. She put on her pajamas, shoved the flash cards under her bed, and lay down on a pile of soft pillows. It was good to be home.

She felt for the little medallion around her neck. She rubbed her thumb over the words "Protect us." Catherine wanted to be protected. And she wanted to find peace. She was ready for a new year and a new beginning with no more stress, no more sleeping pills, no more of the stomach churning. She closed her eyes as the moonlight poured through the slats of the shades in the window at the head of her bed. The thought of God kept coming back to her. She didn't know how to pray, but how hard could it be?

"Help me," she whispered. "If you're out there. Help me and protect me this year."

Chapter 12

JACKSON

Jackson leapt out of bed. He decided to skip his morning walk to Caviar & Bananas, and he dressed without asking Mary Lynn or Anarosa to iron his shirt.

Mary Lynn was on the porch stretching before her jog. He paused on the doorway to admire her as she pushed against the piazza railing and stretched back her calf. Jackson was a lucky man, and he knew it. Not only was his wife beautiful, but she had a kind heart. And she gave him enough room to be him.

"Off to wrangle with the Reverend." He leaned down, gave her a kiss, and repositioned the little stack against his hip that included *The Message*, the *New King James*, and a legal pad on which he'd been writing questions during the entire flight home.

Mary Lynn wrinkled her brow. He knew he sounded a little cavalier, and that tone never sat too well with her—another reason he loved her. She could settle him down without so much as a word. Kind of like his mama used to when he was a kid and getting a little rowdy at the dinner table. Plus, Mary Lynn liked that priest and his family, and she was also warming up to the whole God thing—she was a softy that way, his sweet girl. But now that he had faced this whole subject of God for the first time as an adult and taken the time to read the Bible, he could say once and for all that he had given it a good look, he had heard God out, and it was time to move on. Time to get back on track with the mission statement. Something like this could derail the mission for good, and he could never let that happen.

"Hope it"—Mary Lynn looked at his notebook and back to him—"goes well."

He leaned down and kissed her forehead. "Don't worry, Mary Lynn. I won't be too hard on the fellow. Just want to say my piece and put this thing behind me."

She walked him to the piazza, and he could almost feel her eyes on him as he walked briskly down South Battery, then hung a left on Meeting Street toward St. Michael's church.

Oh, he had some good questions. Some stumpers. He was kind of looking forward to the priest talking his way through these, he had to admit it. He looked down at his notebook and recalled a few:

1. If God is good and all powerful, why is there needless suffering and violence in the world? Either God is not good or not all powerful, or worse, lacking in compassion.
2. Why does the mention of Jesus upset people? Every time it is on my tongue, I feel uncomfortable to the core.
3. Why are so many Christians cruel and judgmental?
4. Why do so many professing Christians turn a blind-eye to the suffering in the world?
5. I now see the Old Testament prophecies and how they were fulfilled in Christ, but why are we all still here two thousand years later? What's the hold-up with this second coming?

● ● ●

It was a sunny January day. Still a little cool this morning, but with the sun at Jackson's back as he walked down the pristine Meeting Street South of Broad, he was starting to warm up. He had a spring in his step. Jet lag didn't set him back too much this time. He was full of energy and ready to start 2010 off right. There were the French and music courses he would be tackling at the college. He needed to deal with some business on the board at Mark Waters Development—a shopping center on Daniel Island had more vacancies than stores and a high-end set of condos in mid-town was hardly selling at all. The banks were getting antsy and they'd have to raise the interest on the loans unless Waters forked over some serious kind of guarantee—maybe a few pieces of commercial property on John's Island to settle them down. Jackson wasn't worried. He and Waters had done very well in the ten years leading up to the recession. They could take a big hit, even a couple of big hits, without breaking stride.

As he walked with the sun on his back, he relished the usual cacophony of hammers and drills and leaf blowers that filled his ears like a kind of post-modern symphony. People took pride in their homes in this historic and exclusive part of town and maintenance was noisy, wonderfully so. Nothing like the calendar flipping to a new year to make you want to give the house a fresh coat of paint or relandscape the garden. Beauty didn't exist without effort. And in the case of South of Broad where most of the houses were over two hundred years old, a lot of effort was required.

A young woman in a jogging suit whizzed past him and he thought of Catherine and how much he enjoyed watching her run cross country, her hair whipping behind her, her strong legs pounding the ground. She reminded him of his mother who had lost the battle to breast cancer when he was nine years old, leaving him and his dad to fend for themselves. She was a runner too. Not in any competitive way but just for fun. She'd loved running up and down the tomato fields, loved to chase him and tackle him. She was strong and healthy, and he could remember her lifting him high above her head after one of their mother/son races on the dirt road that led to their house before she got sick.

He didn't like keeping Catherine from running competitively, but he didn't see how the mission could be achieved any other way. She needed a serious incentive to raise her SAT score. She was bright—not much of a test taker—but smart and savvy. With a little more work she could get in a higher percentile. If they could just raise it two hundred more points, a whole host of colleges would be open to her. And while he had only attended a technical college until he made enough to go back to the College of Charleston, he knew that a degree from an exceptional institution usually led to a graduate degree from an even better one, and he wanted that for her. He wanted it for all of his girls.

Catherine was a sensitive one. He could tell she was worried about the upcoming test. She was also worried about letting Coach Christiansen down—and that son of hers—but you couldn't please everyone if you were going to reach your goal. As he nodded to a fellow member of the symphony board who was cruising by in a new sports car, Jackson recalled Catherine's fourth-grade spelling bee and how she threw up on his shoes when he went backstage to wish her luck and to remind her that *monosyllabic* had two l's.

Pressure was good for Jackson. He performed under pressure. He remembered how his dad wouldn't let him crack a book until he'd harvested as many tomatoes as his crew of migrant workers. But pressure didn't always seem to work as well with his girls, or Mary Lynn for that matter.

As the young woman raced ahead hanging a left onto Lamboll Street, he thought about Catherine racing out of the car last night to see her teammate Bryan. Seeing her standing with him beneath the street lamp by Colonial Lake, the thought had occurred to Jackson that his eldest daughter was no longer a child. It would be a short year and a half before she was out of the nest and off at college. He had to do everything in his power to give her a strong lift-off, even if it meant tough love.

Now he spotted Father Roy Summerall a few blocks ahead. The hefty priest was coming out of the rectory, crossing over the alley and heading toward the church. He stopped to talk to a sweet-grass weaver on the street. Then he gave the elderly woman a hug. Next he stopped under the portico of the church and did a kind of double take before heading into the sanctuary's narthex.

Jackson was near the rectory at this point and he decided to walk slowly. Somehow, he was curious about this priest. He had always closely observed men of the cloth with a strange blend of awe and skepticism. *Why?* he thought for a minute. Then, before he could stop it, he felt the shadow of the preacher standing on the dock next to him the afternoon they laid his mama in the ground beneath the largest live oak tree on the property.

Jackson watched Father Roy come out of the narthex and make his way onto the portico with a disheveled-looking man leaning on his arm. He recognized the man. It was one of the homeless guys who slept in White Point Gardens from time to time. Once, last summer, when the guy stopped to sit on the Scovilles' front stoop on a hot summer day, Jackson had come upon him on his way home from his morning walk to the café with Mac and had said in a firm tone, "Can I help you?"

The man had opened his eyes slowly and

stared into Jackson's in what appeared to be a half stupor. Then he had stood, turned slowly, and shuffled back to the park as Mac tugged on the leash and barked.

"This is the coldest corner of the city, Edgar." Father Roy was pointing toward the signs that said Meeting and Broad Street where his church stood. He stepped out into the cross lane and hailed a cab. Then Jackson watched as Roy patted the man's back and said, "Better get on over to the shelter for a hot breakfast and a shower, man."

The man turned to the priest and nodded slowly. Then the priest helped him into the car before pulling out his wallet to give the driver a few bills. The priest knocked on the window and hollered, "Sunday evening service—bring your friends. Free pizza dinner afterward."

The homeless man, still glassy-eyed and shivery, attempted to look up. He gave the priest an unenthusiastic nod.

"Bless you, brother." Father Roy tapped the glass, then waved as the car drove down Meeting Street headed toward the Cooper River bridge.

Jackson hung back and Roy never noticed him but turned down Broad Street and headed to the church office building that was just behind the sanctuary. A minute later Jackson pushed through the church office door and the receptionist pointed up the stairs to the rector's office.

"Happy new year, Jackson." Father Roy shook his hand vigorously in a hallway of offices on the second floor. Between Jackson's height and Roy's width, they nearly filled up the narrow space.

"Same to you." Jackson nodded, drawing back his shoulders in a posture that he hoped communicated, *This meeting will be all business.*

"Come on in." The priest nodded toward the door at the end of the hall with the large square glass pane.

"All right." Jackson strode into the room and took a seat on the light brown herringbone couch opposite Roy's desk.

Jackson looked around the room. He scanned the bookshelves—the Bibles, the lectionaries, the theological books with names like Chesterton and Lewis and Barclay on their spines. He made note of the brightly painted cross and the framed pictures of Roy, his wife, and his daughter at the top of the steeple on what looked to be Roy's wedding day. Must have been a second marriage for him. *Hmph,* Jackson thought. On the window sill there was large wire sculpture by a local artist Jackson recognized. It was of a woman reaching out to touch the hem of a man's robe.

As Jackson took in the sculpture he could feel Roy smiling at him. He quickly turned back, repositioned his stack of books, and pulled his notebook out. "I apologize for calling you so early the other day."

Roy gave a good-natured shrug. "It's fine. Anne and I were just so glad it wasn't bad news."

Jackson furrowed his brow. "I suppose you have to deal with a lot of bad news in your line of work."

"Not always," said Roy, "but sometimes." The priest rubbed his thick hands on his khaki pants and leaned forward in his seat. "The flip side is that I get to deal with the best news in the world."

Jackson couldn't help but smirk and then he raised his dark eyebrows. He looked up and into the priest's face. "Well." He picked up the Bible he bought on his trip and shook it once. "I don't know about that."

Father Roy nodded. Then he sort of leaned back in his chair as if to say, *I'll give you a wide berth, if you need one, boy.* The priest tugged at his stiff white collar, which looked a little snug for a man his size. "Tell me what's on your mind, Jackson."

Jackson looked down at the Bible. He raked his hand through his salt-and-pepper hair.

"I've been reading this"—he held up the book and set it back down—"for the last week or so." He tapped his fingers on his thigh and was surprised by how clammy his hands felt. "And I gotta tell you, it doesn't jive with my experience or the God I've always heard about."

Father Roy nodded. He sat back and crossed his ankle over his knee. "Tell me what you mean by that."

Jackson shook his head. "Truth is, Father Summerall, I've never had any use for God. Gotten along just fine without Him." He looked up at the priest who tugged on his collar again. "No offense, of course."

"Go on," Father Roy said.

Jackson swallowed and he felt his ears pop. His energy had evaporated and he was suddenly feeling the jet lag. He shook his head and returned the priest's gaze. "I've worked hard, Reverend, I've stayed out of God's way and expected Him to stay out of mine."

The priest repositioned himself and his chair made a little squeak. "Why?" he asked. "Why do you want Him to stay out of your way?"

Jackson rubbed his clammy hands on the knees of his tweed pants. "Because I'd rather be on my own." Then he looked at the window and back to the man's eyes. "And I've never thought He could be trusted."

Father Roy inhaled deeply. He nodded slowly and rubbed his chin. "Go on."

Jackson thumped the Bible beside him. "So I've read this book. It's a crazy read. Stubborn people, a tough God who gets softer as it goes along. There's some crazy, graphic stuff in here."

The priest chuckled and made a little tent with his thick hands. "Yeah, it's something. Anyone who claims the Bible is boring sure hasn't read it, right?"

"The people are just rotten for the most part," Jackson said. "And God goes back and forth from chastening them to forgiving them and then He goes supersoft in the end when Jesus arrives on the scene." He scratched his fresh-shaven chin. "It just doesn't ring true, Reverend." He looked around the room and his eyes settled on the sculpture that the morning sunlight was now filtering through so that it left a shadow on the carpet beside the priest's desk. "And it doesn't compute with the world I see around me." Jackson looked up again. "Even the world of the church-goers."

Father Roy rolled his shoulder forward. Jackson knew he had played a little pro football and wondered if he had an old injury. A great but brutal sport. "Describe the world around you," the priest said as he winced a little.

Jackson rubbed his hands together and leaned forward. This was a subject he'd thought long and hard about. He was catching a second wind now, and he was not afraid to speak his mind to a man of the cloth. "The world is dangerous and unpredictable." He licked his lips. "But the more resources you have, the more control you have. The more education you have, the more control you have. And the more exposure to the mental and emotional luxuries of this life—the arts, music, poetry—you have, the more sane you'll stay and the better off you'll be."

The priest leaned back in his chair. Again, it

made a small squeak compared to the bulk of his weight. He brought both of his index fingers to his mouth, and Jackson had the eerie feeling that the man was praying for him. Then the priest cocked his head and spoke gently. "So, why do you think you're here, Jackson?"

Jackson narrowed his eyes. Was this a trick question? "Here in this office?"

"No." The priest shook his head. "Here on earth. Why do you think Jackson Scoville exists?"

Wait a minute. That was his question. *What are we all doing here?* Jackson sucked his teeth. He picked a piece of lint off of his tweed jacket and wondered how to answer the question. He looked at the colorful cross and again at the statue on the window sill and then back to the priest. He could feel his temples pulse. He was rankled for some reason, and he had the sudden urge to go bolting out of the office and down the stairs and out onto the street. He breathed in slowly. "I don't know why I'm here, but I know dern well what I'm going to do while I'm here."

"What's that?" The Reverend made eye contact and kept it.

Jackson leaned forward and curled his right hand into a fist. "I'm going to do right by my three girls. I'm going to take what we have and hope it takes us far enough. Hope that it leaves them in a better place for their kids and the ones after that." He didn't want to offend the priest, but it was crucial for him speak his mind. "Mary Lynn and I both grew up with little—little education, little exposure. Now we've got the chance to change all of that for them." He released the fist and rubbed his forehead, which also felt clammy. Had he picked up some germ on the flight home? He looked up at the priest. "That's why I'm here. To protect them and give them a better life."

Father Roy cleared his throat and leaned forward. He was only a few inches away from Jackson, who was also leaning forward. He said in a tone that was both gentle and firm, "So what about when it's all over? Your life and theirs. If you're lucky, you've got ninety years or so, and so do they. Is that all there is?"

Jackson felt the shadow of the pastor on the dock, the way he had put his hand on the young boy's shoulder nearly thirty-five years ago. He could still smell the dark, pungent earth his father and his crew had dug. A wave of fury came over him, and he tried to keep it in check.

He blinked, then he looked up and met Father Summerall's gaze. "So what are you going to tell me, Reverend? That there is life after this? That the book of Revelation is true and not some psychedelic dream John—or whoever the heck he is—had on that island of prisoners, and that we're all going to be circling around God's throne singing His praises?" He scoffed. "You really believe that?"

The priest exhaled. He rubbed his palms together and Jackson sensed his concern and his desire to shoot straight. He sat back in his chair, narrowed his eyes, and Jackson stared back at him. "Jackson, I believe that this life is a shadow of the world to come." Father Roy's words were both clear and measured. "I believe that all of the pain and suffering of this life will be restored and returned and reversed. I believe that new life starts right here through faith in Jesus. If I didn't believe that, I wouldn't be here, Jackson. There'd be no point." He looked to his desk and thumped his own well-worn Bible. "St. Paul said in his first letter to the Corinthians, 'If in this life only we have hope in Christ, we are of all men the most pitiable.' And what he meant was that this life is just the first page of the prologue or the first bite of the appetizer."

Jackson squinted. He could feel his face redden and he shook his head. He felt like he did last year when he came down with the flu. "It's crazy," he said. "To work hard, to do right by your kids. That's all there is for me." He stood up. It wasn't even a conscious decision. He was just on his feet towering above the priest. He couldn't do this anymore. This conversation was over. He didn't want to go over his questions. He just wanted to get out of this building.

He must have caught the Reverend off guard because he back-pedaled in his chair for a moment and finally got to his feet. Jackson held out his hand and said, "Thank you for your time. I've got a class to get to at the college." The priest shook his hand hard.

"Hold on." Father Roy walked over to his bookshelf, pulled out *The Everlasting Man* by G. K. Chesterton, *Mere Christianity* by C. S. Lewis, *The Reason for God* by Timothy Keller, and *The Case for Christ* by Lee Strobel.

He handed them to Jackson. "Read a little more if you're so inclined," he said. "A book can't hurt, right? And you seem like you've got a mind that's not afraid to wrestle. Call me if you ever want to talk some more."

Jackson looked at the books. He didn't want to read them. He was getting ready to major in French and music. He had to convince two national banks that he and Waters would make good on their loans. He had to get a daughter into a fine college. There was no time for this. How pitiful, Jackson thought as the priest held out the stack. However, something in him—maybe it was some sort of politeness his mama had instilled in him—wouldn't let him refuse. He took the stack, added it to his own, and strode out of the office.

As he crossed the street he looked back up at the church building. He could see the metal sculpture and beyond that Father Roy kneeling now at the little stool on the other side of his desk. He set his jaw, then turned and strode with one foot in front of the other to the corner where he took a left on Meeting, and before he arrived home he had recalled much of the summer between third and fourth grade, the summer his mama had died.

He could see her refusing to eat or drink except for the ice chips Aunt Hilda crushed in a kitchen towel with one of his daddy's hammers. He could envision Aunt Hilda gently guiding them to her mouth with a long teaspoon.

Only once did his mama rise from the bed that he and Aunt Hilda had dragged into the den the day his daddy drove to the Medical University Hospital in Charleston to pick her up. It was toward his bedtime, and he was sitting in his room playing with the battery-operated train set his aunt had brought him when she first arrived three months before.

He remembered noticing the hall light through his mama's well-worn nightgown as she stood in the door and watched him play. And then, how unusually thin her legs looked—like two sticks from his Tinker Toys joined by a circular disc.

They were no longer the full, sturdy legs of the mama who had sat him on her lap not so long ago to read *Swiss Family Robinson* or their favorite, *Robinson Crusoe*. They were not the same legs who chased him down the dirt road when he raced out toward Highway 17 on the afternoon of his fifth birthday to see if his present, a rock polishing kit, had been delivered to their mailbox on the other side of the road. He had not been allowed to cross the highway on his own, and she had spanked him good that day. Then she had carried him back over her shoulder like a sack of potatoes trying hard not to swing him playfully or kiss his dangling arm too many times to show her relief.

"Hey there, conductor." She had tried to grin, but he remembered it looked more like a wince.

"Hi, Mama." He looked down at the engine and flipped the switch. The grinding motor slowed to a stop.

She moved slowly and carefully across the room toward his single bed and with effort pulled back the covers. He stood, stretched, then climbed beneath the covers. She pulled the sheets up to his chin, then she lay down beside him, resting her arm across his chest the way she did most every night before she got sick. He was almost ten, he could whittle a spear head from a long stick with his pocket knife, and he had even shot one of the raccoons that kept nibbling on her special patch of heirloom tomatoes with his Crosman 764 BB gun, but he still liked the feel of his mama lying down beside him at bedtime.

He remembered wishing she would read to him or say the Lord's Prayer like she usually did, but she had fallen asleep almost instantly. She had not even turned out the bedside lamp. It must have been tough for her to muster the strength to walk to his room.

Then, he took hold of her forearm. It wasn't the usual weight anymore, but it was enough. It was his mama in the flesh, and though no one had spelled out what was to come, he knew he needed to hold on tight.

The next morning she was back in her bed in the den where she refused the ice chips all that day and the day after and the day after that. The preacher came with the Eucharist and went. The neighbors came with casseroles and went. His third-grade teacher came with a bowl of banana pudding, embraced him, and went. He ate the pudding and the casseroles piled high in the freezer night after night. The casseroles all had chicken and were held together with mayonnaise and soups, but he recalled—even now—that all he really wanted was Mama's summer burgers, fried in a pan and topped with cheddar cheese and a thinly sliced heirloom.

School was out, and he had a lot of free time. He skipped rocks on the water. He tied chicken necks to a rope and caught some blue crabs in the tidal creek. He climbed the oak and pine trees around his house. He lit a match and set fire to a tick crawling on the cement slab where his aunt's jade green Oldsmobile was parked. He spent two weeks building a fort deep in the woods across the highway until his daddy went looking for the ax, found the fort, and told him to tear it down. That property wasn't theirs.

One day when he was digging in the dirt beside the creek, he found an arrowhead that was intact except for the smallest chip off the very tip. He washed it off in the murky water. It fit just right in the palm of his hand. Then he raced back to the house and brought it into the den where he held it up before her.

She couldn't speak by that point except through her pale green eyes. They softened when she saw him. They said what he wanted to hear: "Good for you, son. Good for you, my boy." And he squeezed the arrowhead tight before laying it down on the table beside her bed.

Every few nights he'd set up the train set at just the same time—a quarter 'til eight—and flip on the switch. As the engine made its way round and round the track, he'd wait for her to come, to alight in his doorway and grin and call him the conductor. He'd stay awhile that way on his knees, eyes on the engine and ears attuned to every creak in the old clapboard house, until the clock struck nine and Daddy or Aunt Hilda realized that he was still up.

"Lights out, Jackson," Daddy would call.

"Yes, sir."

Her funeral was on a Thursday in late July. His daddy and some of the migrant workers dug a grave by the tidal creek beneath the largest live oak tree. The service was by the hole in the earth and he could still smell the soil, almost sweet, almost reassuring.

The preacher read from a black book with gold-lined pages. His voice was warbly like a bunting and he kept scratching the back of his neck. The neighbors swatted away the mosquitoes and rubbed their sweaty heads with their handkerchiefs as a faint breeze made its way across the marsh toward them. When the breeze died, the no-see-ums started to buzz around his ears so bad he had to cup his hands over them.

He remembered, even now decades later, looking up at his daddy standing tall beside him. He noticed that his old man didn't swat at anything, though surely plenty of insects were biting. Instead, the towering man set his jaw and his eyes took on the same fierceness they had the afternoon he dug the hole with his crew. Not a pure fierceness but a gritty, bitter one. As if grit and anger were the only sources of traction that could help him regain his footing.

Aunt Hilda's shoulders were slumped, and she kept her eyes on the creek in front of the hole. This was her baby sister by nine long years going into the earth. Things were out of order. He had heard her say this more than once to the preacher and to Daddy. "Out of order. Out of order."

After the service, nine-year-old Jackson walked out onto the dock and watched the ripples of the outgoing tide. He could hear Aunt Hilda calling him into the covered-dish luncheon, but he didn't turn back. He'd rather the sun bake him hard than fill his stomach with the rich food everyone had brought by for the occasion: fried chicken, deviled eggs, homemade biscuits, macaroni salad, and brightly colored gelatin rings filled with grapes and melons. He watched the fiddler crabs darting in and out of their holes, bearing the unbalanced weight of their one large claw. He threw an oyster shell at them and watched them dart back in their pluff mud caves. He turned back to watch the water.

Before long, he heard the creak of footsteps on the dock. Then he felt a light pat on his back that was all fingers. It was the preacher, and he was following the boy's eye toward the water. Watching the pull of the ripples like gliders or boomerangs. One right behind the other pushing toward the sea.

"I sure am sorry, son," the man said without stooping down. Jackson watched the man's long thin shadow on the slats of wood. He was scratching at his neck again. Jackson could tell by the elbow jutting out from his head. The preacher looked out toward the green marsh grass before searching the thick white sky. "I reckon' God needed another angel in heaven." He nodded his head. "Don't you?"

Jackson had narrowed his eyes and focused on a school of mud minnows flitting in the water near the other side of the creek bank. He didn't speak, but this image crossed his mind: God scanning the earth before spotting his mama, shrinking her good, and then reaching down.

He remembered not wanting to envision her hands pressed together like the front of some Christmas card, her wings large and white. She'd looked too tired to be an angel. Too thin legged, too dry mouthed. Too hollow boned. He'd rather picture her lying down in a soft bed with a book in her hand, a great adventure that made her eyes grow wide and her heart beat fast. Or in the little garden behind their house tying her tomatoes up to the stakes with the thin white string she always had him hold and cut. But most of all he wanted to picture her pulling back the covers of his bed and patting the pillow. He wanted to feel her hand on his cheek. Her kiss on his forehead. That was the right order. That much he knew.

The preacher softly blew his nose into a cloth handkerchief and put it back in his pocket as an eating-sized trout broke the water's surface for a moment. The man patted the boy's shoulder once more before turning back toward the smell of fried chicken and deviled eggs and biscuits. "Come on in and have some lunch," he called back over his shoulder.

Jackson turned slightly to watch the thin man walk toward his home. A neighbor, Mrs. Smoak, was holding a full plate for him. "This way, Pastor. Sweet tea for you, right?" Then the boy turned back toward the water.

By the time Jackson came back to himself he was sitting on a park bench with the stack of books on his lap. Two dogs were chasing a ball over by the Civil War statue on the corner and a group of college kids were throwing a Frisbee on the green beside the angel water fountain. In a live oak tree to his left a mother was calling up to a boy who had climbed a little too high. The boy's father, who had been taking pictures of the harbor, came over and lifted up his hand and the boy shimmied down low enough for his dad to grab hold of his ankle. The boy jumped into his dad's arms, and once he was on the ground he scurried over to his mother, who tousled his hair and rubbed his back.

Jackson looked at his watch. He had better snap out of this or he was going to blow the whole day—music class, French class, and meeting with Waters. He picked up the load of books. Why did he agree to take them? Why did he even feel the need to talk to a priest? He knew that he knew who God was. As soon as they had a quiet moment this evening he would ask Mary Lynn to return the stack. He would tell her it was fine by him if she went to church as long as it didn't interfere with their plans and goals, but as for him, it was no use. She shouldn't ask him again.

Chapter 13

MARY LYNN

Mary Lynn had watched Jackson take a turn onto Meeting Street toward St. Michael's church pumping his free arm, and she hoped that he wouldn't eat the nice Reverend Summerall alive. Whether Jackson chose to believe or not, she still wanted to be able to go to her women's group and to go to church when she could, and while she knew it would be pretty hard to burn a bridge to any church, Jackson could have a cocky way about him, and she'd seen him ruffle a few feathers in his life when he wanted to win an argument. He always wanted to win.

Mac, who was watching Jackson longingly beside Mary Lynn, started to whine. He was anxious for his morning walk. Mary Lynn bent down and patted the Labrador beneath his soft, black chin. "He's a little distracted, buddy." The dog stared at her with his dark marble-like eyes. "C'mon, you can take a jog with me."

He turned around twice and started to yelp. "Shh," she snapped. She didn't want him to wake the girls; they needed a good morning's sleep to get over their jet lag and get ready for school tomorrow. Too late, she thought as Catherine bounded out onto the piazza in her running clothes. "Want a partner?" The girl flashed one of the biggest, broadest smiles Mary Lynn had seen on her in months.

"You bet I do." Mary Lynn walked over and gave her daughter a kiss on the forehead. "You stretch while I get Mac's leash."

"Okay."

They started off walking quickly down South Battery toward Lenwood Boulevard, Mac pushing them forward as he caught wind of some smell or the sight of a squirrel and then slowing them down as he insisted on relieving himself in the yard of every home that had a dog.

"You seem awfully chipper this morning," Mary Lynn said. "I thought you'd be exhausted."

Catherine blushed and offered to take Mac by the leash for a little while. Once they started to jog she said, "Got an invite to the prom."

Mary Lynn smiled. She didn't look over to her daughter or make too much of a fuss. When your teenager decided to talk to you, you couldn't be too eager. It was a tricky balance that she was still trying to feel her way along.

"Well, I'm not surprised," Mary Lynn said finally, looking ahead. "Has to be either Tres or Bryan." They turned onto Lenwood and started running a little faster along the water. Mary Lynn looked over to her daughter who was bright-eyed and seemed to be enjoying the fresh air and a run in her neighborhood. "But I'm guessing Bryan."

Catherine couldn't contain her grin. She nodded.

"Well, I guess that must mean he's gotten over you not running this year."

The girl swallowed hard and stared ahead as she pointed at a porpoise fin breaking the surface of the water in the middle of the harbor. "I'm not sure he's over it. He's blaming Dad and you."

The sun on the water on this mild winter day was stunning. Mary Lynn couldn't remember when she'd seen a bluer sky. Most of the houses along the battery had taken down their Christmas decorations and it was nice to be back to normal. Like a fresh slate.

Mary Lynn was glad Bryan had asked Catherine to the prom. He was a much better option than Tres King. If Tres spiked his drink at a Christmas party right before her eyes, who knew what he was up to when the parents weren't around.

"He seems nice," Mary Lynn said as she panted.

Catherine nodded. "He is." Then she turned to her mother and back toward the stairs they'd have to run up to get to the High Battery.

"Let's sprint to the yacht club."

"Okay." Before Mary Lynn got to the "kay" Catherine bolted ahead. There was no way Mary Lynn could catch up, but she didn't mind. She ran as hard as she could as her daughter's golden ponytail whipped before her. She felt a kind of peace watching her child run. She knew there was nothing Catherine would rather do. She was built for it somehow. To run. And Coach Christiansen was right, she was like a gazelle, graceful and remarkably fast. She had been that way for as long as Mary Lynn could remember. She would never forget watching her run through Uncle Dale's cornfield when she was a little girl, maybe three or four. Once Mary Lynn even had to call to Jackson to catch her as she sprinted toward the road. The girl had always been fast. Too fast for Mary Lynn to catch up with.

Catherine looked back. "C'mon, Mama!"

Mary Lynn took a big gulp of the harbor air and mustered a little more energy. She got closer as they approached the Yacht Club.

Mary Lynn had been worried about her child. She couldn't quite put her finger on it, but she had a sense that something wasn't quite right. However, seeing her now pumping her arms, racing and smiling, she had a feeling that everything was all right. That those worries that woke her up in the night were really nothing in the light of day. She hoped this was true. She prayed it was so.

They slowed after they passed the Yacht Club.

Mary Lynn patted Catherine on the back. "You won."

"Oh yeah." Catherine did a little dance and spun around.

"No gloating," Mary Lynn said. "I'm an old woman."

"Right, Mama." Catherine rolled her eyes. "You're the youngest looking mom around, and you know it."

Mary Lynn smiled. "That's a sweet thing to say."

Catherine shrugged her shoulders. "I can be sweet sometimes." She pulled the rubber band out of her hair and twisted it up again with the flick of her wrist. "Plus, it's the truth."

Mary Lynn took her daughter's hand. She could feel her child's pulse as she held it. How amazing that the infant in your arm grows to be taller and faster than you. It was a beautiful and satisfying turn of events. "I wish you'd run with me every morning."

"Once I get this dreaded SAT behind me, I will."

They checked for traffic and crossed over East Bay onto Broad Street. Mary Lynn thought of Jackson for a moment. They'd be walking right by the St. Michael's office. Oh, she hoped it was going well. She hoped maybe Roy had a way of blinding Jackson with the truth like Paul on the road to Damascus. Anything was possible.

She squeezed Catherine's hand. "You're going to do fine." She turned to her and watched her child blow a loose strand of hair out of her face before shifting her gaze downward. Mary Lynn squeezed her hand again until Catherine looked over to her. "You are, you know?"

Catherine rolled her eyes and released her

hand. "I hope so, Mama. I really want to run cross country next fall, and I think I will genuinely lose my mind if Dad drills me with questions all summer."

Mary Lynn inhaled. The city was starting to wake up as cars lined Broad Street and men and women in dark, well-pressed business suits made their way into the post office and mayor's office and banks while tourists walked around glassy-eyed with cameras swinging from their necks.

"You'll do fine, Catherine." Honestly, Mary Lynn thought Catherine had done fine before. She was sure to get scored in a higher percentile than Mary Lynn had when she was in high school, and with Cat's foreign language skills, her running, and her music, she'd get into a fine college. Honestly, she wondered if it really mattered where Catherine went as long as she was challenged and happy. It was one of the conversations she had with Jackson in her brain, though never could quite muster the strength to have in real life.

"I hope so." Mary Lynn noticed Catherine wringing her hands as they approached St. Michael's, and she reached over and massaged her shoulders. "Hey," she said. "I was thinking you could do a test run to school with your sisters today. Give your new car a spin and time yourself so you know just when you should leave tomorrow and what route you should take. What do you think?"

Catherine looked over to her mom and bit her lip to once again contain her smile. "That sounds good," she said.

Mary Lynn noticed there was no sign or sound of Jackson when they rounded the corner of Meeting and Broad Street, and she wondered if the meeting had ended quickly and if she would find him sitting at the breakfast table poring over the *New York Times* when she got home.

She and Catherine were discussing various routes to school as they turned from Meeting onto Battery where they noticed some hired hands waxing and buffing Tres King's black Range Rover as well as the Kings' other cars—Bev's silver convertible Mercedes and Hollis's Jaguar sedan in their driveway.

Mary Lynn turned to Catherine. "Don't get any crazy ideas, sweetheart. You know where the hose and the dust buster are. You're going to be washing your own car."

"I know, Mama," she said. "We're spoiled, but we're not *that* spoiled."

"Let's hope not," Mary Lynn said as Bev King shouted, "Welcome home!" from her piazza and waved her over.

"I'm going to head on in and shower," Catherine said.

"And wake your sisters." Mary Lynn patted her child's back. "Tell them about the test run."

"I will."

Mary Lynn walked over to Bev's piazza and had to listen to the twenty-minute tale about their post-Christmas trip to Hawaii. Bev had a nice tan and a little photo album already produced, which she whipped out of her foyer to show to Mary Lynn.

"You all have to go with us next time." Bev squeezed Mary Lynn's wrist as she flipped through the pictures of the King clan with sun-burned cheeks in some fancy restaurant and then at a luau decked in leis and brightly colored Hawaiian shirts in front of a pig on a spit.

"It's one of the few places in the world that actually lives up to its reputation," Bev said. "It's stunning, Mary Lynn. Every day it's stunning."

After Mary Lynn told her briefly about the trip to England, Bev ran to the study in the back of the house to grab a little present she had gotten Mary Lynn. As Mary Lynn waited, flipping through the album again, Tres called down the stairs, "Why didn't you get those flippin' car cleaners to come this afternoon, Mom?" He gave a loud scoff and continued from somewhere on the second floor. "The sound of that vacuum is splitting my head open." When Bev didn't answer he came barreling down the stairs bleary-eyed shouting, "Mom! Where are you?" He straightened up quickly at the sight of Mary Lynn. "Oh, hi, Mrs. Scoville. Have you seen my mother?"

"She's in the study."

He rubbed his eyes and blinked a few times, and

she could still see the boy in the teenage body that was growing taller by the day. He was a handsome boy, if an obnoxious one, and she didn't trust him as far as she could throw him, but hoped he would somehow turn out all right.

After thanking Bev for the unnecessary and extravagant gift of a beautiful set of gold earrings in the shape of the plumeria flower, she headed back home to see how the girls were coming along.

At the little table in the kitchen, Anarosa was serving up pancakes as Casey and Catherine wolfed them down. Lilla was eating her usual breakfast, black coffee and a banana with peanut butter, as she caught sight of Mary Lynn and rolled her eyes. "Mama, I wanted to go to King Street, do a little shopping and have lunch."

"It was Mama's idea to do a test run," Catherine said.

"I can't think of anything more boring." Lilla slurped her coffee as Casey looked back and forth at her two sisters before going back to her pancakes. She knew when it was best to lay low.

Mary Lynn remembered about Lilla's punishment. She cleared her throat and they all turned to her. "Lilla, have you forgotten about being on restriction?" Jackson had spelled it out in Stratford-Upon-Avon. No allowance and no shopping for two weeks. No *Twilight* sequel either. Not until Lilla read the real version of *A*

Tale of Two Cities and composed a five-page paper either comparing and contrasting the English and French peasantry and aristocracy leading up to the French Revolution or discussing how Dickens uses water as a symbol for the peasant mob.

"Ugh." Lilla rolled her big hazel eyes. Then she let her head fall into her hands and Mary Lynn noticed a strand of her hair landing in the peanut butter jar. "Dickens is a bore!"

Catherine, still excited from the run and for any reason to drive her car, poked her sister's arm. "This may be your only opportunity to get out of the house today, L."

Lilla looked up and sneered at her sister. "A drive to school on our last day of break. Just the kind of outing I was hoping for."

Casey giggled, and when her sisters turned to her she stared back down at her pancakes and kept eating.

After the girls got dressed, Mary Lynn timed them as they lugged their backpacks into the car and drove the fifteen blocks across the peninsula to school. They texted her as soon as they hit the school gates, then they drove back.

It seemed to take them twice as long to get home. In the driveway, Catherine had a startled look on her face.

"What's wrong?" Mary Lynn leaned into the rolled-down window.

"She got a ticket." Lilla bit the inside of her cheek and squinted her eyes as if to look into the future.

Casey nodded. She looked like a puppy who knew there was trouble but didn't fully understand what it could be; her dark blue eyes were big and dilated.

Catherine's face was pale and she started to weep with her head on the steering wheel. "That's it," she said. "Daddy said the car goes back if I get a ticket."

Mary Lynn exhaled. Jackson did say that. And he always followed through.

She took the crumpled blue ticket out of Catherine's hands and sent them all to their rooms.

"What should we do?" Lilla asked.

Mary Lynn put her hands on her hips. "You have a British classic to read, young lady." The three girls walked slowly with their heads down up the back steps and into the house.

Mary Lynn looked at the ticket. Catherine had been going 35 in a 25 mile zone. Mmm. Well, the car would be returned. That was almost certain. Poor Catherine. Thanks to Facebook, most of her friends knew she had a new car, and now to go back to school with her tail between her legs and the car turned in to the dealership . . . that would be pretty tough, even though Mary Lynn had her reservations about a sixteen-year-old having her own set of wheels.

Mary Lynn was sitting at the dining room table with Anarosa making the menu for the week when Jackson came home. He put a little stack of books on the table, grabbed his bag from the foyer, and called back, "If I hurry, I can still make it to my music theory class."

She stood and followed him toward the front door.

"How did it go with Roy Summerall?"

He rubbed his neck. "Like I expected. He believes this stuff, and I don't." He shook his head once, then met her eyes. "I know you do, and I can't stop you from it, Mary Lynn. But I hope it won't get in the way of our life and the plans we have for our girls."

She tried not to sigh too heavily. He had read the Bible. He had been to see a priest. Maybe God couldn't cut through the stone that was Jackson.

He turned back suddenly. "What's been going on around here?"

"Well." Mary Lynn bit her lip. She shook her head. "Something not so good."

"What?" he asked.

She put her hand on his forearm. "I better let Catherine tell you."

As soon as she started to call up the stairs, Catherine appeared on the staircase, her eyes red and her cheeks puffy.

"Uh-oh," Jackson said. His chest seemed to deflate. "What happened, sweetheart?"

Catherine rubbed the wooden rail, and Mary Lynn could hear Lilla and Casey tiptoe out of their rooms. She imagined them crouched down behind the banisters of the third-floor landing.

"I took the car out to take a test drive to school. It was Mom's idea. And I got a ticket on the way home."

Jackson furrowed his brow and nodded his head. "Where?"

"On Rutledge Avenue, just after Calhoun Street."

"Let me see it."

Mary Lynn walked over to the mantle, pulled it from beneath the beautiful Chinese vase she had bought from Seabrook Childress when he decorated her home a few years ago.

Jackson stared at the thin, crumpled blue paper for a whole minute. Then he looked up, held out his hand, and said, "Bring me the keys."

There was a collective gasp up on the third floor. Catherine let out a horrified yelp and ran up the stairs to get the key. She was trying to catch her breath between the weeps as she brought the black key down on its preppy ring and handed it to him.

He looked firmly at her. "We had an agreement."

"Yes, sir," she said.

"You weren't ready for this. I see that now."

She nodded.

He put the key in his pocket. "I'm sorry."

"Me too."

Then he turned and walked toward the kitchen where Anarosa was standing on the threshold, wiping her hands on a kitchen towel and shaking her head on behalf of Catherine.

He turned to her and held up his hands, palms up. "Teenagers," he said.

Anarosa sighed. "Yes, sir," she said.

Jackson turned back to Mary Lynn. "I'm off to the college, tardy to my first class."

"Don't worry," Mary Lynn said. "It won't take long for you to catch up."

He kissed her cheek. "Make sure the girls practice their strings for an hour, will you?"

She nodded her head as he made his way through the back door.

Mary Lynn watched him hop on his bicycle and punch open the code for their electronic gate, then she turned toward the foyer where the echo of Catherine's weeping was loud and steady. She headed up the stairs to see about her.

Chapter 14

CATHERINE

Catherine spent the day bawling, studying SAT flash cards, practicing her Mozart sonata, and then bawling some more.

She had posted on her Facebook page about her

ticket and her dad taking her car away. Bryan called her. He wasn't too good on the phone. There were a lot of pauses. She felt embarrassed. How could a day that started off so beautifully, a year that seemed like it was going so well, come crashing down? Her stomach hurt the way it had before Christmas break.

Alyssa called her. She told her she was thinking about her and would be praying for her. Catherine knew Alyssa's family's financial woes, and she realized she probably sounded like such a brat whining about her new car being taken away when Alyssa's dad was now driving a taxi for a living.

Catherine thought about God the way she did from time to time when things were bleak. She had been to church with her mother a few times. Alyssa, her best friend, took her to youth group once or twice as well. She remembered once being over at Alyssa's house when they were about ten and seeing a picture of a Christmas pageant framed on her bedside table. When Alyssa had gone to the bathroom, she had picked it up and stared. There must have been fifty children in the pageant at the altar. Little girls in angel costumes, little boys in sheep and cow costumes, older kids dressed up like shepherds with beards drawn on their soft cheeks, and a teenage couple standing before a manger where it looked like a real baby was kicking, red-faced and crying. She remembered thinking how beautiful it was. As she glanced back over the faces, she spotted Alyssa, who was the star that year. She had a huge piece of cardboard in the shape of a star tied to her torso. It was covered in gold garland. She had gold glitter on her rosy cheeks and she was glorious. As she heard Alyssa coming down the hall she had put the picture back down and walked over to the chalkboard where they were playing school, but every now and then she would look over to the picture and wonder what it was that made it so beautiful.

She thought of Bryan and Coach Christiansen. She had seen them pray before the meets. And once, when they won the lowcountry regionals, he had gotten down on bended knee and looked down at his sneakers for a long time. She knew what he was doing.

He and Alyssa both attended Camp St. Christopher out on Seabrook Island. She knew it was a Christian camp because she'd seen evidence in Alyssa's room: fish on rainbow strings with the camp logo, T-shirts with scripture, and even a baseball cap that said "Where the glory of God meets the glory of His creation to revive the glory of His people."

Once she had looked up the camp online and showed it to her mother, but they had already signed her up for a French speaking camp in Quebec that year and they were going to

178

Tanglewood in Massachusetts for intensive string instruction and a family retreat so it wasn't going to work out.

She loved that word *revive,* and she thought of it quite often. She wondered about God. If He did have the ability to revive, how could she figure out how to get Him to do that for her? How could she find her way to Him?

That night Tres texted Catherine via Lilla's phone. "Meet me."

She knew she shouldn't meet him, but she also knew how badly she wanted to—not because she liked him but because she needed what he could give her. "OK," she texted back. "Bring A & D?"

"Yep."

Lilla furrowed her brow as she relayed the second text to Catherine. She touched her sister's shoulder and looked her in the eye. "I'm glad you're getting out, Cat, but that stuff can mess you up, you know?"

Lilla was social, she liked a good time, she cut up with her friends, snuck around with the cell phone after hours, and snuck out from time to time, but she never drank or pharmed. Her release valve was her social life, laughter, joking around with friends, sarcasm, chick flicks, junk food. She might have had a sip of a beer from time to time, but Catherine was sure she had never taken any medication. However, Lilla had no idea where Catherine was right now. She had no idea how much those two little pills could get her through the week. She needed them now more than ever.

Catherine climbed through the window in her room and Lilla reached out and squeezed her hand.

"I'm okay." Catherine looked up into her sister's eyes. She had to have the dex to relax and she'd need the Adderall to focus in school tomorrow and take her father's drillings that would begin again anytime now.

When she reached the first-floor piazza, she felt a hand steadying her ankle and reaching for her waist. Tres helped her down, and as soon as they were out on the sidewalk he ducked beneath an oleander bush, pulled her close, and kissed her hard. His lips were cold and tasted like metal. His thin brown hair seemed longer than she'd remembered and he shook his head to get it out of his eyes. She hadn't really kissed him back, but he didn't seem to notice.

"I missed you, neighbor." He embraced her. Then he took her hand, squeezed it, and said, "I've got good news."

"What?" She pulled back to get a good look at him. Even in the dark she could see the raccoon eyes from his Hawaiian vacation. He must have stayed out in the sun in his shades a little too long.

"Got my Yale acceptance letter."

"Wow." She blinked. Honestly, she couldn't believe he'd gotten in. She'd overheard his mother telling her mother how unlikely it was even in their circumstance, whatever that meant. "Congratulations."

"Thanks." He led her out from beneath the bush and over to the darkened park. He turned to her beneath the street lamp. "Now that I'm in, this semester is going to be all about blowing off steam. I know next year is going to kick my butt so I might as well have fun while I can."

She cleared her throat. "If you got into Yale, college is not going to kick your butt."

"Catherine." He stopped and looked at her as if she were a little girl. It was a look she had seen him give his younger sister. "You're sweet, you know that? That's what I like about you."

By sweet, she had the sense that he meant naïve or dense or some combination thereof.

She took a step back. "What?"

He pulled her close, and they walked over to the large live oak tree on the far side of the park. "My dad's on the board. The business school is named after my great-grandfather."

He sat down and leaned against the tree, and she took a seat next to him. "So they *let* you in? Is that what you're saying?"

"Let's put it this way." He licked his lips and turned to her. "Neither Sara Hughes nor Bryan

Christiansen got in." Everyone knew that Sara and Bryan were competing against one another for the Peninsula Day School's class of 2010 valedictorian spot. They were the brainiacs of the grade above Catherine and everyone else was a far second, especially Tres, who was known for being more cocky than bright and more unprepared than not.

Catherine nodded. She was just beginning to see how the world really worked for some people. And she was beginning to understand why it was up to her to get a high score on the SAT if she ever hoped to bypass all the applicants with deep pockets and old school connections. Her parents couldn't help her there. Her father had attended Trident Tech to learn about farming and her mother had attended USC-Beaufort, a small satellite school with only a few basic majors. They were self-made. They didn't have any connections or sway at any big institution, but they wanted her to have a shot out there. It was up to her to make that happen.

Catherine knew she needed to tell Tres about Bryan and the prom. She didn't want to mislead him. She suspected he was just bored or lonely, and she was someone to hang out with. Someone to kill a little time with before he left for Connecticut in the fall.

She decided to wait. He was kind of jumpy and had probably taken something before he snuck out of the house. If she upset him, he could storm off, and she had to get her hands on the dex and the Adderall. She needed it. It had been an awful day, getting a ticket and then having her father take her car away. She needed some rest and then enough energy to focus at school and on the test and music tomorrow.

"So your old man took your car away?" He pulled a Ziploc bag of pills out of his pocket.

She scoffed. "Yeah."

He spit and handed her a couple of Robitussin pills and a little bottle of water. "Man, he's tough."

She put the pills on her tongue and swallowed. Her ears popped.

"The toughest." She rubbed her knees. She would be feeling relief soon.

"Why?" Tres took a few pills and threw his head back to swallow them. "What's his deal?"

She had thought about this a lot before. Why was her dad so rigid and intent? She knew he was smart, and he'd never really gotten a chance to do anything with that until his father died. If it weren't for inheriting a little money and then having Mark Waters help him know how to invest it, where would they be? And he had lost his mom when he was nine. That had to do something awful to a kid. She thought of Michael Parsons in her class whose father was killed in a hunting accident. He had a hardness about him that reminded her of her father.

183

She turned to Tres and instead of examining her father asked, "Do you believe in God?"

"Oh, man." He turned away and spit out a loogie, then turned back to her. "I don't know, Catherine. What kind of question is that?"

She shrugged. She had seen them going to church from time to time on Sunday mornings, Mrs. King in some designer suit and Tres and his brother in navy blazers and bow ties, their little sister in some precious silk dress.

He flared his nostrils and looked out over the water as a late-night cyclist sped by. "We go to church just because it's the"—he held up his fingers to make quotation marks—"thing to do."

He spoke about his parents with such contempt. *If he loathes them so much, then why does he want to follow in their footsteps?*

She yawned and began to feel a nice tingling in her fingers. "Have you ever prayed?"

He shrugged. "Not really. Maybe when I was a kid and I was afraid. Never really needed to."

Just then Catherine could hear the slightest snicker behind them. She heard the flick of a switch and just as she turned back she saw a knife come around the tree toward Tres. A young man held it right up to his suntanned neck.

"Where you been, King?"

Tres, trembling, looked over and his face registered that he knew this guy. "Out of town, man. On a trip."

There was another kid behind him who said, "C'mon, TJ. I think I saw a cop driving by."

The man, this TJ, pulled Tres close. He looked back at the fellow beside him and said, "Grab the girl."

Her arms felt light and tingly, but someone grabbed her by the shoulders and pushed her forward and she landed face-first in the grass.

"Nice," the young man with the knife said. "What is a little wuss like you doing with a fine piece like that?"

"What do you want, TJ?"

"You know what I want." He pulled him closer and brought the knife flush to his Adam's apple. "I want your business."

"How about an advance, man." The boy eased off a little and Tres groped for his wallet. He pulled it out and handed the guy two fifty dollar bills. TJ grabbed the wallet and saw that there was no more. He threw it on the ground and it landed with a soft thud. "You owe me twice this much, King. And I'm expecting you to be a regular. I paid a lot to stock up for you, and I'm expecting you to buy."

"I'll keep buying," Tres said. "Meet me here tomorrow, and I'll have the rest of the cash plus more for a purchase."

Just then a beam from a car light crossed over them and TJ eased up and put the knife back in his pocket. He shoved Tres forward, but the boy caught himself. "You better," he said. "And don't think I don't know exactly where you and your pretty little girl live."

"C'mon," TJ called to his friend, who let go of Catherine's wrist and darted toward the street, then over a stone wall of some High Battery home, taking a shortcut to a nearby alleyway.

Catherine sat up and rubbed her wrist. She was tingling all over and her heart was pounding.

"Who the heck was that?" Her voice was hoarse and she couldn't stop her shoulders from shivering. There was an ache where her chin had hit the dirt and it throbbed. She had never seen the guy before. What she really wanted to know was how in the world she had found herself in this situation, in the dark, in the middle of the night, held down by some creep, a knife to her neighbor's throat.

"Relax," Tres said. "It's just this low-life from the projects. I'll get him off my back tomorrow night after I visit the ATM."

"I want to go home," she said. "I can't do this anymore."

"C'mon, Catherine. You're wound tighter than my granddad's pocket watch." He reached over and massaged her shoulders. She recoiled at his touch.

"You're going to get yourself hurt, Tres, or you're going to take one too many of your dad's painkillers and then where are you going to end up? It won't be Yale, that's for sure."

He shook his head and rubbed his throat. "Oh, and you don't need the meds?" He held up the bag that had the dex and the Adderall. "You're above all this?"

She swallowed hard and looked down. She needed those pills to get through the week. "No."

He threw them into her lap. "C'mon," he said. "Let's get you home, little girl."

She grabbed them and put them in her pocket, and she let him take her hand as he walked her across the park and the street and over to her house where he hoisted her up on the first-floor railing where she could hook her leg on a piazza spindle and climb up to the next floor and the next to her bedroom window.

Chapter 15

MARY LYNN

Back to her decade-old role of playing chauffeur, Mary Lynn carted the girls to school, then came home to meet with Anarosa and finalize the menu. Then she opened her calendar and took a deep breath as the machine that was her life kicked into high gear. She would sit in on Lilla's and Casey's strings lessons after school today, then make sure Catherine got off to Mandarin after doing a good hour of homework. Wednesday was ballet for all and Thursday was cotillion, and she needed to take Casey to get a new pair of ballet slippers as she seemed to be having a growth spurt.

In just this week alone she would be leading the Peninsula Day School board meeting, hosting a junior class Parents Guild meeting, heading to the women's prayer meeting (actually looking forward to that one), and planning the very important Charlestowne Garden Club luncheon that was just six weeks away. She needed to call the florist, the caterer, and Seabrook, who said he'd lend her fifteen place settings of one of his hand-painted sets of antique china that he bought at a market in Salzburg a few years ago.

Her cell phone rang and she saw Mark Waters's name flash across the screen.

She clicked the green button of her BlackBerry. "Hey there."

"Hey yourself," he said. His voice seemed more gravelly than usual, and she wondered if he'd been out making a night of it. Late nights were becoming a regular part of his extended midlife crisis, and his rough appearance was beginning to chafe Jackson a little.

"What's up?" Despite his wayward ways, Mark was like an older brother and she could talk with him the way she talked in high school, without all of the pretense and manners. He was a wealthy, powerful man, but he still had a sort of casualness, even a folksiness to him that Jackson had tried hard to shed as if it were a putrid skin.

"Got these tickets to a Joni Mitchell concert that I can't make."

She smiled. His father, Cecil, had introduced her to Joni Mitchell when she was a thirteen-year-old girl and he'd been in love with her mother who worked for him. He had taken her and Mark to a concert in Columbia back then, and she would never forget the way tears filled Mark's eyes when Joni sang "Blue" as an encore, her flip-flopped foot keeping time as she sat on a stool and strummed her guitar on stage. It seemed like another lifetime ago.

"When is it?"

"February 17th in Atlanta."

Mary Lynn consulted her calendar. That night looked free. "Let me get back to you. I might want to take Catherine." Catherine needed to relax and there was nothing like a little soulful Joni Mitchell to help with that. Music had been Mary Lynn's joy as a child. Catherine was well-versed in classical music and seemed to appreciate it, but she had no idea what it was like to relax into a soulful folk song and tap your toes and let the lyrics beat down the door of your closed heart.

"Okay. Where's your hubby?"

"Probably in the college library studying his French." She didn't mean to sound so sarcastic.

"He sure is an academic, isn't he? Reckon he'll

be getting his PhD in nuclear physics before it's all over."

She chuckled. "He's making up for lost time, I suppose."

"I guess. Well, have him give me a call when you see him. We need to go over some items before this week's board meeting."

"Sure."

"Mary Lynn?"

"Yeah?"

"I hope this is a great year for you."

It was probably the most personal, kind thing anyone had said to her in weeks.

"Thanks, Mark," she said. "You too."

She knew that without Mark they never would have come this far. He had taken Jackson under his wing, advised him how to invest, brought him in on the big waterfront project and the midtown condos, and connected him to Chet Hunt, who had sold him low-rent apartment units all over the lowcountry, most of which Jackson had never even seen.

When Mary Lynn headed upstairs to cross reference the school calendar, she realized that Casey had left her backpack and she bolted over to the school to deliver it to her fourth-grade teacher, Mrs. Tate.

On her way through the campus, Mary Lynn spotted Betsy Flanagan, the Head of School, who was flagging her down. Betsy was in her usual dark suit with a serious look on her face that if you didn't know her better, you might take as a scowl. Her hair was jet black and thinning on the top, and she teased it and sprayed it good to give it a little bulk in the back. She was Mary Lynn's age, but she was so bone thin that her body looked like a little girl's and her face looked large and weary. Her husband had been ill with kidney failure for months, and on top of that she'd hit wall after wall in the much-needed campus expansion project. At last she was able to acquire two new lots adjacent to the campus. Now she had plans to build two enormous buildings, one for the high school and another for a fine arts wing. She was gearing up for a capital campaign, but with the economic downturn, there was not as much enthusiasm from the parents and alumni as she had hoped for.

"Happy new year, Betsy." Mary Lynn smiled. "I hope you had some time to relax."

She grimaced. "A little. A little."

"Well, do we need to get together before Friday's board meeting?"

"Yes," she said. "But there is something even more pressing, Mary Lynn."

"What's that?"

"A lot of parents are sending e-mails about the new building projects and there's some concern about an increase in tuition as well as campus security as we bring in these building crews, so I was hoping to plan a sort of town hall meeting for February 17th to present the parents and teachers with our building and economic plan. The architects can be there to show the final drawings, and it's one of the few nights there isn't a basketball game or another major conflict."

No Joni Mitchell, Mary Lynn thought. Oh well. "Great. What can I do to help?"

Betsy put her hands on her hips and leaned forward. "The problem is, I can't be there."

"What?"

"My husband's nephew has received the green light to donate his kidney, and it looks like we're going to have to be at Duke that week for the surgery."

"Oh, I see. Well, let's reschedule the presentation."

"No," she said. "I thought you could give the presentation to the parents. We need to get this show on the road, and I thought you and Jackson could do it together since he's serving on the capital campaign committee."

Mary Lynn's heart jumped a bit. She was always a little uncomfortable speaking publicly, but maybe she and Jackson could do it together.

"All right. Maybe the three of us can sit down and go through it all. He's more articulate than I am."

"Great. I'll have my assistant e-mail you a few times and you can get back to me."

"Sounds good." Mary Lynn walked to her car as

two wrens chirped to one another in the beautiful oak tree in the center of campus. What a world. One moment you could be living on a rundown farm, the love child of a quirky, beautiful woman who captured the town's negative attention for decades, and the next you could be the chairman of the board of a prestigious private school less than fifty miles away presenting building project plans to parents, faculty, and alumni.

The presentation was the same day as the Garden Club luncheon so it would be a little nuts. Her heart started to pound as she wondered if she could pull it all off. And yes, she couldn't help but think of Weezie Pruitt, who would surely be attending both gatherings just around the time that the debutante club of South Carolina was voting on its new members and sending out their annual invitations to join. If Mary Lynn ever wanted to get into her good graces, that would be the day.

She felt the sudden need to go shopping with Bev King and spruce up her winter wardrobe. Maybe a new dress for the luncheon and a new pantsuit for the presentation at the school. She had heard there were some great sales at Saks, or maybe they could take a quick trip to Atlanta. She hoped Bev was free tomorrow.

Her cell phone rang—Scottie. "Want to go to lunch tomorrow? I want to hear about your trip, and I miss you."

"You know," Mary Lynn said, "I'm feeling a

little overwhelmed with all I have to do in the next few weeks. I think I'm going to have to pass."

"What's going on?"

"It's that big luncheon I was telling you about, and now I have to do a big presentation at school the same day."

"Ahh," Scottie said. "Well, I'm here if you need anything. How about Wednesday's study? Do you want me to pick you up?"

"Thanks, Scottie. But I doubt I can make that. I've got this junior class meeting at my house and knowing the moms, it will go way over."

"Well, if it gets out early, come on over. It's not the same without you."

Mary Lynn smiled. "I will."

She hung up the phone, then dialed Bev King, who agreed to meet her at Saks the next afternoon.

Bev hounded Mary Lynn the entire shopping trip as she tried on one brown pantsuit after the next along with brown beads and brown leather pumps in every shade and with every kind of heel. Would Jackson put in a good word for them with the yacht club? Would Mary Lynn put in a good word with the debutante club if she was invited? Did she need help planning the garden club luncheon? Bev was still a member of the Symphony League of Manhattan, and she would fly up for a luncheon and meeting every quarter, so she was full of fresh new menu ideas that might impress Charlestonians.

Over a latte on King Street, she grabbed Mary Lynn's wrist and confessed, "If we don't start making more social in-roads, Hollis is threatening to move back to the northeast."

Mary Lynn furrowed her brow. "Well, I hope it doesn't come to that." Then she leaned forward. "I mean, is all the social stuff really that important?"

Bev drew in a big breath. "Of course it is, Mary Lynn. Especially since we both were brought up in the world of the social elite. What would my children do if they didn't have a group in which to set themselves apart?"

Mary Lynn chuckled. Yes, she enjoyed seeing how far she and Jackson could fly on nothing but a little education, a little money, and a little charm. But if they hadn't been invited to join one group or club, would she still have been happy? She hoped the answer was yes.

She wouldn't say this to Bev. It was crazy talk to someone like her. But she said it to herself, and she would find herself wondering about it more seriously as the January days ticked by.

The next morning she hosted the parents of the junior class meeting. She served coffee and black currant scones from Caviar & Bananas with clotted cream and lemon curd and butter.

The parents chatted about the same subjects they'd been stewing over for years—college applications, the maintenance of second homes, spring break vacation spots, and summer camp options. South America was a good choice for spring break. You could do the Buenos Aires/Punta Del Este combination trip for quite a good rate. Of course, skiing was still good in Utah and Idaho in mid-March, and the Caribbean was always an agreeable spot where one could go just to get away and relax.

In the midst of all the chatter, Mary Lynn suddenly realized that she couldn't stand the thought of missing today's women's study at church. She quickly ran through the business of planning the junior/senior prom and helping to host the Senior Lunch, which was a responsibility that always fell to the juniors. She hurried everyone out of the door and raced over to St. Michael's.

Scottie and the other women greeted her with a light in their eyes. They read a passage from Galatians about carrying one another's burdens. When they went around with prayer requests she finally spoke up. "Pray for Jackson," she said and that was all she could say. They sensed her anguish, and they prayed a special prayer for him aloud and an overwhelming peace flooded Mary Lynn's heart.

After carting the kids to dance class and riding them hard on their homework, she felt weary, and she snuck to her room and read her *Message*

Bible. She almost felt as though she couldn't read it in front of Jackson, so she did it when he was at school. She prayed. She couldn't stop herself. She needed it. It was like water to her soul. She wondered, often, what a life would really look like if you followed God and loved others a hundred percent of the time. Very different from hers, she was sure. Very different. This made her heart sink, and the hardest part was that she couldn't share her inner conflict and questions about their life with Jackson. She was beginning to wonder if you could be one flesh and have such a different view of God.

As for their children, it occurred to her that what they were teaching their girls was the opposite of the gospel. They were teaching them that their hard work, their behavior, their intellect, their know-how, these were the things that kept them in good standing with their parents, their teachers, and by implication, God.

But this wasn't the truth. She'd recently read in Romans 3 of her *Message* Bible, "But in our time something new has been added. What Moses and the prophets witnessed to all those years has happened. The God-setting-things-right that we read about has become Jesus-setting-things-right for us. And not only for us, but for everyone who believes in him. For there is no difference between us and them in this. Since we've compiled this long and sorry record as sinners (both us and them) and proved that we are utterly incapable of living the glorious lives God wills for us, God did it for us. Out of sheer generosity he put us in right standing with himself. A pure gift. He got us out of the mess we're in and restored us to where he always wanted us to be. And he did it by means of Jesus Christ."

Help us, she prayed. *I don't want to waste it.* She knew it was up to them to show their children a different way of life, and she hoped it wasn't too late. But how? How could she do it without her husband leading her? And what would happen to their marriage if she pushed ahead without him? As she drew closer to God, would he get further from her?

She looked at the little stack of books Roy Summerall had given to Jackson. She had moved them from the dining room to Jackson's bedside table, but they appeared untouched. She sighed.

Then she took Mac around the corner to White Point Gardens where they played a game of catch. She saw Jackson coming around the corner on his bike with his backpack over his shoulders, but he didn't seem to notice her.

If he didn't change course, he'd be majoring in every subject the college offered for the rest of his life, and to what end? Could all the knowledge in the world, could all the unreached potential of his childhood finally fulfilled in midlife, really make a difference to his soul?

• • •

That night as they got into bed, he pointed to the stack of books on his bedside table. "Will you deliver those back to Roy Summerall tomorrow?"

She looked at him and thought her heart would sink into the pit of her stomach.

She nodded. "Sure." She reached over and squeezed his hand. Then Lilla called from upstairs, "Mama, will you call out these questions to me?" She had a big test on the constitution tomorrow and needed to be drilled.

When Mary Lynn returned, Jackson was reading one of the books, *Mere Christianity* by C. S. Lewis. He looked as though he was already a good fifteen pages into it, and she suspected it was not the kind of book you could put down once you started.

Her heart beat fast. She decided not to say anything. She lay down and picked up her *Southern Living* and fell asleep halfway through an article titled "Welcome Friends with a Beautiful Table," where a preeminent hostess from Richmond shared tips on her five cardinal rules for setting the perfect Southern table.

Chapter 16

JACKSON

Jackson was agitated. He drove Mark Waters back to his office after a tough meeting with one of their lenders over the mid-town condominium project. They had borrowed five million dollars to build the luxury condos on upper King Street and more than two-thirds of the finished building were sitting there empty and had been for over twelve months. The bank was nervous and needed Jackson and Waters to further secure the loan with a hefty collateral, otherwise they'd be receiving a foreclosure notice in the next few months.

Mark wasn't afraid of a foreclosure notice. He'd received more than one in his career and so had his father, who had been one of the most prolific developers in the state, and he always found a way to work with the banks, make a profit on the property, and land on top. But Jackson didn't have the stomach for a foreclosure and what it would do to his credit, not to mention the media coverage. He and Mary Lynn were on the verge of reaching a sort of summit in the South of Broad society, and a mar like this could cause some second-guesses and grumblings among some in the community, who, no matter how many times you had attempted to prove yourself as cultured and civilized and devoted to all matters that benefitted Charleston, remained wary and skeptical of come-yas.

Jackson had agreed to give the bank a deed to the one thousand acres he owned and used for deer and dove hunting in Round O. This seemed to satiate the lenders for the moment, and he and Waters were going to have to sell the heck out of those condos in order for him to get back his recreational land. He was grateful for the bread and butter of his income, the apartments Hunt managed, and if he got out of this luxury condo business without taking too much of a significant hit he was going to stay out of the high-end real estate development from now on.

But even the Hunt housing was not without its challenges. He had seen the paperwork for each and every property. The buildings were well-built and up to code, though truth be told, there were several he had never had the chance to lay eyes on around North Charleston and Orangeburg. However, one resident was blaming an electrical fire on Hunt management and was threatening to sue Hunt and Jackson, and another resident said she had suffered physical and emotional damage from a chest cold she had not been able to shake after moving in to this unit. Chet Hunt assured Jackson that he was on it, that some bottom-dweller lawyers had roused these tenants in their effort to sniff out an extra buck and that he had the paperwork to prove that everything was up to code.

Jackson was drumming his fingers along the dashboard as he drove, and Waters checked his e-mail on his iPhone. He knew the source of his agitation wasn't really about the bank or the property, nor was it about the paper he had due in three days on Louis the XIV and the advancement of art and culture in seventeenth-century France, or about trying the new set of sample SAT Critical Reading tests out on Catherine. Instead, the source of his anxiety and frustration centered on that blasted book, *Mere Christianity*, which Father Roy Summerall had given him to read. He couldn't shake the stirring in his gut after the line he'd read last night long after Mary Lynn had fallen asleep with the magazine on her chest: "If I find in myself a desire which no experience in this world can satisfy, the most probable explanation is that I was made for another world."

That line infuriated him, and he couldn't stop running it over his mind like a finger scratching at a scab. Jackson's whole adult life had been about trying to fulfill the desire, the craving he had in his heart. The way he went about filling the craving was to taste from every apple he could get his hands on, especially the ones he'd never had the chance to taste as a kid. He had had some remarkably fulfilling experiences—his studies, his travels, his deeper understanding of art and

202

culture, and his social strides. But he had never actually admitted the fact that the craving in his soul—even after he'd made a good deal of money and could nearly guarantee his family's security —had left him with a kind of hunger that he had not yet satiated.

He had to admit that an immense yearning still existed. He had always assumed it would eventually dissipate, that the sum of all of his strides, efforts, and experiences would collect to such a height in his soul that he would one day nod and say, "Yes, I am full now. I am home. I am at peace." He expected it would be fully realized in the success of his children and their reaching adulthood, but now he wondered, after reading the passage in *Mere Christianity*, if anything would ever fully satisfy the yearning.

He had Googled Lewis last night and come across his famous sermon, "Weight of Glory," and this quote had also stuck out in his mind: "As long as this deliberate refusal to understand things from above, even where such understanding is possible, continues, it is idle to talk of any final victory over materialism." Well, he'd never had a problem with materialism so that didn't stump him, but what got him was this: a deliberate refusal to understand things from above. For a man who was determined to understand everything, he had to admit that he had deliberately refused to understand anything about God, anything about a world beyond child rearing, social climbing, business, academia, and the arts. Even in art, when a piece of music moved him to a point that almost felt transcendent, he would anchor himself in the history of the composer, in the shape of the piece and the arrangement of the notes so as not to let his feet be lifted off the ground. He was, he could see now, a stiff-necked sort. And he wondered if this mattered. If there was some entirely separate piece, some frontier, some part of existence that he had never experienced because of his deliberate stubbornness.

He turned to Mark. "Waters?" he asked. "You believe in God?"

Mark looked up from his iPhone and grinned his side-angled grin. He had aged a lot with this second divorce and the economic downturn, and he looked rather fragile despite his large build as the sun lit up his tan face and the white hair that was overtaking his thick brown mane.

The man bit his lip and his teeth looked surprisingly yellow despite the bleaching. He shook his head. Jackson knew Mark attended First Presbyterian, a prominent church downtown. He had given a lot of money to its recent building project, so much so that the new parish hall had been named after him.

"Here's the thing, Jackson." Mark gritted his teeth and looked over to his partner. "I give a lot to church."

"Yeah. I know that, but—"

Mark cleared his throat long and hard and tapped Jackson on his wrist before looking back to the road. "And I pray like the devil that God'll let me be."

Jackson turned back to the sunlit road. There were tourists walking aimlessly down Meeting Street, stepping in the road, not paying a bit of attention to the traffic lights as if it were all Disney World and it wasn't really a town but a commercial façade. Jackson let a group cross over Cumberland Street even though he had a green light. "Yeah, I see what you're saying."

While Jackson never really observed it, he had a hunch that Waters was adept at the unsavory art of greasing palms. He was known about town for taking a special interest in certain politicians and organizations, and Jackson sensed that this was why they'd never had to fight too hard to put a set of condos on the harbor or enclose a block with a brick wall for a gated community in midtown when other developers had to overcome all kinds of zoning restrictions, not to mention wary residents. While Jackson tried to steer clear of any of that kind of behavior (and made a real effort to overlook it in Mark), he was inextricably linked to Waters and he had Waters to thank for his financial security. No doubt about it. But Mark was just a man, and a mighty flawed one at that. Surely he didn't think he could buy God off?

Jackson looked at Mark, who was back to his iPhone, pressing the touch-screen with his large fingers. Sometimes Jackson wondered why Mark had taken him in. They had grown up in the same small town and Mark's father had made it from nothing, nearly marrying Mary Lynn's mama, his secretary, for his fourth wife before he keeled over on his desk with a heart attack a few weeks before their wedding. Mark seemed to have a soft heart toward Mary Lynn and anything that meant a lot to her. He'd never asked Jackson to cross a moral line, and he almost always brought him in on deals that were low-risk and paid high returns, for which he was grateful. Jackson had never thought to look a gift horse in the mouth or judge a generous man who seemed to have good intentions despite a few unsavory methods.

After Jackson dropped Mark off at their State Street office, he decided to work out his agitation with a drive. He was out of town and twenty miles down Highway 17 South before he realized that he was headed to his childhood farm in Meggett. Since he'd bought the new hunting properties around Round O, he hadn't been out to Meggett in a year or maybe even two. He'd leveled the homestead long ago and built a cabin and a new dock a few acres away, and he rarely ventured over to the old spot where his house had stood or the simple stone grave markings beneath the live oak tree where his mama was buried. (His daddy had remarried when Jackson was in college, and he was buried in the graveyard of the church that his second wife still attended down the road in Hollywood.)

Jackson parked the car by the cabin, but he found himself walking through the avenue of oaks and over to the spot where his old house was, where there was now just a concrete slab and a little grave marker and a crumbling dock with barnacles reaching all the way up its pilings at low tide.

It was a crisp winter day. The sky was bluer than blue and the light filtered through the live oak trees and each strand of the Spanish moss like soft, white beams. Beneath the tree where his mama was buried he noticed a snake skin caught on a large two-pronged limb that must have fallen in a storm. The nine-year-old kid in him would have been in awe of this. He would have grabbed the skin up and run it into the house, and Mama would have helped him determine what kind of snake it belonged to by pulling down one of the encyclopedias they kept in the den. Once she was gone, his daddy didn't do much of that. Home-work was up to Jackson. His daddy's life was the farm and surviving, and he made sure that Jackson understood that hard work, follow-through, and a devotion to cultivating the land were of the supreme importance. More important than a curiosity over nature or a love of stories or an education.

Jackson stared at his mama's little gravestone remembering how his father had curled his hand into a tight fist as the neighbors lowered her in. It was a tight fist that never knew how to release itself. Now Jackson walked out onto the rickety dock where a school of mullet skittered on the surface at the water's edge, and he let the memory of the rest of his nine-year-old summer wash over him without attempting to beat it back as he had in the decades that followed.

Three days after they buried Mama, Aunt Hilda was gone. She had told him that she had to get back to her husband and her job at the public library in Pierce County, Georgia, not to mention Ticky, her one son who had been expelled from tenth grade and needed a firm looking after. She had offered to take Jackson with her, but Daddy wouldn't let him go. "Time for us to settle in," Jackson had heard his father say to Aunt Hilda the night before she packed her bags. "No use prolonging it."

The next week his daddy woke him up before sunrise. "Let's get to work, son," he said. Jackson poured himself a bowl of cereal and a cup of coffee with a lot of milk and sugar, then followed his daddy out to his mama's little garden on the edge of the commercial field. "Pick the last of the heirlooms, then cut the string and pull up the stakes," Daddy said. "I'll check back in the afternoon to see how it's coming."

Jackson spent the morning twisting off the last of the ugly, ripe tomatoes. He stopped in the afternoon to boil himself a hot dog and then he went back out to pull up the stakes that had rotted in some places and broken apart at the bottom. He'd had to get a shovel from the tool shed and dig the bits of dark wood up, but he'd had trouble getting every last piece, especially the smaller ones, and he wondered if they just might break down in the soil over time.

When his daddy came back from the fields to inspect the work, he shook his head and pointed at little bits of rotten wood jutting out from the open soil. "No use doing it if you don't do it all the way."

Jackson nodded. He understood. "Yes, sir," he said. And he got back to work with a gardening shovel, digging up every last bit of wood until he had sores between his forefinger and his thumb.

Two days later he followed his daddy out to the main fields where the migrant workers were already pulling up the large, thick stakes. His daddy handed him some scissors and pointed to the black plastic pulled tight like a drumhead over each bed. "Cut the plastic corners on these eight rows," he'd said. "Then we'll start bush hogging 'em."

"Yes, sir," Jackson said. The sun was rising and he could feel the heat, then the buzz of the black flies as he bent down at the edge of the row and started to cut. Every few inches was a missed tomato, its skin torn, its edges starting to darken. To this day, he couldn't stand the smell of a rotting tomato.

Pretty soon he worked eight-hour days in the main field where he followed alongside the migrant workers, digging up remnants of rotten stakes, swatting flies, and learning cuss words in Spanish as his dad rode the tractors up and down the rows, getting the soil ready to plant the next crop, corn. The air was thick and the days were long, and on particularly hot afternoons his daddy would tell him to go on in and rest. If his hand had a new blister or his neck felt sunburned, he'd go on in, take a shower, and watch television with a grape soda and the window fan directly on him. He still liked "Road Runner" back then, but his favorites were "Tarzan" and "Land of the Lost."

Some days, he'd stay out until dusk, until the workers climbed up on the trucks and waved good-bye, talking and laughing and spitting tobacco juice as they pulled out warm colas from their coolers and pulled back the metal tabs. *Kshshsh.*

After the men rode off down the dry dirt road, Jackson would walk slowly through the still fields toward his house, looking up at the sky at the formation of the thick clouds, wishing for rain. He thought of his mama. No—more than thought.

He longed for her. He wondered on many afternoons like that how light she was now. He wondered if she floated or flew up there with the heavenly hosts. He pictured her skin as translucent as the one a caterpillar left on his window sill after the molting process, but he hoped there was something still inside the shell.

He knew that from here on out he would be the opposite of light. He would be a rock in a quarry or a pebble in the back reaches of a cave. In September, once the ground was plowed up, Jackson picked up the *Robinson Crusoe* book on his bedside table and started to read it to himself. It wasn't the same, of course, and he no longer imagined making his own life in the cave of a deserted island the way he had when she'd read it to him. This time he imagined being the cave, rock hard and carved out, and he wondered if Daddy was thinking the same way, as if a hard and quiet life could protect you from the roving eye that had the power to reach down and pluck.

When Jackson awoke from the recollection he felt a kind of warmth in his gut. For a minute he thought he might be sick right there on the old rickety dock, but it passed and what it left in its wake was a question, an intense wondering. Had he cut himself off from something a long time ago when they put Mama in the ground? Had he cut himself off from anything spiritual, any life beyond the one you could see and feel and work in? Had he cut himself off from God at age nine? Another school of mullet jumped and skittered along the far edge of the shallow tidal creek and a white heron waiting at the curve in the marsh bend bent down quicker than a flash and caught a late lunch. A dog barked in the distance behind him and another answered back.

Now Jackson had the vaguest recollection of an Easter Sunday morning when he was really young, maybe four or five. He remembered him and his mama cutting some azaleas out of the bushes around their house and her wrapping them in a wet paper towel and tin foil and instructing him to put the flowers on the cross at the back of the Hollywood Baptist Church when they arrived. The thought occurred to him that he may have been baptized. He didn't know for certain, his daddy had never mentioned it, but he had the feeling that God and church were important to his mama and maybe even Daddy before her death.

Mary Lynn had mentioned getting the girls baptized a few times through the years, but they had never done anything about that. God was not part of the mission, and He had never figured heavily into the plans. Should He have?

Before Jackson realized what was happening he was back in his truck heading over to the First Federal Bank in Walterboro where he still kept the lockboxes his daddy had rented for as long as

Jackson could remember. He had never looked carefully through them, though he suspected that all there was to see were some old coins and documents, maybe a marriage certificate or a social security card.

The bank manager greeted him with a smile. She knew who he was and had remembered his daddy, who had passed away only a few years ago.

She grabbed a set of keys from another room and motioned for him to come on back, and he followed her to a vault where several boxes stood in rows. She handed him the key and pointed to one numbered 505. "Here it is," she said. "I'll leave you alone, but you just holler when you're ready to leave."

"Thanks," he said. He noticed there was mud caked on his loafers and he hoped he hadn't tracked it onto the plush carpeted bank floor. If so, he'd write the manager a check to bring in a cleaning service. He took the little key she had given him and inserted it into the little box, which he pulled out and put on a table in the center of the vault.

There was his daddy's small thin wedding ring in a little Ziploc bag on the top and beside it he noticed another ring with a diamond so small you could hardly see it. It must have been his mama's engagement ring, and there was a thin gold band with it that must have been the wedding band. Beneath that were a few old pictures of his mama's parents and his father's brothers in their World War II uniforms. One of them died in the South Pacific at the age of nineteen and the other was never quite right in the head and spent the rest of his life in Columbia at a sanatorium battling both syphilis and the mental toll of whatever he saw during his tour in Italy. There was a picture of Jackson as a toddler on a rocking horse dressed in a cowboy outfit, and he smiled at the memory of it and wondered why it—out of all of the family pictures—had made it into the lockbox. Beneath some coins his father collected and a copy of the deed to the farm as well as some bookkeeping from the 1970s was a manila envelope that was folded over and smudged with something dark like ink.

Jackson unfolded it, pulled it out, and flipped through documents: his birth certificate, his parents' marriage license, a record of his immunizations, a ribbon from winning the second-grade science project, and then a small piece of white paper with a dove with outstretched wings engraved on the top. It read,

This is to certify that
Jackson Everett Scoville, Junior
Who was born on
May 19, 1965
Was sealed by the Spirit
In Holy Baptism

And Marked as Christ's Own
Forever in St. Paul's Episcopal Church
on August 8, 1965
Signed The Reverend Arnold H. Hughes,
III

Jackson blinked several times. Then he ran his hand over the words and became aware of a firm pounding in his chest. He could hear it in his ears and feel it in his fingertips, the feel of his heart pumping blood through his body. A reality so amazing yet so constant that he hardly noticed it as he went about his busy life, reaching up for another apple, devouring it, then setting out to reach for another.

He turned over the small certificate and noticed the signature of his parents as well as his Aunt Hilda, who must have been his godmother, though he never knew it. He took the small certificate— it was no larger than his hand—and tucked it inside the pocket of his vest and called out for the manager to let her know he was finished with his business. He put the other papers, the coins, and the rings back in the box and he thanked her as she walked him to the door where he made it to his car before pulling out the certificate and examining it again as the lump in his throat grew and a tear streaked his chiseled cheeks.

For once in his life he was speechless, without a plan, without any way to process this new finding. He put his head on the steering wheel and tried to pull himself together. He had been set apart. He had been sealed. He had been marked as someone else's in an Episcopal church just down the road. What did this mean now that he knew? Could he ignore it and get on about the business before him?

As he pulled out onto the two-lane road that led back to Charleston, he glanced at the digital clock on the dash board. It was five p.m. He had missed a French class, he had missed quizzing Catherine, and if he didn't hightail it back he would miss supper. The sun was setting behind the pine trees, but its light was nearly blinding as it ricocheted off the oncoming cars and the road itself. Everything seemed bathed in a blinding light, and he remembered one of the stories he found most compelling from the New Testament that he had read on their trip to England: Paul on the road to Damascus.

Chapter 17

CATHERINE

It had been a rotten day. She woke up with a bruise on her chin, which her mother wanted an explanation for at the breakfast table. She said something about falling out of her bed while reaching for a book and Lilla cleared her throat dramatically and rolled her eyes, but her mother and Casey didn't seem to clue in.

Her mother lent her the car to drive, and as she pulled up to the school parking lot, Casey and Lilla had run ahead to beat the tardy bell. While she was pulling her heavy load of books out of the trunk, Tres came up behind her and put his hand on her hip, patting it as if she were his.

She pulled away as soon as she hoisted her book bag over her shoulder, but just as she did she noticed Bryan Christiansen standing behind them with his mother They must have parked in the next row back, and when she looked into Bryan's eyes, Tres put his hand right back on her hip and Bryan shook his head once and walked past them with his eye on the school building.

Coach Christiansen gave Catherine a concerned look and then she too walked by as Catherine squirmed away from Tres and said, "Stop putting your arm on me, will you?"

Tres stepped back and put his palms up as the three-minute warning bell rang from the school yard. She would be late. She knew that much.

He furrowed his narrow brow. "I don't get you, Cat. One minute you're hot, the next you're frigid."

She felt tears welling up in her eyes. She knew she wouldn't be going to the prom with Bryan anymore, and Tres was right, she had been sending him mixed messages.

"I'm sorry." She blinked back the tears and tried to shake off the weariness she felt even though the day had hardly begun. "I just want to be friends, okay? I didn't mean to send you any other signal."

He flipped his hair back and tucked his tanned hands into his designer blue jeans. "You didn't mean to send me any other message?" He put his finger to his mouth in a mock form of pondering, then he raised his thin, dark eyebrows. "I get it," he said. "It's all about the meds." He swallowed hard and gave her a side-angled glance. "You're hot when you need them. Am I wrong?"

How had she gotten to this place? Hanging out in the middle of the night with a guy she didn't like to get high on over-the-counter and prescription drugs? This wasn't her, but Tres was exactly right. That was why she had been hanging out with him.

He turned sharply on the balls of his loafered feet and walked toward the building without another word. She inhaled and flung the backpack over her shoulder. It felt like it weighed a ton. She was an awful person. There was no denying it. She was selfish and conniving, and she felt now as though she could hardly stand to be in her own heavy skin.

She walked toward the building and was not surprised to find her biology professor writing up a detention pass for her that he placed on her desk with a flourish for all the class to see as she took her seat on the front row.

Later that night she was waiting for her father to quiz her on the reading comprehension for the SAT, but by nine p.m. he hadn't mentioned it, and she was grateful for the reprieve. She had a test in French tomorrow on Proust's *Swann's Way*, and she had read the book carefully so all she really needed was a good night's sleep to do well.

She took two Tylenol PM and waited for them to kick in as she picked up her SAT vocabulary flash cards that her dad had replenished last week and mixed them up so they weren't in alphabetical order: *futile, disdain, indecorous, eulogy*. When she got through forty and the medicine didn't kick in, she decided to take two dex and one more Tylenol PM. She put down the cards, put her ear-buds in, and turned on her iPod. "Born This Way" by Lady Gaga blared through the buds. *Ooo, there ain't no other way*, she sang, *Baby, I was born this way*. Before the Gaga collection was over, her limbs felt as heavy as lead and she fell into a deep, dreamless sleep, unable to turn off her bed-side lamp, unaware of her father coming up to apologize for not quizzing her, and unconscious when Lilla came in with her cell phone to relay a message from Tres.

The next morning she couldn't hear sound, but she could just barely feel someone shaking her shoulders. It seemed as if she were in the bottom of a deep well, and while she knew something was coming out of both Lilla's and Casey's mouths, she could not make out the words or even the noise of them. Something pulsed slowly in her ear. Her heart beat slower and slower. She tried to move her fingers and her toes, but she couldn't seem to find them. She was suddenly aware of saliva building in the back of her throat, but she didn't think she could gain enough control of her body to swallow and for a moment she thought she might drown.

Help, she wanted to say, but her lips wouldn't move. There was a dull ache in her belly and a throb in her head as her adrenaline kicked in. Lilla leaned over and pulled back the hair in her face and seemed as though she were screaming at her, but she still couldn't hear. Then their mother came up the stairs, walked into the room, and started calling her name as if from a great, great distance. As if from the far end of a city block.

Help me, Mama, Catherine wanted to call, but she couldn't find her voice or her lips. When her mother came back with a cold wet rag and placed it on her head, it shocked her, finally, and she was able to sit up and she leaned forward and vomited all over her silky white down comforter. She looked around the room like a cornered animal. Had she hidden the bottle of pills? She didn't see it anywhere. She must have hidden it and all of the little casings with the green capsules in them.

She was smarter than that, wasn't she? She wouldn't have left them out. Her mother gently grabbed her elbow and helped her to the bathroom where she collapsed on the cold tile floor and retched more. It was an awful blackness that came from her stomach. It looked like something from the bottom of the oyster beds along the edge of the harbor.

"She must have the stomach bug," her mother called over her shoulder to her sisters as she held back Catherine's long, golden hair. "Go ahead and get ready for school, girls. I'll drive you."

But this was not the stomach bug and Catherine knew it. She had taken too many of the pills. She had found herself in a well that she didn't know if she could climb out of. How could she stop this dangerous habit? How could she tell her parents?

When her mother left to take the girls to school, Catherine rose from the bed, found the medication in the second drawer of her desk, emptied them all in the toilet, and flushed. *I want to end this,* she prayed to the God Coach Christiansen and Bryan believed was there. *Give me the strength to stop it. I cannot do it alone.*

Chapter 18

JACKSON

"So," Jackson said to a wide-eyed Father Roy Summerall early one Wednesday morning.

He was sitting in the same spot on the sofa of the priest's office where he sat five weeks ago. He was holding well-worn copies of the four books he'd been given: *Mere Christianity*, *The Everlasting Man*, *The Reason for God*, and *The Case for Christ*, and his Bible—the spine was good and cracked and had multicolored sticky notes carefully arranged all around the edges. It looked like a rectangular peacock.

On his left he had another stack of books, new copies of the very same apologetic books to add to the priest's library because he'd been so hard on the original ones. Plus, now that he'd underlined in them (often in the same places as the priest had), he was hoping to keep them for himself.

Jackson leaned forward and narrowed his eyes toward Father Summerall. He was excited, scared to death, but excited. "So, Reverend, why do *you* think we're here?"

The priest smiled and Jackson wondered what he was thinking. He had a kind of strength and certainty about him that seemed different than the usual ego-based type that he sensed in most men around town. He tugged at his tight collar and said, "To receive God's unmerited favor and love through the shed blood of Christ." He cleared his throat and continued, "To love Him back, to love our brothers and sisters, and to spread the gospel to the ends of the earth so every soul will have the chance to hear and know and believe."

Jackson shook his head and smiled. "Not about living a good life, is it?"

The priest rotated his shoulder forward. "Nope. That's the big misconception." He leaned forward to meet Jackson's gaze. Jackson could tell he was sizing him up, maybe assessing if he could move from milk to solid food. Jackson met his eyes as if to say, *I can. Let's get to the heart of the matter, Father Summerall.*

The priest blinked, then said, "Nine out of ten people who come to my office in need of counseling or help don't know that, even though I attempt to preach it every Sunday . . ." He shook his head. "Rather unconvincingly, I reckon. Anyhow, I'll say to them, 'What puts you in good standing with God?' and they say, 'I've lived my life the best way I can, I try to be as good and morally upright as possible.'"

"That's the law speaking," Jackson said. "They don't get grace."

The priest's eyes got as big as the skeet Jackson shot at the farm in Round O. Jackson knew the priest saw that he understood. "Either they don't get it or they don't want to, Jackson," Father Summerall said. "I'm not sure which."

"Well, it is awfully counterintuitive, don't you think?" Jackson shook his head. "It cuts against the grain of everything I've ever been told or taught in my life."

The reverend nodded firmly and Jackson could tell he was working hard to suppress a full-blown smile. "Yeah, Jackson. But it is the only way out of our condition. And it is the only thing that can set us free."

"I've been fighting this since my mama died," Jackson said. "I've been deliberately fighting this."

Roy nodded. "Why do you think that is?"

Jackson exhaled and rubbed his hands on his khaki pants. "Because God took her." He swallowed the lump in his throat. Where had that come from? He'd been facing this full on, hadn't he? "I was nine years old, and the preacher told me God needed another angel in heaven."

Roy shook his head in dismay. "That's not right, Jackson. That's not why she died."

Jackson swallowed. "I'm beginning to under-stand that now." He tapped his hands on the books. "It's a messed up world. I knew that. But it's not God who causes it to be a messed up world. In fact, as far as I can tell, He's done what needed to be done to bring us all home to the world we were built for." He shook his head and continued, "I've made some mistakes, Reverend. I've been stubborn as all get-out and selfish too. And some bigger ones than that, but I'm trying to right them the best way I know how."

There was a long silence between them. Jackson didn't know until the words came out that he really meant the part about God doing what He could to bring us home. But somehow he did. Somehow he was beginning to believe this was the truth. He was starting to know it the way he knew the tide would shift every six hours, the way he knew how to saw a piece of wood along its grain, or that a buck's stamp and snort beyond the trees meant that a second buck was nearby just beyond the first line of trees.

He felt he was falling, and he couldn't break the fall. Or maybe it was more of a leap, but a leap he didn't have any choice about. As if a Cape buffalo had chased him to the edge of a water hole that could be full of crocodiles. If this was what would fill him, finally, should he take the risk? But more importantly than the risk, he wanted forgiveness for his stubborn, self-centered life. He couldn't stand the thought of delaying that any longer.

He looked up at the priest and rubbed his hands together. "So here's the deal. I want to go all in." He made like he was putting a stack of poker chips in the middle of the table.

"You mean you believe?" Roy cocked his head.

"Yes." Jackson nodded once. "I told God on my morning walk here that I'm ready. So go on and tell me what to do next."

"Does your family know?"

He crossed his arms and furrowed his brow. "Mary Lynn suspects it, but she doesn't know for sure." He raised his eyebrows and nodded. "I think she'll be happy about it. She's the one who has been wanting us to come to church."

"Good." The priest nodded encouragingly. Jackson wondered if maybe Mary Lynn had talked to him about this before. "I bet she will be delighted," the priest said. "Please call me Roy."

"Okay, Roy. And I'm going to tell my kids today." Jackson crossed his legs and tapped his fingers across his shin. "This is going to change everything for them." He sat back. "And my guess is, they'll be glad."

"This may be the best news I've heard all year." Roy smiled and rubbed his own large palms together. "What joy."

"Thing with me, Roy," Jackson said as he pointed to the priest, "is that I don't do things halfway. I'm not bragging or anything, it's just the way I am. I'm usually all in or I'm all out, you know? I'm terrified by what that means, but I'm even more terrified to turn away from it."

"I'm glad to hear that, Jackson." Roy leaned forward and patted the man on the shoulder. "I could use your help. I could use someone who's all in. You'd be surprised how tough that is to come by, even at a church."

"So will you meet with me regularly? I need to start figuring out what to do. There's my money to think about, there's what role I can play in sharing the gospel. There's a new family mission statement I need to come up with. There's the suffering in the world I can't ignore any longer." Jackson felt his own heart beating fast. By the look on Roy's face, he was wondering if anyone ever before had been so straightforward.

"All right," Roy said. "How about we meet this time every week. Let's read a book of the Bible before each meeting starting with the New Testament. We'll go through it, we'll pray, and God will reveal His plan to you."

Jackson stood up quickly and shook Roy's hand hard, maybe as hard as a linebacker. Roy shook back with the same force and they both nodded their heads, and as he looked at the light in Roy's eyes he felt something like an electric light fill the room. Words came across his mind like a picture. They were from Ezekiel 36:26: "I will take the heart of stone out of your flesh and give you a heart of flesh."

Chapter 19

MARY LYNN

It was the Wednesday before Mary Lynn's big week. In one short week she would be hosting the Charlestowne Garden Club luncheon and presenting the new building plan to the parents and teachers of the Peninsula Day School. The South Carolina Debutante Society invitations would be mailed this week (according to Bev King, who had just lent her Nantucket cottage to the club's secretary over the holiday).

Mary Lynn hoped she would be receiving the engraved invitation she'd secretly dreamed about ever since they were invited as guests to their first debutante ball eight years ago. There was something about imagining her girls in the white dresses with the long white kid gloves curtsying on the polished hardwood floor of South Carolina Society Hall that filled her heart with a kind of hope and joy. It meant a lot to her. That was the truth. She'd admit it. A counselor, she was sure, would point out that it was merely her own need for social acceptance after a childhood of chuckles about the scandalous way in which she came into the world. A way to compensate for watching most of the girls in her fifth-grade class put on their fluffy tea-length dresses and white gloves and walk over to the little Meggett Country Club every Wednesday after school to learn the waltz and the fox trot and the proper way to greet an adult or get in and out of a car. She wasn't the first child not to know her father or to suffer the consequences of an illegitimate beginning, and she certainly wouldn't be the last. But she was thankful that her daughters never had to know that kind of shame, and somehow imagining them in beautiful white gowns gliding across the Society Hall dance floor in Jackson's arms—for all the world to see—was like a salve to her old heart wound.

She had her outfit for Wednesday, a pantsuit from St. John's that she stumbled across on the way to buy a new pair of brown loafers for Jackson at Gucci after Mac had chewed both of the heels of his old ones to bits. It was a gray and black eyelash knit-tweed blazer with three quarter sleeves and a rosebud print with the same rosebud print in a chiffon tank to match and pleated wide-leg wool pants. It was tastefully elegant, just dressy enough, and she would wear her silvery Tahitian pearl strand Jackson had bought for her at Cartier the last time they were in New York.

It was mid-morning and she was still in her running clothes with her hair pulled back in a ponytail. She was laying out the hand-painted china from Germany Seabrook brought over for the luncheon as Anarosa examined the silver serving pieces, deciding what needed to be polished, when Jackson walked through the door.

He bounded into the room, reached across the table, and put his hand on her back with a gentle firmness. "We need to talk, Mary Lynn."

She looked up at him, tucked a loose strand of stray hair behind her ear. She was so focused on getting ready for the big day that she had almost forgotten he was meeting with Roy Summerall this morning after having read those books.

"Okay," she said. Anarosa, who always tried to stay out of Jackson's way, held up a handful of tarnished forks and said, "I'll start polishing these."

"Great. Thank you."

Mary Lynn followed Jackson up the stairs to their bedroom and into the little sitting area over-looking the harbor.

"I did it, honey." He had a grin from ear to ear and his flushed face reminded her of his teenage years when he'd show up on her front stoop, his dad's maroon-colored pickup in the dirt driveway, to ask her on a date.

"Did what?" Her heart welled up thinking of those old days when they were young and in love. What a sweet time that had been. It seemed like the sweetness faded through the years and she just had to be thankful that she had at least experienced it. Now she had to savor the steadiness instead. She looked into his eyes and noticed a kind of light in them. There was something new about them. Or maybe it wasn't new so much as restored. Not a restored she had ever known in him, but a restoration nonetheless. She furrowed her brow and chuckled. "What do you mean?"

"I'm a Christian."

"What?" She felt her jaw drop. He had been reading the books, but she thought it would likely be several years of the truth working its way through his skeptical mind and his hardened heart before it came to pass—if ever.

He nodded his head excitedly and took both of her hands in his and rocked them gently back and forth. "I believe it, Mary Lynn. The whole kit and caboodle from Adam and Eve to the birth, life, death, and resurrection of Christ."

Her eyes widened. She thought of the prayer she uttered on Christmas Eve just two months ago.

"You *believe* it? *Really,* Jackson?"

"Yes. I do, Mary Lynn." He looked out of the window. "And I've never felt more alive."

A large sailboat was headed up the Ashley River toward the drawbridge. She watched him watching and then he turned back with soft, wet, fiery green eyes. "This changes everything, Mary Lynn. You know that, right?" He shook his head as though he was shaking off a blow. "The mission statement, what's important, it all shifts now. The whole trajectory turns."

Her heart beat rapidly. She could hardly believe her ears. She liked the idea of everything shifting dramatically. It had been her secret yearning for some time now. She hoped it would be good and right.

"That sounds great to me." She shifted her weight, sat down on the love seat, and patted the seat next to hers. "How do you envision it changing?"

He sat down and put his head in his hands. "Well, I'm not sure." He squared his shoulders and turned to her. "As far as I can pinpoint, the whole reason that we are here is to love God back, love our neighbors because He loved us, and share what Jesus did to reconcile us to our Father to the ends of the earth. Anything that doesn't feed directly into that needs to go. Some of the business stuff doesn't seem right anymore either. I probably need to separate from Waters."

She had drifted for a moment. The sound of the gardener trimming the hedges reminded her of the time he got carried away and made the bushes so bare they looked like bald heads lined up against the fence. Had she reminded him not to cut it too close this time?

She turned back to Jackson, who was eager for her to respond. "He's not going to like that."

"I know," Jackson said. "But he'll get over it. I think I know enough now for us to do well and not be wrapped up in his ventures. All right?"

She nodded and swallowed hard. Mark could certainly survive without Jackson and maybe, just maybe, he could be drawn to God too, over time. "So what are we going to tell the girls?"

He rubbed his large, strong hands together. "Well, I'm going to share the gospel with them tonight and then we'll go to church on Sunday."

She breathed in and out. She thought of Scottie and the other ladies laying hands on her at the Wednesday gathering. The Lord had answered her prayers. She could hardly believe it. What would they say when Jackson walked into church with her and the girls?

She embraced him, and he held her tight for whole minutes. She wanted to rest, rest in his arms. She wished she could stop time for a moment. *Thank you, Lord. You are amazing,* she thought and she closed her eyes until the sound of the trimmer woke her from her praise. She stood, opened the window, and called to the gardener, "Not too close!" She wanted everything to be just so. This was the big week. This was it. Everything was coming together.

That afternoon when the girls arrived home from school, lugging their backpacks and instrument cases, Jackson was waiting at the door.

"Family meeting, gals," he said. "Put up your stuff and come down here as quickly as you can."

Lilla rolled her eyes slightly and Catherine

blew a strand of golden hair out of her face. Casey looked to Mary Lynn, who gave her a reassuring grin, then she ran upstairs and put up her backpack and viola.

"Wow," Lilla said when she walked back into the den. Jackson had gone to Krispy Kreme and come home with a dozen of their favorites: the chocolate-covered donuts stuffed with custard. He also had a big pitcher of chocolate milk. Jackson had always wanted them to eat a healthy after-school snack so they could focus on their homework, usually cheese and nuts and fruit. Mary Lynn had to chuckle.

Catherine looked at the spread and then at the time on her cell phone. "We have twenty minutes to get to our strings lesson."

"No, no, no." Jackson swatted a hand in her direction. "We're going to skip that today."

"What?" Catherine shook her head while Lilla raised her eyebrows nearly as high as her hairline. "Our recital is in two weeks." Sweet little Casey just giggled, grabbed a donut, and looked at her two sisters with an expression that said, *Has Dad flipped his lid?* Suddenly Catherine looked a little worried. The last time they had skipped practice it was because Mary Lynn's mama had passed unexpectedly in the night from a stroke at the retirement community in Hilton Head. "Did someone die?"

Jackson grinned. "Well, yes, they did, Catherine

Scoville." He pulled out an evangelism cube he'd bought at the Saints Alive bookstore. "Two thousand years ago someone extremely important to us died. And His particular death was a sacrifice that saved the lives of you, me, and all of mankind."

"Huh?" Lilla's nose crinkled as if something smelled bad. She looked to Catherine and made that *Dad might be nuts* face. Then she grabbed a donut and sat down next to Casey.

Mary Lynn could not help but smile. She felt as though she were living a dream. She couldn't believe the words coming out of Jackson's mouth. Life would be better from here on out. Oh, she hoped it would.

Casey stopped petting Mac for a moment. "Are you talking about Jesus, Daddy?"

"Why, yes, I am, pumpkin. How did you know?"

She nodded at the book on the coffee table. He glanced at the Bible and then back to her.

" 'Cause you've been reading that lately."

He held up the EvangeCube so they could all see it. The first side had a man on one side with a black background and then a rip in the middle and a bright light on the other side of the rip. "Pour yourself some milk and get comfortable, girls. I'm going to tell you all about it."

That night Mary Lynn called Scottie. She told her what had happened and Scottie squealed with delight.

"Did the girls respond positively?"

"They were caught a little off guard," she said. "Catherine never seemed to get her mind off of her violin lesson. But he shared the gospel in a very straightforward, compelling way, and he told them why he believed and that he was ready to say the prayer with them anytime they wanted. And that we were going to go to church and we were going to read the Bible and rethink what was important and what wasn't. They didn't have much to say, but I could tell they all liked the sound of rethinking what was important."

Mary Lynn chuckled. "He's such a task master. Maybe he'll relax a little now. I want that for them . . . for all of us."

"I'm sure he will," Scottie said reassuringly.

"Anyway, Casey took the EvangeCube up to her room and she was opening and closing it when I came in to check on her."

"This is good, Mary Lynn," Scottie said. "This is unbelievably good."

"I know," Mary Lynn said. "Now pray for my busy week. This is a really important one."

"Sure thing," Scottie said. "Tell me all about it."

Late that Thursday afternoon Mary Lynn and Casey walked in after an hour-long viola lesson. "Daddy, want to hear what I learned at my lesson?"

His nose was deep into the Bible, and it looked as though he was taking down all sorts of notes.

He looked up at her and smiled. Then he closed the book and put his arms out. The little girl walked over and he pulled her close.

"I'd rather just hold you for a minute." He tucked a strand of black, silky hair behind her ear. "How was your day today, sweetheart?"

She looked up at Mary Lynn as though she thought this was hilarious. He rarely wanted to sit and chat about anyone's day.

"It was okay." She squinted her eyes as if rewinding a little video of her day in her mind.

"Tell me." He patted her back. "I want details."

She shrugged and Mary Lynn detected a half smile forming. "I played a little four square on the sport court and then a little basketball. Mrs. Yancey wants me to try out for the basketball team, but it would kind of mess up my Mandarin and viola schedule."

He rubbed his chin, then pulled her close. "Maybe that would be okay. Would you like to try out?"

"Are you serious, Dad?" The little girl pulled up and looked back at him. "I've always wanted to play a sport."

"I didn't know that." He looked at Mary Lynn, who rolled her eyes. Casey had been asking her dad if she could play basketball and soccer for the last five years now, but it had always interfered with the foreign language and music schedule. Where was he?

He turned back to his youngest daughter. "I think you should, Case. I think you should try out for the basketball team this year. Why not?" She embraced him and Mary Lynn chuckled.

"What's happening to you, Daddy?" Casey asked.

He stared at his notes and then back to her. "I'm not sure. Maybe I'm just getting old."

Mary Lynn squeezed his shoulders. "Maybe you're getting a little soft." She looked at Casey. "That wouldn't be the end of the world, would it?"

Casey's eyes lit up. "No, ma'am!" she said. "That wouldn't be bad at all." And they all three laughed at the truth of the matter.

"What are you reading about?" Casey asked him.

"Grace," he said. "Do you know what that is?"

"You mean like dancing real lightly at ballet?"

"Nah," he said. "It's a much better definition than that. Let me show you how it works."

"Okay," she said.

He stood and called up the stairs to Catherine, who came down and walked apprehensively into the den.

"What is it?" she asked. "I have a huge calculus test tomorrow."

"Catherine," Jackson said. He pulled out the Vineyard Vine key chain from his pocket and handed it to her. Her jaw dropped and her eyes grew wide. "Even though you messed up, I want to forget it all. I want to pay the ticket and give you back your car." He winked at Casey and looked back to Catherine. "Because I love you deeply."

Catherine looked at Mary Lynn and then back to her father. Her posture seemed to say she was a little wary. He pointed out the window where the car was parked. He'd gone to get it back from the dealership.

"I don't know what to say, Dad."

"Say thank you," he said.

"Thank you!" She ran over and kissed him. "Thank you! Thank you!"

Mary Lynn watched her precious daughter who was certainly a young woman now. She had been worried about her, and she knew the car wouldn't solve the anxiety she had over taking the SAT test. He pulled back and squeezed her shoulders. "Now I still want you to try your best for the SAT. But if you think you can take on track and field this spring, I want you to do it."

Catherine turned back to her mother and then back to her father. "Really?"

He nodded. "Yeah. I know you love it, and I don't want to keep you from it. Plus, you're really good."

Mary Lynn could almost visibly see something fall off of Catherine. Like whatever worry she had been carrying around could be unzipped like a body bag and she could step out of it.

Mary Lynn looked at her husband. He was smiling gently at their eldest daughter. She wondered if he could see it too. Catherine stepping out of whatever had been containing her these last months since the SAT scores had come in. Whether he did or not, it didn't matter. He was giving her life. Mary Lynn didn't think she had ever loved him more.

Catherine's hands trembled. "Dad, I don't know what to say."

Casey was beaming beside her, watching her big sister fill with joy. "Say yes, Catherine!" the little girl said. "Say yes, and go drive around in your car with the windows rolled down and the music playing!"

"Yeah," Jackson said. He stood and embraced his eldest. "Casey's got it. Just say yes and then celebrate."

"Yes." Catherine squeezed him back. She breathed deeply and took the keys from his hand as Lilla walked into the room.

"What did I miss?" She looked around at everyone smiling, Catherine through tears.

Catherine held up the keys to show Lilla, who squealed. "Want to go for a spin?"

"You bet!" Lilla said and they both bolted out of the kitchen door with Mac barking behind them.

Now Jackson turned to Casey, who was bouncing up and down in all of the excitement. "Well, it's not the perfect metaphor, but it gives you an idea. God loves us not because of anything we do or don't do, but because He just loves us."

The little girl nodded. "I think I'm starting to see."

He leaned over and kissed her forehead. "He loves us so much that He sent His Son to die for us, not while we were well-behaved, but while we were misbehaving—terribly."

"Wow." The little girl hugged him. She could barely reach his waist. "Thanks for making Catherine so happy." She squeezed him as tight as her thin little arms could. "For giving her grace."

He rubbed her back. "Thanks for understanding it, Case."

Chapter 20

JACKSON

The next Sunday morning as the bells from the St. Michael's steeple rang out through the city streets, Jackson took a deep, satisfied breath and straightened his bow tie in the mirror. Something about the other afternoon and giving Catherine back the car and telling her she could run track had gotten the girls excited about going to church. Mary Lynn didn't have to tell them to get up and get ready more than once, which was a minor miracle in and of itself.

He could hear their hair dryers going and their leather shoes click-clacking on the third floor just above him, and when they walked out onto the sidewalk, all dressed for church with fresh faces and pressed dresses, he felt more proud and purposeful than he had ever felt. As if maybe the longing could be satisfied through this new life of faith. And it had to do with them doing it together. With him leading and them following. It was a purpose, a real purpose, and he could feel his chest puffing up at the thought of it.

He took Mary Lynn's hand and it felt warm and soft and delicate. Did she have any idea how much he adored her? How he had her to thank for this spiritual awakening? Through the years he hadn't paid her the attention he should have and he was sorry. He wanted to make up for the lost time. He wanted to know her completely, to give her a safe place to be herself; he wanted them to grow on this spiritual journey together.

He leaned over and kissed her tenderly on the cheek the way he had when they were teenagers and he'd be walking her up to the front-door stoop of her Uncle Dale's late at night, returning her home after a long walk along Edisto Beach or a movie in Charleston.

She looked up at him, and he wanted to tell her how beautiful she was. How fantastic she looked, how good her heart was, but he thought if he started right now on the way to church he just might break down. As soon as they were alone tonight, he would make time to tell her everything. He hadn't ever consciously decided to take her for granted and he hadn't ever been unfaithful to her, and yet there had been a wall between them from time to time. He squeezed her hand and he hoped she could sense the hope and the promise in the squeeze. He was passionate about her. They were going to enter into this second half of life hand in hand, and he would do all in his power to make the latter part of their marriage even more full of love than the first. He was going to love her with all of his heart and make time to show her.

As they made their way down Meeting Street toward St. Michael's, the air smelled sweet. The last of the camellias were blooming and Jackson reached out to touch one of the soft, satiny petals as they crossed over a lovely garden on Tradd Street.

As they passed by South Carolina Society Hall, he spotted Roy Summerall a block and a half away standing under the church portico with the crucifer and the choir. The priest was praying aloud before the service commenced, and when he looked up, Jackson gave him a big wave. "Hi, Roy!" he called. He was nearly a block away now, but he thought the priest had spotted him and his family. Roy squinted for a moment and then waved back and smiled a hearty smile. *God is good. God is good. God is good,* Jackson said to himself as they approached the church.

When they reached the portico, Jackson shook Roy's hand firmly and Mary Lynn gave him a big kiss on the cheek before reintroducing him to the children who, with the exception of the youngest, seemed a little unsure as they looked to one another and looked at all of the congregants greeting one another as if it were old home week.

Jackson observed Roy taking note of Catherine's and Lilla's nervousness. He watched him signal a handsome chap in a jacket with a nose ring and flip-flops who came over immediately and introduced himself to the girls. He was the youth minister, Keith Jennings, and he invited them to the Wednesday night youth group.

The girls nudged one another. Catherine shrugged and nodded her head. "Okay," she said. "If we can get our homework finished in time, we'll come by."

"Great." Keith smiled his sincere smile and headed into church. Then out of the corner of Jackson's eye he spotted Bryan Christiansen, Catherine's friend from the track team. He wondered if she had told him the good news. As he nudged Catherine to point Bryan out, he watched her quickly stare down at her feet. By the time Jackson looked back up he noticed Bryan glancing their way and then turning briskly into the church. *Kids,* he thought.

Later that morning, as the Scovilles sat in a pew

in the front, fumbling through the prayer books and hymnals to find their place, Roy came over and gave them all hugs during the peace. "Don't worry about keeping up with everything," he said. "It gets easier each Sunday."

Jackson loved the sermon. An old football buddy of Roy's from the Clemson days, Shep Douglas, was the guest preacher. He had gone to seminary after selling insurance for a few years, and he talked about the life he had chosen to lead in inner city Atlanta where he and his family ministered in a rough neighborhood and coached all sorts of inner city kids in church sports. It was a real testimony about stepping off of the worldly track and into a life of service, and he beamed as if to say, *Don't you see. This is the abundant life.*

Jackson immediately thought of how he'd been spending his time and energy over the last decade. Certainly it wasn't in giving. It was in taking and taking some more, and he wondered how one could make that kind of shift to a life of serving others. *Show me the way,* he prayed in his pew during communion. Yes, he was scared, but he was ready to try.

At the coffee hour in the parish hall just after the service, Roy waved Jackson over and introduced him to his old buddy. "Wow," Jackson said. "That was some sermon. I'd love to come to Atlanta and help you sometime. I'm ready to go all in. I'm serious about it."

"Great." Shep shook his hand hard. He handed Jackson his card. "We're planning a Vacation Bible School for spring break, and I could use you then."

"All right." Jackson smiled and felt as if he'd landed his first fish or performed the Haydn quartet without even the faintest of bow screeches. "Let's do it." He pointed to Mary Lynn and his daughters, who were pouring lemonade into little wax cups for each other. "Maybe my girls can help too. If the spring breaks align."

"Oh yeah," Shep said. "We'd put the whole gang to work. Last year over two hundred kids showed up." He leaned toward Jackson. "It's not like these folks are headed to Disney World or the Bahamas. Their parents, or I should say their parent, because most of them only have one, have to work and they like to know their kids are safe and off the street during the day, even if they are skeptical about church, especially a big, goofy white guy's church." They all laughed. "Anyhow, we try to make it a good time for the kids with all kinds of games and crafts and prizes and the more help we have the better." He grabbed Jackson by the shoulder and nodded firmly. "Especially from folks who are all in."

As they shook hands, an older man with a hook for a hand walked over with a cup of piping hot coffee to bend Roy's ear about something. Jackson remembered his name as he approached.

Colonel Simmons. He had met him in the back bar at the yacht club a few months ago. Jackson heard Roy say, "We're not going to budge on that one, Colonel. Even if Anne and I have to cook the casseroles ourselves, it's important for the believers to break bread with the seekers. Something miraculous happens when you share a meal together. We've talked about this. You know we can't give that up."

"Mmph." The colonel furrowed his brow.

"How about we hold off on that paint job in the parish hall." Jackson watched Roy look around at the room they were standing in. "We really don't have to do that every three years. If you ask me, this place looks fine."

Colonel Simmons grumbled. "It looks great because we take good care of it. Without a well-maintained building, what happens to the church?"

Roy raised his eyebrows and Jackson was getting pretty good at reading him. He had something good to counter with and Jackson smiled as he heard him say, "That's a great question. And it kind of gets to the heart of what the bishop suggested we focus on during our upcoming vestry retreat."

"What's that?" The colonel gave a stern eye toward Roy.

"What is the church?" he asked. "Is it the building or is it the people?"

The colonel shook his head. "We've been able

to boast of some of the best maintained buildings on the peninsula for generations, Roy."

Roy took a deep breath. "I'll look forward to hashing this all out at the retreat."

After Shep turned to greet some other parishioners, a group of boys from the youth group who had football questions cornered him so Roy introduced Jackson to the colonel.

"Good to see you again, Colonel Simmons," Jackson said. "I've been anxious to get together with you."

"That so?" Simmons blew air through his nose. He reminded Jackson of Colonel Hathi, the pompous old elephant in Disney's animated version of Kipling's *The Jungle Book*, and he tried not to chuckle imagining Colonel Simmons inspecting his trunk.

"Yeah." Jackson nodded eagerly. "So what's the plan?"

"I beg your pardon?" Colonel Simmons asked.

"To spread the gospel to the ends of the earth," Jackson said. "That's what we're about, right? So what's the game plan? I want to get in on it."

The colonel looked off for a moment, bit his lip, then looked back at Jackson and to Roy who was standing firmly by Jackson. "Well, first we have to get this budget under control. Giving is down."

Roy nodded.

Jackson crossed his arms and said discreetly, "By how much?"

"Seventy-five thousand dollars." The colonel raised his furry eyebrows.

"We can take care of that." Jackson turned to Roy. "Roy and I are going to meet this week, and I'm ready to tithe. I get it now. It's not my own. I've got to look at my finances, but if I start today, I think it will be somewhere in the neighborhood of two hundred thousand we can give this year."

The colonel shook his head in disbelief. "Don't tell anyone, of course," Jackson leaned in to say. "Can't let the right hand know what the left hand is doing." He turned to Roy. "Which gospel is that?"

"Matthew 6." Roy smiled.

"Right," Jackson said. "I apologize, Colonel. I'm new to all this. But anyhow, once that's taken care of, what next? I'm ready to go. To make disciples of all nations baptizing them in the name of the Father and the Son and the Holy Spirit."

Roy gave a deep belly laugh. The colonel turned to Roy and elbowed him. "Where'd you find this one?"

Roy smiled. "He's a neighbor. Just called up and wanted to meet a few weeks ago."

Jackson nodded eagerly and called Mary Lynn over. "I want you to meet my wife. She's been coming here for Bible study for a few years."

Mary Lynn shook the colonel's hand, then called

the girls over and introduced them to him. "Well, what a beautiful family," he said. "Welcome to St. Michael's." He seemed a whole lot more chipper than he had a few minutes ago.

After Scottie came up to say hello to Mary Lynn, the girls headed back to the cookie table where someone had laid out a fresh tray of home-made chocolate chip oatmeal cookies.

"Anyway," Jackson said to the colonel and Roy, "I know y'all have a plan so I don't want to step on any toes, but I did want to share that I found this website called Operation World and I had their book overnighted. Got it yesterday and it contains real detailed information on every nation in the world including statistics on the religious makeup of every country and updates on gospel work in every country. It also includes a prayer guide that you can follow, and if you follow it over the course of a year, you will pray specifically for every nation in the world. It tells us where all the unreached places are and everything."

"Great," Roy said. "Bring that in on our Tuesday morning meeting."

"All right." Jackson turned to the colonel. "This is all subject to Roy's approval, of course, but I want to evangelize in the city and I'm not afraid of street evangelism. Then I want to go at least two or maybe three times a year to an unreached place overseas." Jackson gripped the bulletin firmly and noticed his knuckles turning white.

"I want to make up for lost time. Jesus said go, and well, I'm ready!"

Colonel Simmons looked rather stunned. He didn't seem to know what to say.

"Let's all get together sometime soon," Jackson said to Roy and the colonel. "I'm going to take the confirmation class and we're going to join the church as soon as we can."

"Very well," the colonel said. He stuck out his hand. "Pleasure to meet you and your lovely family, Mr. Scoville."

"Oh, you too, Colonel Simmons."

On the way home Jackson couldn't help the spring in his step. He was so frisky he was walking ahead of the girls and Mary Lynn, who could hardly keep up in her heels.

"Wasn't that great?" he said. "Going to church. I loved it."

When no one answered he turned back and noticed Mary Lynn comforting Catherine, who seemed to be crying.

Lilla and Casey caught up with their dad.

"What's wrong with Cat?" he asked Lilla. He was usually the last to figure out when the girls were upset.

"Bryan rescinded his prom invitation, Dad. And he didn't even talk to her today after church."

Jackson shook his head. "Prom invitation? I didn't know he had extended one."

Lilla shrugged. "Yeah. He did. Anyway, he thinks Catherine is all into Tres King so he told her to go with him."

Girls. There was always a little drama. Well, while he didn't understand it and could hardly fathom that he had a child old enough to go the prom, he wanted to make sure Catherine knew he loved her and even though this was small potatoes, he cared if she was upset.

He walked over and rubbed her back. She turned away from her mother and into his arms, and he squeezed her tight and rocked her back and forth. He should have spent a lot more time doing this than he had over the last few years. He said the only thing that seemed to help with the girls. He was finally beginning to realize that they didn't want things to be fixed right away, they just wanted you to commiserate.

"I'm sorry, sweetheart. I'm so sorry, my love."

Chapter 21

MARY LYNN

On Wednesday, less than an hour before the guests arrived, the doorbell rang. It was the UPS man, and he dropped ten boxes, each the size of a file storage box, at the front door and was pulling back onto the road before Mary Lynn could get his attention. She didn't need to deal with another thing this moment and was hoping that whatever it was, he could leave it on his truck until tomorrow. As the brown truck sped away, she looked down at the stack of cardboard boxes taking up a good fourth of her piazza. When she looked at the return address it said Campus Crusade for Christ. *Jackson.* What was he up to now? He was getting awfully zealous as he looked at his globe and prayed about the world. He'd been doing this for the last few days. She was thankful, of course, but she hoped he might slow down a bit. They had a life here in Charleston, and today was a day devoted to the society that they had tried so hard and diligently to become a part of.

Jackson had bolted out of the door so fast this morning to meet with Roy that she didn't even have a chance to remind him that today was the big day and she needed him to stay out of the way at lunchtime and then be there by her side at the Day School this evening to help present the building plan. Surely he remembered. He couldn't have missed the flower arrangements all over the house or the stacks of china and silver trays in the dining room.

Mary Lynn was dressed impeccably, and she didn't want to lift the boxes that were already a little damp from the trickle of cold rain that was coming down. It had been raining off and on for the last twenty-four hours. She looked around for someone to give her a hand. The girls were at school, Jackson was at the church, Anarosa and the catering crew were in the kitchen putting the garnish on the silver platters of shrimp salad and loading up the tiered silver trays with crab cakes and quiches and chicken salad tarts and asparagus wrapped in prosciutto and fresh berry kabobs and little cheesecakes. And Carlos had run to get more ice from the convenience store. Mary Lynn shrugged grudgingly, then she carefully unbuttoned her thousand-dollar jacket, slipped it off, and laid it on the joggling board, then lifted up a box that was surprisingly heavy and carried it into the house. It took ten trips, one box at a time, and she shoved them all in the storage closet under the stairwell.

She went back onto the piazza, grabbed her jacket, then ran upstairs to roll the lint from the cardboard boxes off of her trousers. Mac, whom she had stowed away in Casey's room, had been barking up a storm ever since the doorbell rang and she could hear him scraping his paws on the hardwood floor. She ran up the next flight of stairs, opened the door to Casey's room, and called, "Settle down, Mac. I'll let you out soon." Just as she turned to leave, he bounded toward her, leaving a string of slobber and snot on the back of her perfectly pressed pleated wool pants.

She closed the door, took a deep breath, and

willed the perspiration burning beneath her arms to cease. She'd been planning this day for a year. Oh, she hoped it would not only run smoothly but that it would be an especially nice and memorable event. She put more into coordinating this luncheon than she had into her own wedding, which was under the live oak trees near the dock of her aunt and uncle's home.

She quickly wiped the slobber off of her pants with a damp hand towel, ran the hair dryer over the wet spot, and headed back downstairs to survey the elegant room. Her florist, Tiger Lily, had created a gorgeous centerpiece in her tall silver urn bursting with white calla lilies and pale green hydrangeas and peachy roses with auburn edges. Everything in the room sparkled, and she smiled at the new portrait hanging above her fireplace. It was of an elegant but rather buttoned-up English woman from the early nineteenth century. They had bought it at the Portobello Road Market over their Christmas vacation and named her Aunt Flossy. When they hung it above the mantle a few weeks ago, Casey had said, "Aunt Flossy looks a little bit bossy." And Mary Lynn had trouble looking at it without imagining Aunt Flossy coming to life and wagging her finger at them for hauling her across the sea to a nouveaux riche stranger's house in the terribly obnoxious United States of America.

She put her jacket back on, reapplied her lipstick, and tucked it into a drawer in the sideboard just as the doorbell rang.

"Hi there!" Bev waddled into the room in a snug brown tweed suit with large gold buttons and kissed Mary Lynn on the cheek. Mary Lynn thought again that Bev simply refused to move up to a size 8.

She surveyed the dining room. "Everything looks gorgeous, Mary Lynn. Just perfect."

"Thank you." Mary Lynn blushed. "I'm glad it came together."

Bev formed her brown painted lips into a tight smile and reached out and squeezed Mary Lynn's forearm. "Me too." Then she took a step closer. "The debutante club invitations were mailed yesterday, and word is there is one addressed to you."

"Really?" Mary Lynn took a deep breath and held it for a moment. She pictured the white gloves in her locker at Meggett Middle School and imagined herself pulling them out and stomping on them for Claire and all of the ugly girls who laughed at her to see.

"Yes." Bev winked. "Georgia Franklin came over for cocktails last night and after two cosmopolitans she spilled the beans."

Mary Lynn clapped her hands together. She was living a dream.

When the first guests arrived, Mary Lynn stood at the door and welcomed them in. Everyone was offered mimosas and peach iced tea and coffee or Perrier. Once everyone mingled for a while, they were invited to go through the buffet. Then they took their places all around the living room, dining room, and den until Mary Lynn rang a bell and invited them to the living room where the presentation would take place. The presentation was always a sort of afterthought—anticlimactic to the annual luncheon itself. This year they had invited Eunice Simms Quattlebaum to talk about her recent book, *Hidden Gardens of Charleston.*

Weezie Pruitt, the president of the South Carolina Debutante Society and a fifth generation member of the garden club, was all smiles. She'd had two mimosas and two cheesecake squares, and she took Mary Lynn aside just as she was walking into the living room for the presentation and whispered, "Be on the lookout for a special letter this week."

Mary Lynn blushed and nodded. She was speechless.

Just as Eunice came to the conclusion of her presentation, the front door opened and a man who looked like he lived his life on the street walked through the door. His clothes were stiff with frayed edges and he had a stench—a cross between a dank watering hole and a port-o-potty —that was palpable. He looked at the ladies as though he happened upon this kind of scene daily, and he scratched at the stubby, splotchy

257

beard that was growing all the way down his neck.

The women closest to him squinched up their noses and turned to Mary Lynn with a look on their faces that was a blend of shock and disgust.

"Can I help you?" Mary Lynn raced to the foyer, the fringe on her jacket fluttering up around her forearms.

"Not to worry, honey," Jackson said as he popped around the door. He was dressed surprisingly down in jeans and a gray fleece pullover. "He's with me. This is Edgar." He looked to Mary Lynn and then back at the group assembled in straight rows in the living room. "Hi there, ladies." The women looked to one another and then back to the scene in the foyer. Mary Lynn thought she detected the slightest smile on Bev's face as if this were a movie she never thought she'd have the chance to see.

Mary Lynn excused herself and then pulled Jackson out in the foyer as several ladies cleared their throats and readjusted their posture and Eunice waved her hand and said, "I'd be honored to answer any questions about the book."

"What are you doing?" Mary Lynn's eyes bore a hole into Jackson, but she could tell he didn't seem to notice. He leaned toward Mary Lynn. "We were looking for a delivery from Campus Crusade for Christ. Has it come?"

"Jackson." Her voice was hushed but terse. "I want you to get this man out of here right now.

I've been planning this luncheon for a year. What are you thinking?"

Edgar looked up from the dining room. He was helping himself to a few chicken salad tarts on one of the unused gilded china plates, and he cocked his head and gazed at Mary Lynn as if to say, *I may live on the street, but I do have ears.*

"We'll get out of your way in two shakes, sweetheart," Jackson murmured good-heartedly. He walked toward the hall closet, located the boxes, and asked Edgar to give him a hand loading them in the truck.

"Don't worry," he said to Edgar. "Anarosa can pack us up a nice to-go box before we hit the streets."

Hit the streets? Mary Lynn didn't even want to know. She just wanted them to get the heck out of here as fast as they could. She cleared her throat, straightened out her jacket, and walked regally back through the foyer and into the room.

Several eyes flashed in her direction and then back to the speaker who was showing a photo of a Japanese garden abundant with delicate ferns that very few people knew existed just beyond the gates of 32 Church Street.

Everyone clapped after the speaker answered a few more questions and the garden club president, Marney Pringle, made several announcements about the upcoming garden tour in April. Then the guests filed out, thanking Mary Lynn with a certain look on their faces that seemed to say, *Well, it was almost perfect, dear.*

Mary Lynn followed the last guests out onto the piazza to bid them farewell. Bev King was hanging back. Mary Lynn was sure she was going to have much to say about Jackson's abrupt appearance. As Mary Lynn stepped out onto the sidewalk to give the final cheek kisses and good-byes, she noticed Jackson backing his pickup through the electronic driveway gate with the boxes in the back of his truck. He had forgotten to secure the tailgate, and as he hit the little dip at the end of the driveway, it fell open and one of the boxes fell out, spilling shrink-wrapped containers of little yellow tracts titled "Four Spiritual Laws" all over the wet sidewalk and into the street.

Mary Lynn tried to point the women in the opposite direction as Jackson and Edgar hopped out of the pickup and tried to salvage the packages, some of which had fallen into a fairly deep puddle at the end of their driveway. When Edgar bent down to pick up the tracts, his pants nearly fell down, and Mary Lynn thought she might faint at the sight of his underwear, just as Weezie Pruitt grabbed her arm and said, "The luncheon was divine, Mary Lynn." She kissed her cheek. "I'll look forward to tonight's presentation."

Mary Lynn pulled her shoulders back and spread her legs a little wider, trying to block Weezie's view of the men scrambling to salvage their mess.

"Oh, thank you, Weezie," Mary Lynn said. "It was an honor." She breathed a huge sigh of relief as Weezie turned the opposite direction and headed north on South Battery toward her car.

Chapter 22

MARY LYNN

By the time the girls arrived home that afternoon Mary Lynn had gone over the Day School presentation three times. The Head of School, Betsy Flanagan, had sent her a text that a reporter from the *Post and Courier* would be there as well as a representative from the mayor's office. She felt the butterflies in her stomach as she tucked her notes into the file folder while the girls trudged up the stairs with their instruments and book bags. Lilla was bemoaning the fact that she had to write an essay tonight (after a week of procrastination) about the relationship between reason and faith in Dante's *Inferno* while Cissy was asking Catherine to drill her on her times tables for the fourth-grade competition tomorrow.

Mary Lynn had been so busy this last week that she hadn't stayed on top of the girls' work or checked in on them the way she usually did, and Jackson, who was usually relentless about checking and double-checking their homework, had all but dropped any interest in it since he started reading his Bible and meeting with Roy Summerall.

Just on the heels of the girls, Jackson came through the front door like a ball of energy. His face was wind-burned, his clothes were droopy, but his eyes were sparkling like the midday sun on the harbor. He called up to them, "Girls, tonight is youth group at the church."

"Dad, I have a big essay due tomorrow," Lilla said. "The *Inferno*, remember?"

"Essay?" He swatted at the air. "That's *this life* stuff. And this life is *short*. What we need to keep in mind is that eternity is sure and goes on forever. You've got to get focused now, Lilla. Let Dante and hell worry about themselves."

The thought suddenly crossed Mary Lynn's mind that Jackson might be drunk. He was hanging around that street fellow, and even with his newfound faith she couldn't imagine him encouraging Lilla to blow off a major essay.

"Mama," Lilla called as she bolted down the third-floor stairs toward the master bedroom. Mary Lynn could feel the roll of her daughter's eyes before she even hit the threshold of the bedroom door. She lowered her voice slightly as Jackson walked up the stairs toward them. "Please talk some sense into Mr. Jesus Freak, will you? This paper is worth forty percent of my overall semester grade."

"I want to go, Mama," Casey said. She scooted around Lilla and hopped up on the large antique four poster bed. "I like youth group. But I've got to know my times table through twelve by tomorrow. Can you drill me?"

"I wouldn't *mind* going." Catherine came down with her violin and bow in hand. "I mean, I kind of like it . . ." She shrugged. She looked at her bow and back to her mother. "But does anyone remember that on top of my SAT in two weeks, my violin recital is next Thursday? Mr. Shue said that if I don't practice at least an hour a day between now and then, there is no way I'll be able to pull off the Mozart piece." She twisted the knobs and ran the bow over the strings in an effort to tune the instrument. Mary Lynn never could tell exactly when an instrument was properly tuned. Truth be told, she still favored the sound of her Uncle Dale's mandolin or the acoustic guitar.

Catherine looked to Jackson. "And did I mention that he's already printed the program, Dad?"

Mary Lynn looked down at her Peninsula Day School file folder and then over to the mounted maps of the new buildings and the overall campus once they officially acquired the new property and the additions were complete. She still didn't fully understand how much green space would be left on campus nor did she have a clear sense of how the children would be able to focus and stay out of harm's way during the school year as the steel pilings were hammered into the ground and the new buildings constructed, and she knew that question would be asked. Her stomach flip flopped again and she noticed a sour taste in her mouth.

She was still furious with Jackson for his intrusion at the luncheon today. He had most certainly marred an otherwise flawless event. And what had he been doing with that strange man? She hoped he wasn't giving him money so he could fund whatever his habit was. Surely Jackson wasn't that naïve even in his new born-again state. As he made his way into the room, the girls held their noses. He smelled like gasoline and smoke and bacon and sweat. Did he even remember about the presentation this evening? And yes, youth group was important, but so were violin recitals and school and grades and GPAs. College was just around the corner for Lilla as well.

Mary Lynn was becoming more livid by the moment as she thought of all of his missteps, and she didn't even know where to start once she had a moment alone with him.

She felt her knees buckle and she thought she just might faint as her family crowded around her calling simultaneously, "Mama!" "Honey." "Mo-o-o-o-m!"

Her stomach ached and she clapped her hands over her ears and closed her eyes. "Stop it!" she screamed. Everyone got quiet and took a step back. She opened her eyes and took her hands just half an inch away from her ears. Then she fired off orders in a manner and tone that was decidedly Jackson. "Catherine, go drill Casey on her times tables and then get to work practicing for the recital. Lilla, get up to your room and work on that paper. I want to read it when I get home tonight. Jackson, stay right here. I need a word with you." She cleared her throat and adjusted her posture. "And by the way, *no one* is going to youth group tonight." Everyone's eyes widened and she could see all three girls looking back and forth between her and Jackson. Jackson didn't say a word and she had the eerie feeling that he was praying for her. Praying! Who did he think he was now? She turned back to the girls. "Your dad and I have a meeting so you will all focus on your work until we get home. Anarosa made a pot roast that can be eaten anytime."

Jackson rubbed the back of his neck as the girls quietly filed out of the master bedroom and up the stairs to their rooms. Once they were out of sight, she could hear them whispering to one another in short, breathy hisses.

He closed the door quietly. "What's wrong, Mary Lynn?" He walked over and took her hand. And he took it in such a tender way that it reminded her of the time she had suffered a migraine headache on their honeymoon at Surfside Beach, and he had gone to the drug store and come home with five different kinds of aspirins and pain relievers and brought her a cold, wet washrag from the motel bathroom that he folded carefully and laid across her head.

"I hate to see you suffer," he had said that day.

She took a deep breath, pulled her hand away from his, and tried to stop seeing red. "Now look, Jackson. I'm glad you've found God. In fact, I was the one who *wanted* you to find God." She pointed to her chest. "I'm the one who *prayed* for you to find God." She put her hands squarely on her hips. "But I'm worried that you're going a little overboard here." Her eyes darted around the room and back to him. "I mean, you bring a homeless man to our house during the most important event I've ever hosted, you've probably forgotten that we have a major meeting at school tonight, you don't seem concerned with the girls' grades and homework and music, something you've insisted was crucial all of their lives." She balled both of her hands into fists and slowly blinked as if to gain focus. "I think we need a little time here. You can't just expect us to flip a switch and change our entire life course. It doesn't work like that for most people."

He nodded his head slowly. He looked beyond her shoulder toward the window overlooking the harbor. The sky was already beginning to darken and the light in the room was fading by the moment. A flock of ibis in the shape of a wide arrow were heading across the water toward James Island.

"I see what you're saying, Mary Lynn." He looked at her until she met his sparkling eyes. They looked more alive than she could ever recall. "I'm just *excited*." He took a step closer and gently took her by the shoulders. "I finally figured out my real purpose, and I want it to be *our* purpose." He rubbed her arms and then he took both of her hands. "I just have this kind of assurance that if we move full steam ahead in this direction, we'll have the existence we've always yearned for. It's like something we wanted, but we didn't even know how badly we wanted it. And we were hoping all this other stuff would be it, but it wasn't." He squeezed her hands, and she could feel a heat in them. "We've just uncovered the path to joy and the honest-to-God abundant life." He kissed her forehead and interlaced his fingers with hers. "It's the truth. I can feel it. Why should we wait or hold back, Mary Lynn?"

She took a deep breath. Her hands felt cold and clammy compared to his large, smooth, hot palms. Something in her was repelled by what he was saying though she wasn't sure why. She narrowed her eyes and released her hands from his. "Did you ever stop to think there is a balance, Jackson."

A look of deep concern crossed his face. He seemed almost to hold his breath before he exhaled. He said in a whisper, "No, I guess not,

Mary Lynn." He breathed in again and she watched his tall chest rise and fall. "I guess I didn't stop to think of that." He stared at her until she met his eyes. "And I'm sorry."

She looked to him and then at her cell phone. They had twenty minutes before they needed to be heading to the school. "Go take a shower. We've got to be walking out the door at five o'clock sharp."

He took a step away from her, and she watched his tall frame pause for a moment.

"Hey." He turned back toward her. "I love you. I know you're going to do great tonight."

"You actually remembered that I have to give the presentation?"

"Of course."

She softened a little and looked down. He headed toward the shower and she called after him, "You might like to know—I heard today that we're going to get an invitation to join the debutante club."

He peered from around the bathroom door. "That's something you still really want?"

She let out a guffaw. Wasn't it what he wanted too? "I thought you'd be happy. I mean, who would have ever dreamed that our girls would be making their debut in Charleston?"

He shrugged his shoulders. "It's just that . . ." He looked at her for a moment and she felt as though he could see right through her. It was an eerie feeling. "Never mind. Let me get ready."

• • •

Fifteen minutes later he came down the stairs looking handsome in a tweed coat from Brooks Brothers, a crisp white shirt, pressed pants, and his Gucci loafers. Now there was the Jackson she knew and loved. He had the littlest dollop of shaving cream below his chin that she wiped away with her index finger. They embraced. He was back.

She called good-bye to the girls, who were each in their own rooms doing their homework. "We'll be back around seven. If you're hungry, go ahead and help yourself."

Casey ran downstairs to give them a kiss.

"What's eight times eight?" Jackson said to her.

"Sixty-four." She grinned.

"That's my girl," he said. He smiled as she bounded back up the stairs with Mac on her heels.

On the way to the Day School, Jackson told Mary Lynn about the street evangelism he and Edgar had done under the bridge. Edgar was a friend of Roy's who knew Jesus but was battling an alcohol addiction.

Surprise, surprise, thought Mary Lynn. She felt callused and judgmental, but she couldn't seem to help herself. If he wasn't going to use his brain, she would.

He was gesticulating with his hands so much while he drove that she had to point out the stop lights and a student crossing the street illegally between the fraternity houses on Coming Street.

"We took a bunch of bottled water and granola bars and set up in the parking lot of the Crisis Ministry Shelter." He smiled. "And we made this poster that said, 'Got Jesus?' and I tell you, Mary Lynn, I was shocked by how many people walked up to talk and read a tract and receive prayer."

She swallowed hard. She just wanted to get to school and get this thing over with. "I've never felt more alive, Mary Lynn," he said.

"Hmmph." She sucked her teeth. "And Roy thinks you're ready to do this? I mean, how long have you been a Christian? A week?"

"Strike while the iron is hot, Mary Lynn." He pounded the steering wheel excitedly. "I've got a plan, a big one. When you're ready I want to share it with you. I want to reach out and really help people in need in concrete ways—not just give them a tract. It's going to be awesome. Anyhow, when we were calling out to folks walking under the bridge, a lot of folks with very meager means, it was like this thing came over me. Like a desire . . ." He shook his head as if he had been hit. ". . . like a fiery thing." He turned to her. "It was the Holy Spirit, I guess, like in the book of Acts. It had to be."

She pointed to the road and he continued, "Anyway, I could hardly stop myself from hollering, 'Come find out about the One who loves you and is making all things new.' I was talking about the cross and the resurrection and folks on the street were walking toward us and listening and receiving a hug, a tract, a snack, and a prayer. It was the most exhilarating thing I've ever done."

She almost prayed to God for him to stop talking, but even in her angry state, she didn't feel right about that prayer. The timing was bad, that was all. This was a crazy week. An important week. Why didn't he see that?

"It's like I sense this sort of, I don't know, urgency." He turned to her as he pulled into the parking lot. "That's what I felt, Mary Lynn. Urgency. Like if I don't go on and share this good news, my lungs are going to catch fire. I'm going to explode." He patted her knee. "It's not fear. It's joy. There's a big difference. And it's more than just how I feel, it's that—"

"Can you get the posters out of the back?" She interrupted him. He needed to get focused.

"Sure," he said.

As they walked toward the school auditorium, she told him about the reporter from *The Post and Courier* and the representative from the mayor's office. They went over all the information Betsy Flanagan had given them about where they stood with purchasing the property, the preliminary architectural plans, the loan, the capital campaign. He understood this kind of thing a lot better than she did, and he promised to step in and help if need be.

The auditorium was filling up steadily as Mary Lynn and Jackson set up the posters on the stage and the Assistant Head of School, Daniel Cohen, set up a PowerPoint presentation about the upcoming capital campaign and the different levels of giving.

With the exception of a microphone glitch that was taken care of quickly in the beginning, it all seemed to run rather smoothly. The reporter had questions about the Lead-Safe Certification for the building and what was going to make these structures uniquely green for downtown Charleston. Mary Lynn had studied up on this—there was the rainfall that would be collected from the roof for all of the water needs and the sunlight that would warm the building and fuel the lights. She was able to answer in a way that seemed to satisfy the reporter.

Next, a concerned parent asked about a tuition hike and Jackson quelled the fears and murmurs from a group of parents who seemed particularly worried about that. "The loan is for a projection of tuition at the current rates with our usual increase of six percent a year to reward our faculty and keep up with the cost of living. We do not foresee a significant tuition increase in relationship to the building project."

Now there's my husband, Mary Lynn thought.

There's my tall, handsome Jackson, financially savvy and capable of mollifying unwarranted fears.

There was a collective sigh of relief among the parents, and the teachers seemed happy to know that their cost-of-living raises would not be adversely affected by the extensive building project. Then an alum raised his hand and announced that his great aunt was planning to leave everything to the school and another gentleman said that his neighbor had just contributed fifty thousand dollars to kick off the capital campaign. There was a round of applause and everyone seemed happy.

Daniel Cohen then ran the quick PowerPoint presentation concluding with a piece of music composed by a student and a few photos of the choir, the strings program, the soccer team holding their state championship trophy, the sailing club on the *Spirit of South Carolina* ship, and the sea turtle rescue squad patrolling the beach. Just as the lights came up and folks started to stand up, Jackson took Mary Lynn's hand, walked over to the microphone, leaned down, and said, "Before we conclude, I just can't help but ask this question that is burning in my bones right now." A few people continued to walk toward the aisle but most people sat down.

No, thought Mary Lynn. She quickly released his hand. She wanted to scream or to rip the microphone out of his hand, but she stood stone still like a statue. A worn-out statue in a very expensive pantsuit with a strand of Tahitian pearls from Cartier and a middle-age paunch that no amount of running or sit-ups could eradicate.

"Does everyone here know Jesus?" Jackson asked. He was smiling his friendly smile, and his eyes continued to sparkle. There was a collective gasp and a few other people heading toward the aisle paused and sat back down as if the real show had just begun.

Jackson, unaware of how shocked and entertained the folks were, pulled a little yellow pamphlet from his pocket. "I've got these Four Spiritual Laws tracts, and they break it down so clearly." He shook his head and smiled. "I just committed my life a few weeks ago—I mean, I had been baptized as a baby, but now I've dedicated my life as an adult . . . and I really don't feel right going anywhere without letting people know. It's like having the cure for cancer or finding the fountain of youth and keeping it to yourself, you know?" He stood up tall, as dapper as ever. "I realize this may not be a totally appropriate venue . . ." He turned to Mary Lynn, who thought she might vomit right there on stage, and then back to the audience. "Yet, I just can't help feeling that time is short, you know? These buildings, this school, even this whole city will one day pass away. They are important, but there is something much more significant and something much greater at stake than our children's educations." He smiled a warm smile. "Anyhow, come on up here if you want to know more or just would like to pray."

There was another collective gasp followed by a few murmurs and clearing of throats. Daniel Cohen strode across the stage to the microphone, pulled it away from Jackson as graciously but firmly as possible, and said, "That was not part of the Peninsula Day School program, folks." He looked at Jackson as though he were either the stupidest person he'd ever laid eyes on, or the craziest. He scrunched up his nose as if the Scovilles gave off an unbearable stench. Then he turned back to the audience, pushed his glasses up on his nose with his index and middle finger, and continued. "As you know, this school has no religious affiliation, and many faiths are represented among our student body as well as our faculty and staff. We respect all of the faith traditions as well as the right not to have a faith." He looked back at Jackson as though he were a riddle he did not want to figure out. The thought crossed Mary Lynn's mind that Daniel Cohen was, in fact, Jewish. She had read an article about his role in helping to raise funds for his rabbi's new mid-town home a few months ago in the Faith and Values section of the Sunday paper. She wondered if he were particularly offended by the mention of Jesus.

"Thank you again for coming, everyone," Daniel Cohen said. "We don't want the gist of this wonderful presentation to be forgotten in these last few minutes. We are greatly excited about the building project, and we want your support. Have a good night."

Mary Lynn stood there in shock. She could see Weezie Pruitt boring into her chest while whispering to her husband, and she felt as though she might pass out. *What just happened?* she thought as everyone slowly filed out of the auditorium and into the brisk and starry night. *Surely Jackson didn't proselytize at the Day School meeting . . . did he?*

Daniel Cohen was berating Jackson near the stage curtain as Mary Lynn stood stone still like a statue, partly wondering if and partly assuming that in one unchecked moment their social status had shifted permanently and they might never be able to regain their footing again.

Once everyone was gone except for Jackson and a man who had stuck around to talk to him, she turned to look at her husband, then turned away and walked out the side door of the auditorium and into the school building to avoid the crowd outside. She walked down the hall where her children's papers and art projects were hanging neatly amid all the others, but she didn't stop to pick them out or to take a photo of them with her phone or to even read what they had to say about the Revolutionary War or Important Women in American History or The Need to Recycle in order to save the world. She scurried as quietly as possible out of the emergency exit in the back of the building, and by the time she got to the car she noticed that the Head of School had texted her.

"Call immediately," the message from Betsy read.

She got in the car without her husband and started the engine. "I'm so sorry, Betsy," she said when the Head of School picked up the phone. "I'll resign as chairman of the board if you think that is the best course of action."

"Let me think on it," she said. "I just don't know, Mary Lynn, but I can tell you one thing—I will *not* be looking forward to opening my inbox tomorrow."

"I know," Mary Lynn said. "I don't know what has come over him."

"He might need help," she said. "This doesn't sound like the Jackson Scoville our academic community knows and loves. If you need a recommendation for a psychiatrist, contact the guidance counselor tomorrow."

"Okay," Mary Lynn said as she drove through the city streets feeling more alone, more ridiculed than all of her days at Meggett Middle and High School combined.

She was tucking Casey into bed that night, trying to hold back her tears and hoping against hope that her children wouldn't be made fun of tomorrow and in the days and weeks to come as Lilla screamed from her room. "Mama?"

"Yes?"

"Tell me Dad didn't pull a Jesus freak at that meeting y'all went to."

"I wish I could," Mary Lynn said.

Lilla screamed in horror. "Isabel just posted on my wall, 'What's up with your dad and religion? He like grabbed the microphone at the meeting tonight and started an altar call.' "

"What does that mean, Mama?" Casey said. "Is Daddy okay?"

Mary Lynn hugged her. She could hear Catherine's bedroom door swing open as she ran across the hall to Lilla's room. "Let me see your page!" she could hear her say.

Mary Lynn looked back to Casey, whose eyes were red and watery. She embraced her baby girl. "He's fine, sweetie. A little overzealous, perhaps, but that's all."

The little girl pulled back and nodded. Mary Lynn knew she would take her word for it. "Tell him I said good night and I love him," she said as she lay down and let her mother tuck her in.

"I will, sweetheart." Mary Lynn leaned over, kissed her child on the forehead, and turned out the light. Then she headed toward the third floor.

When she got upstairs she saw Lilla pacing back and forth as two little images of the computer screen lit up Catherine's eyes. Catherine looked up at her. "Has he lost it, Mama?" Her oldest's voice was wavery, and she thought she was going to burst into tears. She tucked her hair behind her ears and Mary Lynn noticed her fingers trembling.

"Are you kidding?" Lilla spewed. "Of course he's lost it. He's totally lost it, and we're going to be the laughing stock of school for *weeks* to come."

Mary Lynn tried to settle them down. She took Catherine's shaky hands in hers and noticed her teeth chattering. "Are you cold, sweetie?"

The girl nodded. "I think I'm just tired."

Mary Lynn looked back and forth between Catherine and Lilla. "I know this is embarrassing," she said. "I was embarrassed too. Maybe I do need to get your father to go see someone, but I don't want y'all to fall apart. He's going to be okay."

They both looked at her and she nodded firmly in an attempt to calm their nerves and give them security. But in truth, she had no idea what was going to happen next.

Jackson walked in an hour after she had gotten everyone down.

"I'm sorry," he said as he came through the bedroom door where she was lying in bed trying not to weep too loudly into her pillow. "I just got carried away."

"Don't talk," she said. "I can hardly stand to be in the same room with you right now, Jackson."

She sniffed the air trying to see if he'd been drinking, but she didn't smell a thing.

"It was that bad?" He rubbed the back of his neck. "Really?"

"Yes," she said as she narrowed her eyes at him. She couldn't remember the last time she loathed someone this much. "Yes. It was horrible, and we will never live it down."

"Oh, come on, Mary Lynn." He rubbed his chin and looked as though he were trying to see her side of things. "I ended up talking to that fellow, Joe Newsome, who came up to get a pamphlet. He's got a child in third grade at the school and he and his wife are separated. We talked a long time and I prayed for him. He's going to meet us at church on Sunday. Isn't that something?"

She stared at him hard, then her eyes filled with tears. What had she done by praying that prayer on Christmas Eve? If she could take it back, she would. She felt betrayed by him, she felt betrayed by God, and she wanted to find a way out of this situation as quickly as possible.

"I want you to sleep in the carriage house," she said.

"Mary Lynn." He tilted his head to catch her eye, but she refused to look his way. He exhaled and nodded. "All right." Then he went to his chest of drawers, the one with his own portrait (Jackson in a suit sitting on the square columned porch at the Greenbrier Resort) hanging over it. He took out a pair of pajamas and headed down the stairs and through the kitchen door.

Now Mary Lynn felt more alone than ever as she saw the light come on in the building behind the kitchen. She couldn't pray. She couldn't read her little black Bible. She was angry with God. She couldn't talk the trouble through with Jackson. He had lost it. She couldn't call Scottie because she would likely defend Jackson, and she couldn't call Bev, who had been strangely absent from tonight's presentation. She was sure Bev had heard all about it by now, and she would get a kick out of hearing from the horse's mouth about just how mortifying it all was.

Mary Lynn wept as quietly to herself as was possible and then she fell asleep with the lights on and her head buried in her fresh cream-colored sheets. She did the opposite of praying—instead she talked to herself. "How can I fix this? How can I find a way out of this situation and salvage what is left for me and the girls?"

The next day, while the kids were off at school and Jackson was out cavorting with street people and saving the world, Mary Lynn spotted Weezie Pruitt lingering on the sidewalk near her front gates. *What is she doing?* she thought.

Within ten minutes, the mailman, Barry,

appeared. He stood on the stoop for a moment pulling out the Scoville mail, lining it up, then folding two magazines and a catalogue around it as he headed to the privacy door of the piazza where they had a big brass slot.

Mary Lynn ducked down beneath the living room window and slowly crept up to get a better look. As soon as he exited and crossed the street, Weezie scooted through the privacy door, grabbed a rectangular shaped cream-colored letter out of the basket, and scurried down the steps, through the gates, and down the sidewalk as she tore the letter in half.

Mary Lynn's heart pounded furiously. What nerve! Not to mention the fact that mail theft was a federal offense! She thought of her girls, her precious daughters and the event they would no longer be able to participate in. They would have to watch and listen and have their noses rubbed in it for a year as their friends went to parties and luncheons and bought white dresses and sent out hundreds of invitations for the state's most influential people to come and honor their coming-of-age, their passage from child to woman, and the promise their adult lives held. It would be as awful as finding a pair of smudged white gloves in a school locker over and over.

Then she went up to her bedroom, locked the door, and screamed into her pillow. She wept so long that she blocked out Mac, who had somehow sensed her sadness and scratched on the outside of the bedroom door with such tenacity that he had cut through the paint in several places and gotten down to the raw wood. Finally, she cracked the door and let him in, and he jumped up on the bed beside her and he licked her tight fists as she buried her head into her pillow and cried some more.

In just one day, Jackson had committed social suicide. She knew she could never forgive him. Not after all the years of exhausting research and work, years of acute observance in all of the social settings, of teaching her children manners and stressing every day to make sure they were well-dressed, manicured, acceptable. Not to mention herself—all of her efforts to look and act gracious every time she walked out of the house and into the world of Charleston. It was like a savings account she had put pennies and dollars in each day for ten years, and then he went and spent it all without bothering to consider her, to consider their children, not even for a moment. It was unthinkable. It was the opposite of the love she wanted from him. It was the final blow after years and years of his self-centeredness, and she would not let it go this time. Even if he tried to take cover under the noble banner of religion.

Now she reached for the phone on her bedside table. She had forgotten to un-silence it from last night, and she noticed that Mark Waters had left her three messages this morning.

She blew her nose, put a warm washrag over her puffy eyes, and called him back. He answered on the first ring. "Hey," he said. "Can you meet me for lunch this afternoon?"

"Yeah," she exhaled. "As long as we go somewhere off of the peninsula."

He chuckled a sympathetic chuckle, and she was sure he had already heard all about it. Word traveled fast around here and there were many clucking hens in the audience last night.

"How about somewhere in Mount Pleasant?"

"How about somewhere in Mount Pleasant that has a well-stocked bar?" she asked. "I've never needed a margarita so badly." She rarely drank except to sample how a wine went with a certain dish when they were traveling or out to a nice restaurant. However, if there was ever a time to cut loose for a moment, it was now.

"Sounds good," he said. "Let's do Shem Creek Grill. It's practically a tourist-only joint and they have a nice, dark bar. Noon?"

"See you then," she said as she clicked the end button and set the phone down.

Mark. He had a way of making everything better. She remembered how he had soothed her mother after she found his father dead on his desk from a massive heart attack. He had rocked her back and forth and promised to take care of her just the way his daddy would have wanted him to. "Poor Cecil," Mama had said. The old man had a soft spot for her mama, but he could be a ruthless businessman and she had confided in Mary Lynn a number of times after his death, "I sure hope he made it to heaven." Mary Lynn had comforted her mama. "I'm sure he did, Mama," she had said, though honestly she could see why her mama had her doubts. "He sure loved you, Mama, and that has to count for something, right?"

Now Mary Lynn wondered, would Mark Waters find some way to put the pieces of their lives back together? Would he help Jackson collect his faculties? Would he make Weezie Pruitt see the light? Would he found his own debutante club that her girls could be a part of? She wouldn't put anything past the man. He could make almost anything happen.

But in truth, Mary Lynn sensed that if there was any hope of getting Jackson to collect his faculties, she had to have a word with the priest who must somehow be brainwashing him. Father Roy Summerall had seemed so nice. He had prayed for her the day she had hurt her leg, and his prayer had worked like no other she had ever known. Did he realize the havoc he was wreaking upon her now?

She picked up the phone again, made an appointment with Roy Summerall's secretary for tomorrow, and then headed into the closet to pick out something nice to wear for her lunch date.

Chapter 23

MARY LYNN

Mark was sitting at a little round table in the back corner of the dim, near empty bar when she walked in. He looked as though he had just taken a shower, his gray hair combed back just so, and he was in a canary yellow Izod shirt with what looked like a newly purchased tweed blazer. He looked up from his iPhone, gave a tentative smile, and stood as she walked over to the table. He kissed her cheek and embraced her tightly. He smelled like cigarette smoke and mints and red wine, and he held her a little longer than seemed appropriate as she relaxed into his broad chest and held back the tears.

She looked ridiculous in her olive green Lela Rose suit with the three-quarter sleeves and tailored skirt to match. She had on her pearls and a pair of taupe Christian Louboutin pumps she'd bought for nearly a thousand dollars at Saks last year. She looked more like Jackie O headed off to a White House luncheon than a desperate housewife meeting an old friend in a dark suburban bar.

As soon as they sat, she noticed Mark nod to the bartender, who quickly brought over two frozen margaritas in thickly salted, wide-rimmed glasses with a big round lime hooked on the side.

He lifted up his glass for a toast and whispered gently, "To new beginnings." She didn't know exactly what he meant, but she did know that she had reached the end of something. Certainly the end of her social status and probably the end of her marriage.

She raised the heavy glass and met his with a soft tap and then she took a hearty sip that nearly gave her an instant headache. She couldn't remember the last time she had a margarita, or any hard liquor drink for that matter. It must have been during the trip she and Jackson took to Mexico to the Cervantino Art and Music Festival in Guanajuato three years ago to celebrate their sixteenth wedding anniversary. He had convinced her to take a bite of his fried crickets dish at a restaurant, and it had so bothered her that she sucked back two margaritas to get the taste out of her mouth before collapsing in their hotel room for a long afternoon siesta, missing Jackson's favorite event, the guitar concerto by the national orchestra.

She remembered thinking, *I really don't care about missing the concert. Go ahead without me and just let me rest.*

"So." Mark tapped her fingers tenderly. "Jackson's lost it, hasn't he?"

She nodded, blinking back the tears. "It looks

like it, Mark. I suppose you heard about the presentation last night?"

He grinned ever so slightly and she sensed that he was trying to suppress a full smile. "Oh yes," he said. "I received two calls and three e-mails by midnight."

Mary Lynn shook her head. "It was awful. Absolutely awful." She took another sip of her drink. "Then this morning I watched Weezie Pruitt snatch our invitation to the debutante club out of our mailbox and tear it up."

He shook his head. "Whoa, Mary Lynn." Then he squeezed her hand hard with his large, warm hand and looked into her watery eyes. "I know that meant a lot to you. I'm sorry."

She swallowed hard, willing the lump in her throat to go away. She shook her head. "I just don't know what to do now. It feels like everything we've been working for has crumbled in less than twenty-four hours, and I don't know if I can ever forgive him. He's humiliated me. He's humiliated the girls. I don't know if he's lost his marbles, and right now I don't even care." She sucked her teeth and looked up at Mark. "Where do I go from here, Mark? Where in the world?"

He sat back in his chair and tapped his fingers on the slick granite table. She noticed the clink of the bartender sliding a glass from his dishwasher tray of clean ones up in the ceiling bin and then the cackling of a few older women in visors and sweat suits with distinct midwestern accents who took a seat at the bar and ordered three strawberry daiquiris.

"Mary Lynn," he said as his large, brown eyes met hers. "You know I've always been in love with you."

She felt herself blush. Yes, she had sensed this before. Her mother had told her more than once how much he adored her. He had come to every bluegrass concert she participated in as a young woman, and sometimes the thought had crossed her mind that his willingness to help them so much was because of his affection for her, though she had never dwelt on it too long.

Her stomach started to churn and she felt slightly dizzy. She had only had a few sips of her drink, but she was scared about what he was going to say next—and yet she also sensed it was inevitable.

She tucked a loose strand of hair behind her ear. "I didn't know," she said.

He leaned forward and his eyes looked soft beneath the puffy pockets that fifty years of life had wrought for him. "You did know," he said. "Surely, you've always known."

She put her hands in her lap. What in the world would he say next? The thought crossed her mind to pray for help. She had turned to God when she was perplexed and afraid, but she wondered if God was far from her now, far from her heart and ashamed by her shame of Him.

"We can start a life together," he said. "You, me, your girls. There is nothing I would rather do."

Her heart pounded heavily in her chest. How could her cozy, safe family life have taken such a dramatic turn?

He cleared his throat and whispered softly, "I know this seems overwhelming to you. You've had to process a lot in the last day, but life is short, and I want to be with you. I've been hoping this opportunity would present itself ever since I was a young man, and now that it's here I have to seize it."

She shook her head. She scooted back her chair as if to stand and leave, but he reached out and took her hand. "Hear me out. You owe me that much, Mary Lynn."

She relaxed back into her seat and exhaled deeply. She nodded and met his gaze.

"We could move to a new place. I have a lot of contacts in Columbia and Greenville as well as Jacksonville, Florida. We could step right into the kind of life you have here and recreate it there—for you, for your girls—I would do anything for you. We could be a new family. We could start over together and live the rest of our days with one another, and I could give you anything you want. Anything."

She bit her bottom lip until it whitened. The older women at the bar were telling jokes and taking a picture of the bartender, who was young and handsome, probably a graduate student at the college.

He laced his fingers in hers and she didn't know whether to cringe or to relax.

"Now I know you've got a lot to sort through, and I'll give you time. But I'm ready. I could leave here tomorrow. I want you to think it through and get back to me."

"But Jackson . . ."

"I'll take care of Jackson," he said. He narrowed his eyes and seemed to focus on something just beyond Mary Lynn. "I know just what to do to get him to let you go." He sniffed the air. "I'm a shrewd businessman, Mary Lynn. There's not a man around that I can't pin against the wall. You know what I mean?"

Her stomach continued to churn. She felt a sour taste in her mouth. How ugly. How ugly it could all become. She didn't really want to know what he meant, but she was sure he had some way to harm Jackson or to make him relent. She was in a wicked web, and there was no escape from it.

He leaned over and kissed her tenderly on the forehead. "Think on it hard," he said. "I'll call you in a few days. As soon as you say the word, we can be out of here."

She watched Mark as he walked over to the bar, nodded at the women, and paid the bill. Then he turned back to her and winked before he walked out of the bar and into the parking lot.

Now Mary Lynn sat back stunned. Mark Waters wanted her, he wanted them to move to a new town and start over, he had what it took to force Jackson to let them go.

She had seen several marriages disintegrate in Charleston over the last few years. While it was a genteel place, it was not without the usual drama of one wealthy man falling in love with another man's wife. It was not without the story of families tearing apart and binding themselves to new ones. Her girls had seen it. Divorce. At least three or four of their friends had been through it, and they had entered into new blended families, sometimes without too much drama or negative consequences, but other times it had seemed awful and full of heartbreak.

She thought of calling Scottie, but what would Scottie say to this? She'd never understood Mary Lynn's deep need for social acceptance. In fact, while Mary Lynn made inroads into old Charleston society, Scottie had purposefully stepped out of it time and time again, marrying a country music man, living at the beach, sending her kids to public school, refusing to join any of the social clubs or to sign her children up for cotillion or any of the other high society stuff.

Mary Lynn straightened out her jacket and took a hearty sip of her margarita. Then she leaned back and listened to the women at the bar tell about their tour of Magnolia Plantation and the Edmondston-Alston House as she thought of her mama chasing her in the cornfields and Uncle Dale teaching her to sing "The Narrow Way" on the back porch and how sweet and simple her life had once been.

Chapter 24

CATHERINE

Catherine's father had been the talk of the school that day. Several people snickered and pointed at her in the hallway, and by the time she met up with her sisters, Casey was in tears after a class-mate called their father unstable and Lilla had a Saturday detention for giving her tenth-grade nemesis, Brook Bennett, a tongue-lashing for writing "Jesus freak" with a Sharpie pen on the outside of her locker.

They drove home in a kind of shock. They had never felt so marginalized. They wanted to talk to their mother, who would surely talk some sense into Daddy and make things right for everyone.

When they arrived home, their mother was nowhere to be found. When their father came into the house he said, "How was your day, girls?" Lilla rolled her eyes and stomped upstairs and Casey fell into his arms and said, "Are you unstable, Daddy?"

Catherine watched him pull back and lift up her chin gently. "I'm a sinner, sweetheart, but I don't think I'm unstable." Then he held her close until she asked to go to the kitchen where Anarosa always had an after-school snack waiting for them.

Catherine's father motioned for her to go outside to the pool so they could talk privately, and she followed him and plunked down on the new hunter green–cushioned lounge chair where she said, "Dad, we were all made fun of today. It was horrible."

He took a seat on the lounge chair opposite her and shook his head. "I'm sorry, sweetheart. I guess I acted too hastily last night." He squinted his eyes. "It's just . . ."

Catherine looked over to him. Her tall, handsome father who had always seemed so in control. "Just what?"

"Just that"—he pressed his hand on his chest— "this is the most real thing I've ever known or felt, and I feel a sense of urgency. It's like if I don't communicate it now to the people around me then I'll never get it out." He rubbed the back of his neck the way he did when he was thinking or concerned. "Do you know what I mean?"

Catherine looked to her father. It had been a good few weeks for her. She had not taken another pill even though Reeves had told her she had a stash and Tres had texted her a few times. Tres was as lonely as she was, she figured, and even though she was hot and cold, he wanted someone to hang out with in the park at night. She had turned down each one of his invitations and was feeling a little stronger.

Of course, Bryan had written her off. The prom was coming soon, and she wouldn't be going, but that didn't bother her as much as she thought it would. She was making ground on the SAT studying. She would focus on that and look forward to track this spring and a fresh start next year, her senior year, where she'd run cross country and try to continue to live a substance-free existence. Truth be told, she did sort of know what her dad meant. God had helped her. He had answered her prayer, at least so far, and given her strength to say no to Reeves and Tres. That was the only explanation.

She cleared her throat. "I'm starting to believe it's all real too, Dad."

He took a deep breath, and she could tell he was trying to temper his excitement by holding back a full-grown grin. "Really? You're starting to believe?"

"Well, I don't know all of the particulars. I just feel like God is real, and He's been helping me." She swallowed hard. "I sure know there's a lot of bad stuff inside me. I get the 'sinner in need of a rescuer' part."

He opened his eyes wide and she noticed something both loving and fiery inside of them. He moved over to her lounge chair and sat beside her. Then he took her in his arms and squeezed her so tight she thought she might crack a rib.

"Dad!" she choked out.

He pulled back and she could see the water filling his eyes. "I'm so glad, Cat. I'm so glad you're starting to see." He blinked hard. "I've prayed for God to make up for the lost time with you girls. I've been giving you a lot of wrong messages throughout your lives, and I knew only He could do the rewiring of your hearts and minds."

She swallowed and fell into his chest. He wasn't crazy. Her dad. He was just in love with God. How could they fault him for that? Even if it seemed ridiculous, even if it offended people?

"I'm sorry," he said to her. "I'm so sorry for all the pressure I've put on you through the years. It's been too much. I've been off base a lot of times."

She breathed heavily, and it was as though the oxygen, the air around them were sweeter and more life-giving than any air she had ever known. She let it fill her lungs, held it in, and exhaled.

"It's okay," she said as she nuzzled into the crook of his warm neck. "You were just trying to help."

They stayed that way for whole minutes as she noticed the trickle of the fountain in the side garden and the coo of two doves calling back and forth to one another. It was February, but it was a warm day and the buds on the azalea bushes were starting to form, dollops of pink and fuchsia peeking through the bright green sheaths.

She felt her father's chest rise and fall, then he pulled back suddenly. "I'm sorry about the cross country last fall. I should have let you join."

She couldn't help the tears that formed in her eyes. She started to sob and bury herself deeper and deeper into his strong chest. "I'm so sorry, baby. Please forgive me."

She wiped her eyes with her wrists and nodded. How could she not forgive him? He was her father, and he loved her—he loved all of them.

"Of course I do, Daddy. It's okay."

"You've worked so hard. It's been too much. It was too intense and off base." He rubbed her wet cheeks with his thumbs and looked into her watery eyes.

"You don't need to take the SAT again if you don't want to." He put his forehead against hers. "You did fine. You did just fine."

She put her head back into his chest. "But I want to," she said. "I'm gaining ground. I want to give it another try."

He rubbed the top of her head. "If you want to, that's fine by me, and I'll help you. But you don't have to, love. You've done good. You've done real good."

She stayed in his arms for what seemed like a

long time, just breathing in the air that made her feel more alive than she'd ever felt. Whatever was happening to her dad, it was good. It might be strange, it might be off the beaten path, but she knew for sure that it was good and right and she would stand by him.

Casey came out with a milk mustache and Mac by her side and she pushed her way in the middle so she could be a part of the embrace. Catherine and her father held her tight, and Catherine hoped her little sister could feel the sweet air too and take it in and accept it as the best that life had to offer, as Mac plunked himself on their feet and yawned heartily.

Chapter 25

MARY LYNN

The next day Mary Lynn strode through the door of the St. Michael's Episcopal Church office. She was as polished as she could be, fully made-up in a pantsuit and a fresh haircut and fancy brown leather boots. She knew she looked like she had just stepped out of one of those glossy magazines in Barnes & Noble and she carried a stern, resolved look on her face that she had never worn before.

She was aware that Father Roy Summerall had

been in touch with Jackson regularly through their weekly meetings and daily phone calls, and he probably knew Jackson had been sleeping in the carriage house since the meeting at school. When she saw him in the hall a bitter taste filled her mouth. She suspected he had been praying for her, for her heart, but she gave him a serious look that she hoped conveyed the anger and betrayal she felt toward him and how wrong he had been to stoke the sparks of her husband's newfound faith to a dangerous fire that was consuming her and the children.

He led her to his office where she sat down and burst into tears before she even heard the click of the door close. She tried to stop herself, but she couldn't hold back, not even for the polite niceties of *hello, how are you, lovely pre-spring weather we're having,* etc.

"This is all my fault," she said. He quickly picked up the Kleenex box and offered it to Mary Lynn. She took two and started to wipe her eyes as the tears and mascara rolled down her cheeks. "Remember when I asked you to pray on Christmas Eve?"

"Yes, I do." He nodded reassuringly, and she sensed him staring at her until she had to look back. "I've thought about that prayer many times since then."

She shook her head and blew her nose. Then she wiped a piece of lint off of her pants. "I never should have done it, Father Summerall. I'm sure it's sacrilegious of me to say, but it is how I feel." She bit her lip and tried to hold back the rest of the tears. "He's gone crazy. He's unhinged. Part of me thinks he needs psychiatric help."

"Really?" Roy wrinkled his brow. "That's not the impression I have, Mary Lynn. I've been spending a good deal of time with him, and I don't see it that way at all." He put his forearms on his knees and leaned forward. He said in a pure and gentle tone, "I know he's excited and maybe he needs to temper his evangelism a little. Sometimes if you come on too strong you do more harm than good. However, that's a *good* problem, not a bad one." He took a deep breath. "One I'd like to see with a lot more folks who claim to have a faith. One *I* could even learn from, truth be told." She looked up at him and shot a few imaginary daggers his way, but he continued. "He'll figure out how to temper it in order to be most effective as he goes. He's feeling his way right now, and he has no fear of taking a risk— which is a miracle in my book." He nodded, and she felt her temples begin to pulse with supreme frustration. "I don't think he has a screw loose or anything. He's just allowed himself to be emptied out, to be filled with the Holy Spirit. It's really beautiful. Do you in some way see that?"

She took a deep breath and narrowed her eyes. "Look, Reverend Summerall, we've been in

Charleston ten long years, and we've done our best to become a contributing part of this community. We've respected the culture here, we've not pushed too hard or imposed ourselves, and when we've been invited to walk through certain doors, we've done it with as much grace as we could muster. I'm proud of that."

The priest sat back in his chair. "So you're talking about your social standing?"

"Well, yes. That's a big part of it." She blew her nose and reached for another Kleenex. "We've tried to create a life for our girls. The life we never had. And we were doing so well until all this . . ."

She watched him cross his legs and look at her as he created a little tent with his fingertips. "And you were fulfilled in creating this life? It felt right to you? It was satisfying your soul?"

Mary Lynn swallowed hard. She thought of last Christmas Eve and how much she wanted to go to church. She thought about the girls and their rigorous academic and extracurricular schedules and how she had wished from time to time that they could run away from it all and just be kids. She thought of her fear that maybe, somehow they were missing something.

"I don't know," she said. "It's just we've worked so hard, Roy. We've stepped so carefully and had to learn so much. And I'm too tired to start all over again."

The priest cleared his throat and said softly but

firmly, "Why did you work so hard? Why was this important to you?"

"It was for the girls. We love our girls." Mary Lynn shook her head, and she knew he was forcing her to ask herself the question. *Who was it for anyway, Mary Lynn? Was it really for you?* She felt a wave of resentment wash over her. She didn't need him to hold a mirror up to her. She'd been through a lot, things he surely couldn't understand. And she could start all over with Mark Waters in another place. And who cared what the local priest had to say about this? He was partly to blame for backing her against the wall, wasn't he?

She felt her chest heave as she wept, and she could sense that he cared deeply for her, and she resented him even more for that. If he had cared, he wouldn't have let Jackson get this far out of control. Yes, she did love her girls, that was true, but she knew in her heart of hearts that there was something else behind her longing to be accepted. The old wound, the desperate need for an assurance that if she could reach this level or that in society, she would be safe and well and satisfied. Was that so inherently bad or evil? No, she thought as she reached for another Kleenex and felt her muscles tighten. No, it wasn't.

"Mary Lynn, why don't you and Jackson come meet with me and Anne. We could get together regularly and pray and try to find a way to work this out between you."

She looked up at him and narrowed her eyes. "Do you think I'm wrong to care about his committing social suicide with this overbearing faith?"

She watched him inhale and exhale slowly. Then he rotated his bum shoulder forward. He looked as tight as the tin man, stiff and in need of an oil can.

"I think you are hurting, and your husband wants to know why and wants to love you. I also think that his faith is remarkable, and if you let go of your fears and inhibitions you might be able to enjoy it alongside him."

She bit her lip and corrected her posture. "No," she said. She pushed back her shoulders and looked beyond Roy to the window overlooking Broad Street. "I've followed Jackson for over twenty years now," she said. "I've written down his mission statement for our family and done most everything I could to help it come true. Now he's taken a huge left turn on me, and I just don't know if I can go along with it. My heart was attached to where we were going. How am I supposed to tear it away now? And how are my girls? They didn't ask for this. They are being made fun of at school. Their grades are going down. Everything that they've been told is important is being disregarded. They miss their father. I miss him."

She looked at Roy hard. She swallowed and said, "I had a feeling you wouldn't understand."

"Mary Lynn," he said, leaning forward.

She shook her head. "I've got to go." Then she stood and added, "I can't be blamed for not being able to live this way. It's not fair to me." The anger in her heart was overwhelming—she had never felt anything like this. As he stood and opened his mouth to say something, she turned and walked briskly out of his office, closing the door behind her.

Walking home, her cell phone rang. It was Mark.

"Hello," she said through her fury and tears.

"I've got a proposal," he said. "How about you go to Hilton Head next weekend. Tell Jackson you just a need a little time to clear your head. I'll meet you there, and we'll talk this thing through. I'll tell you my plan, I'll let you share all your fears and doubts about it with me. I want a chance, Mary Lynn. I want a chance to tell you about the life we can have together. Give me that."

Her shoulders were tense, she was worn out to the bone. She noticed a few blooms on a dogwood tree at the Calhoun Mansion, and she spotted Weezie Pruitt and Bev King and a few others heading into the mansion with floral arrangements for some kind of meeting for some kind of society that she would never be invited to.

Her stomach was turning flips from meeting with Roy, from the anger she felt toward him and the love she sensed he had for her and Jackson.

"What do you say?" Mark said after a long pause.

"Yes," she said. "I'd like to."

"Great. I'll make the reservation under your name at the Ocean Front Hilton, and I'll meet you there on Friday night around six."

"See you then," she said. As she tucked the phone back in her pocket she noticed Weezie and Bev watching her, their heads tilted together and their lips moving ever so slightly as they murmured to one another. When Mary Lynn caught Weezie's gaze she had half a mind to yell, "Federal offender!" But as soon as Weezie and Bev realized she had spotted them, they both turned quickly on their sling-back heels, their styled hair and skirts swooping as they headed back into the mansion.

Mary Lynn's face reddened the same way it had when she was a kid in school and she would open her locker to see what miserable treat Claire Gustafson had left for her. She took her wide, designer sunglasses out of her pocketbook and put them on, tilted her head toward the sidewalk, and walked quickly home, hoping not to be noticed by anyone.

Chapter 26

MARY LYNN

For the next few days, Mary Lynn did not pick up the phone when either Scottie or Bev called. She didn't go to Bible study on Wednesday nor did she go to the Parents Guild meeting or the coffee for mothers of cotillion students. She kept to herself, thankful to have Catherine, who was able and willing to cart everyone to school. Mary Lynn only left the house very early in the morning for her jog and then again at night when she needed something from the grocery store.

Jackson came to her on Tuesday and stood on the threshold of their bedroom door. He had tried to talk to her a few times since the school incident, but she had refused to hear what he had to say. Now he stood unshaven and in a well-worn pair of jeans he used to only wear when he was doing woodworking in the garage and a fleece with some sort of stain on it. "I've been praying for you." He shifted his weight and she gave him a fierce look.

"And?" she said. "And what did God tell you to do for me, Jackson?"

Three worry lines formed across his forehead. "Mary Lynn," he said in a voice that was more tender than she had heard from him in years—maybe ever—though she knew its source was delusional.

"You know I love you," he said. "I've been trying to tell you that. And trying to tell you that I'm sorry you're so upset."

"You're sorry, Jackson?" She crossed her arms firmly and glared at him. "Well, that's just dandy. That makes it all better now."

His nose flared as if there were an awful stench in the room. She couldn't remember when she had ever used sarcasm with him or anyone, but it seemed completely appropriate and natural to her now.

"I've been praying," he said as he leaned against the doorknob and put his large hand over his heart. "And what I think I need to do is give you some time alone."

"Fine." She blinked hard. "Fine by me." She turned toward her cell phone where she had just received a text from Mark with the hotel reservation number. She caught a glimpse of herself in the mirror above their bed. She had never known she was capable of this level of deceit. The words nearly caught in her throat, but she spat them out by sheer will. "And I've decided to go to Hilton Head this weekend to clear my head. Do you think you can stop saving the world long enough to look after your three daughters for two nights?"

Jackson blinked as he looked at her. She could

tell he wasn't going to get angry and this kind of shocked her. No, the look on his face wasn't anger and it wasn't disgust—though she had felt a twinge of disgust when she glanced at herself in the mirror. He looked at her with the same look he had given her the night he proposed on the High Battery over twenty years ago. It was a look of adoration, and it made her shudder.

"Yes," he said. "I'd be happy to."

She recrossed her arms and felt her shoulders droop. She was like an angry, weary version of her real self. She felt sluggish and heavy, though she'd dropped a few pounds since the school incident because she'd lost her appetite. Sunlight beamed through the open door in the second-floor hallway that led to the upstairs piazza, and just the sight of it made her both irritated and forlorn.

She sucked her teeth and focused her eyes back to him. "And you might remember that Catherine has her SAT a week from this Saturday. You've caused her to stress out for months over it so you might want to actually take an interest in it again." She looked over at a photo of Jackson and the girls with an astronaut at NASA. It was a trip they had taken a few years ago for an educational jaunt one summer. "Maybe you could practice with her. Show her you still care about that? Everyone can't pivot and leave the world behind the way you do." She cleared her throat. "Or should they?"

"All right." He nodded, sort of dipping his head

a little, though she couldn't tell if this was out of deference or pity. He nodded and stared at her until she met his bright green eyes. "I've got the old study guide. We'll get together this weekend and go over it."

"That would be nice, Jackson," she said. "Very nice of you."

He took a step out into the hallway and turned toward the stairwell. She half wanted to shove him down the stairs and half wanted to grab him and cry into his chest and say, *How could you have done this to us, Jackson?* But she didn't. She felt a bitter taste in her mouth, bile rising from the pit of her stomach, and she waited stone still until she heard him take his last step and then open the front door heading out to who knows where, probably with that homeless man.

Mary Lynn couldn't get the thought of divorce out of her mind. It was like an arrow shooting her forward. It was her only destination. She could take the girls and move with Mark to a new town. She could set up a new life, make sure the children were educated, and then hope that strong academics and a good college would set them on a right path. Social status in Charleston, South Carolina, wasn't absolutely essential to their well-being or a secure future. At least she hoped not.

But she would never forget how her husband had forced her to let go of all they had worked so many years to build.

She tried to ignore Jackson, whom she now heard chatting with his homeless buddy as they loaded his pickup with bottled water and snacks and tracts and headed out of the driveway. She had overheard him talking to Roy about setting out with his new best friend and another guy from Coastal Crisis to knock on every house on the other side of town for the next few weeks to present each resident in the poorer, rougher neighborhoods with some fresh produce, a pound cake loaf, and the gospel.

She had overheard him from the living room last night telling the girls that he had signed up with a group from the church who were going to Haiti next month. When she went downstairs to pour herself a cup of coffee, she suppressed the urge to topple the globe he kept in the den or rip up the notebook he was now keeping with a tally of all the souls in the world that needed to be reached.

She didn't crack her Bible on her bedside table or anything other than her *Southern Living* magazines the rest of that week. She felt betrayed by God, by the church, and by her husband, and even though there was a powerful man who wanted to rescue her, she felt very, very alone. On Thursday night the family went to Catherine's violin recital and Jackson handed out tracts to the other students and their parents and then stopped the car on the way home to chat with a scantily clad woman on a corner.

This is crazy. I want out, and I want out now.

She tried to figure out how and when to tell him. She didn't want the word to get to the girls until after Catherine's SAT test. She would tell Jackson after the weekend away with Mark and they would tell the girls the following week.

That night as she lay in bed drifting in and out of sleep, she felt that it all had to be a bad dream, a very bad dream. The word *grace* came to her mind in her dreamy haze. She could see Scottie sitting in a fold-out chair at a table in St. Michael's parish hall saying, *Grace is God's unmerited favor and love.*

Where was grace in her world, she thought? Why couldn't the ladies of the garden club and the parents of the Day School show them grace? They had been contributing citizens of this community for over a decade. How could one moment of poor judgment, even one as big as the one Jackson made at the Peninsula Day School on the evening of the presentation, warrant kicking them out of the circle they'd tried so hard to work their way into?

She woke up at four thirty that Friday morning in February with an awareness that grace would not come. It was a beautiful concept. Maybe it was something God offered. But it sure didn't seem to translate into human-to-human relationships. How could it? It was more natural to resist it. As she sat up in bed, looking out toward the dark harbor through the window on the far side of the master bedroom, she knew she would divorce Jackson and marry Mark and she and the girls would have to begin the painful process of letting go of their old life and starting over. She wasn't the first person who ever had to scrap an old life, and they wouldn't be the first children who endured a divorce. And she knew this much because she knew human beings: none of them would be the last.

The house was quiet, and she felt the great urge to get out of it, at least for a few minutes. It would be dark for another good hour and a half so she put on her jogging clothes, went out on the piazza, stretched her muscles, and went for a long, hard run in the early morning darkness.

She hit the coast guard station at a great speed, then she turned onto Murray Boulevard as the sky started to rumble and lightning flashed in the distance. Clusters of cars were parked along the battery, and she saw someone reclined all the way back in his seat, snoozing.

Just as she bolted toward White Point Gardens and the tip of the peninsula, she looked out to the water that was churning and splashing up over the sea wall. She scooted to the middle of the Low Battery keeping her eye on the water. It must have been forty degrees out, and she didn't want to get splashed. When she looked back to the sidewalk she noticed a couple of college kids who looked as though they'd been out all night moving fast on their bicycles in the opposite direction. They were watching the churning water as well, their lips glistening, their mouths moving and calling out words she couldn't make out in the wind and the churning, and they were headed straight toward her.

She made a quick, sharp turn to the right as they whizzed by and when she did, she felt a shot of pain go through her calf as her muscle ruptured for the second time in two months. Tennis leg. Agh! The back of her leg throbbed as she rolled over on her back. How could this have happened again?

She sobbed as the pain reverberated with each beat of her heart. It was still quite dark, and she was near the steps leading up to the High Battery. Unless another couple of drunk college kids came whizzing by, no one would find her for at least a half hour. She lay her head down on the sidewalk. The concrete was cold and it chilled her jaw to the bone. She scooted as best she could toward the very edge of the railing in case another group of cyclists were headed her way. It was quiet, very quiet except for the sound of the water splashing against the sea wall and the thunder in the distance. When the next splash sprayed cold water over her legs, she started to weep and shiver.

An old brown van was parked near where she lay, and she could see movement within it. When a heavy-set figure opened the van's large sliding door and stepped out, making his way toward her, her heart started to pound even more. She was alone in the deep shadows of the early morning, unable to move, and she could sense almost immediately a dark and nefarious soul moving steadily in her direction.

The heavy man started to chuckle as he walked toward her. "Took quite a spill there, lady, didn't you?" he said. She couldn't make out the features of his face. They almost seemed completely blurred as the water sprayed over her head again. He looked over his shoulder twice, then he reached down toward her and as he did she prayed the first prayer she'd prayed in a long time. *Lord, save me. Lord, Jesus, save me.* As he grabbed her roughly and pulled her up she screamed, "Help! Help me!"

He put his large, fleshy hand over her mouth as he moved toward the dark mouth of his van, and she twisted and turned, trying to break free from his hold. Just as he stepped into the van a figure bolted across the street from the park, kicked him with full force in the back, forcing him to drop her near the sidewalk where she hit her head hard on the threshold of the van.

The man who had come from across the street grabbed her nimbly while kicking the big man again so hard in the stomach that he fell down on the sidewalk and lay there making a muffled moan. Whoever had her now had an awful stench, but she didn't care. She knew without even opening her eyes that she was safe in the arms that held her, and she drifted out of consciousness from the awful pain in her leg, from the knock on her head, and from the shock of it all.

Chapter 27

CATHERINE

Catherine awoke to Casey tapping on her arm. She rubbed her groggy eyes and looked over to her younger sister and then to her clock, which read five a.m.

"Somebody's knocking on the door downstairs." She could hear Mac barking up a storm two floors below them.

Catherine swallowed hard. Ever since she'd had the conversation with her father she'd been able to sleep easily on her own and she was grateful for a night's sleep not induced by Tylenol PM or dex or some combination of the two.

"Where's Mama and Dad?" She reached her arm out to rub Casey's back. The child had a worried look on her face as the dog's bark continued to echo up the stairway.

"They're not here," Casey said. "Neither one of them are in their bed or their room or anywhere in the house, and I'm afraid to open the door."

Now Catherine could hear the knocking beneath the bark and the faint call of a man's voice. It wasn't a familiar voice, and she wondered what to do.

She sprang up from bed, threw a Peninsula Day sweatshirt over her pajamas, and said, "Stay here—I'll go see what's going on."

As she walked down the two flights of stairs, Mac raced up and met her and followed her back down, his tail wagging as if she were going to make everything all right. She could hear the knock and a hoarse male voice calling, "Hello? Help."

Her heart pounded furiously in her chest. She called out, "Mama? Dad?" But no one answered. Then she worked up the nerve to peek through the peephole and she could hardly believe what she saw—someone, a dark figure, was holding her mother in his arms.

She was terrified to open the door, but she was even more terrified for her mother, so she took a deep breath, unlocked the dead bolt, and swung open the door.

The stench hit her right away. The man standing on the doormat of the piazza must not have bathed for days. She recognized him after blinking back the sleep in her eyes. It was her dad's friend. Edgar? She had met him once when he was in the driveway helping her dad unload something, and he was holding her mother, dressed in her black running outfit, her head completely falling back. She was totally unconscious.

"She's hurt," the man said. He looked weary and tried to lift her up a little.

"Let's get her on the sofa," Catherine said. She took her mother's seemingly lifeless legs and helped Edgar get her through the door and into the living room where they lay her down on the elegant pale green velvet Chippendale sofa. Mac raced to her mother's side and started to lick her limp hand.

Her mother was wet and she was completely out, but Catherine noticed that her chest was rising and falling so she knew she was breathing.

Catherine looked into the man's rich brown eyes. She had no idea what had happened, but she sensed in her bones that this man was good, and whatever had happened out there, he had helped her mother.

"I don't know where my father is," she said. "Maybe he's in the garage."

The man cleared his throat and collapsed on a nearby chair. It must have been tough carrying the nearly dead weight from wherever he carried it.

He looked to Catherine and nodded toward the back of the house. "He's out in the carriage house."

"He is?"

The man nodded and stared down at the oriental rug.

How strange that a homeless man knew where her father was and she had no idea. "Okay," she said. "Let me go get him."

Catherine ran through the kitchen and out into the driveway where she knocked firmly on the carriage house door and then, noticing that it was unlocked, shoved it open. Her dad was nowhere downstairs so she raced up the narrow stairs to the bedroom and there he was asleep in the bed, and she noticed that there was a suitcase there with lots of his clothes in it.

"Dad." She shook his shoulders and his eyes opened wide. He shot up straight in the bed and looked at her. "What's wrong?" he said.

"Mom's hurt. Something happened. Come to the living room as fast as you can."

They both scurried down the stairs, out into the cold morning for a moment, and then through the kitchen and dining room until they reached the formal living room on the other side of the stair-well.

Edgar was sitting, still staring at Catherine's mother whose eyes were fluttering ever so slightly as if she was trying to open them. Mac was by her side staring at her, panting.

Her father bent down beside her mother's face. "Mary Lynn. Mary Lynn."

Then he turned to Edgar. "What happened?"

"Don't know for sure," he said as he blew his nose into a frayed handkerchief. "She was on the sidewalk and a man from a van picked her up. I ran over and kicked him, but she dropped. Then I kicked him again, picked her up, and brought her home."

By now Casey was downstairs and Lilla too. They were standing in the doorway looking at the scene with tears in their eyes. Mac ran over and stood between them as if he wanted to take in the scene from their vantage point. Catherine's heart was racing. Her mother was out in the middle of the night at the battery? Her father was sleeping in the carriage house and must have been for a long time? Something was wrong, really wrong, and she felt as though the world were shifting beneath her feet.

Just then her mother opened her eyes. Her daddy turned back to her mother and rubbed her forehead gently with his thumb. "Mary Lynn," he whispered into her ear. "I don't know what happened, but we're going to call an ambulance and get you to the hospital to get checked out."

She couldn't seem to talk, but her eyes moved up and down as if to say yes and then they closed again. Lilla came running over with her cell phone in her hand and Catherine, who heard Casey crying, raced to the doorway and hugged her little sister who was shivering beyond control as their father dialed 911.

The ambulance came and the EMTs placed their mother on a stretcher before rolling her out the door. She had an oxygen mask on her face, and her father said he would meet them at the hospital.

Before he changed, he put his arms around them. "Now, girls, it's going to be okay. Your mother is breathing. Her eyes opened for a little bit. It looks like she went running a little early this morning and somehow had an accident."

Casey was sobbing and he took her in his big arms and picked her up and rocked her back and forth as Catherine looked to Lilla and they exchanged a glance that said, *This is serious.*

"Can we pray for her?" Casey said when she pulled back from her father.

"Yes, we can, Case," their father said, and they all got down together on their knees in the living room where he led them in a prayer for their mother that left Catherine feeling a heat like no other she had ever felt in her chest. While it looked as though their parents' lives were more of a mess than she had ever imagined, she had the sense from the heat that no matter what happened, it was going to be all right.

It was a Friday, a school day, but their father told them to stay home and he would send word as soon as he found out something at the hospital.

"You're in charge," he said to Catherine.

"Yes, sir," she said, and when he left she took Casey in her arms and nuzzled the child as she buried her head deep into her big sister's neck. Catherine stared at Lilla as she rocked Casey back and forth. "It's going to be all right."

Chapter 28

MARY LYNN

Mary Lynn woke up late that morning in the hospital. Jackson was immediately by her side when she opened her eyes.

She felt a dull pain in her calf, and the morning jog slowly came back to her.

"Hey there." He cautiously took her hand. She was surprised by how warm and large his hand seemed. As she turned her head ever so slightly toward him, she felt a pain where her neck met her skull and she remembered falling on the threshold of the van.

Her throat was dry. She could feel a needle in her arm where they were giving her fluid. She tried to find her voice and eventually it came up like a gurgle from the depths of some deep cavern. "Hey."

"You're going to be okay," her husband said. She noticed a shaft of light coming through the tall, thin hospital window washing the side of

Jackson's face and the lower half of her bed with a soft creamy heat.

"Who?" she tried to get up and out of her throat. "Who carried me?"

He rubbed the edges of his watery eyes with his free hand. "Edgar." He squeezed her hand and she thought, *Who is Edgar?* before she remembered the stench and the picture of the man in their foyer on the day of the garden club luncheon.

"Ah," she said as she glanced toward the lighted window and the dust particles floating in the shaft. She was stubborn, she had been hurt, she had been furious beyond measure, but she wasn't so rigid that she didn't see the irony of the situation even as the back of her head pounded. She had prayed for help on the sidewalk this morning, and God had sent the very man who symbolized, in her mind, her husband's descent into lunacy. *Forgive me,* she prayed. *Lord, forgive me. Have mercy upon me.*

She met Jackson's eyes, and he leaned over and kissed her softly on her cheek. "I adore you, Mary Lynn. I would do anything for you."

Whether it was the bright morning sunlight or the tender kiss she did not know, but an electric heat washed over her body, the same heat she had felt in the Christmas Eve service at St. Michael's when she had asked Roy and Anne Summerall to pray that Jackson would have a faith.

What a fool she'd been not to see that God had

answered her prayer and answered it in a mighty way. What a coward she had been not to accept the consequences of a life truly changed by God and give thanks for it no matter what changes it brought. How silly she had been to care so much about what others thought.

To insist, even to the point of murdering her marriage, that social status was of the supreme importance.

"I'm so sorry." She released his hand and patted her chest. "I've done some terrible things lately, Jackson. I've had some terrible thoughts and some terrible plans."

He shook his head and again took her hand into his large warm hands. "It's okay. It doesn't matter. We're going to be all right."

And she told him about her plans to meet Mark in Hilton Head this weekend, about Mark's proposal, about the decision she had made in her heart to divorce and to start a new life in a new town.

Jackson blinked back tears and shook his head. The sunlight was all around him, and he looked more like a ministering angel than a person in that moment. "Mary Lynn, it's all right. It doesn't matter. None of it matters, if you'll forgive me."

He shook his head and stared into her eyes. "I haven't loved you nearly the way I should have. And I understand why you were hurt and angry. But if you'll give me a chance, if you'll think on our vows and give not only me a chance but God who is so clearly calling out to you and me in a way we can no longer ignore, then I know we can have the truly abundant life we've both secretly yearned for. And we can share it together and with our girls. And it will be so much richer than anything we could set out to create."

Her heart beat fast and tears filled her eyes. Could she let go? "It's so much to give up. We've worked so hard. I'm tired."

He leaned closer so that his face was just before hers. "Your strength will be renewed if you go to the source."

She inhaled slowly. Her head pounded and her calf ached. She felt a big scrape on the back of her left forearm and heard the crinkle of a large bandage there. If God was willing to lay her flat like this to get her attention, if He was able to provide a husband with a rewired and forgiving heart—one full of grace and willing to bestow it lavishly upon her—would she be so stubborn to refuse it?

She thought of Uncle Dale and Aunt Josey and her mama singing "Gathering Flowers for the Master's Bouquet" on the back porch many a night, and these lyrics surfaced in her mind as clear as if Mama were right there singing in her ears, "Let us be faithful 'til life's work is done."

It was she who needed her head examined. Mary Lynn Scoville, the woman who had nearly been eaten up with anger and resentment. And it had taken a near abduction and a few painful wounds to knock some sense into her.

Who really cared what Weezie Pruitt or the entire Parents Association of the Peninsula Day School thought of her? Who cared what Mark Waters thought? He had been biding his time, cornering and out-witting Jackson in who knows how many ways, but he would not have the ultimate say in their lives. She was one of God's own, broken, misguided, but still one of His own. She felt it in the core of her being. The Lord had reached out to her and her husband, and it was high time to cut any tie that kept her from following Him.

"I want to go to the source, Jackson," she said as she heard the sweet, familiar voices of their daughters right outside the room now, tapping lightly on the door.

He nodded and a smile formed on his face as the light seemed to shine through each beautiful salt-and-pepper hair on his handsome farm-boy head.

"We'll go together, Mary Lynn." He leaned over and kissed her full on the lips, and she kissed him back.

She nodded and smiled as he pulled away, and before she could say anything more the girls burst into the room.

"Mama! You're awake!" they squealed and

laughed and crowded around her bed. She reached out and made sure her arms were touching every member of her family. Her head throbbed and she could hardly make out all that they were saying—questions about her health, comments on the hospital room, nervous giggles, but she had never felt joy quite as deep as this.

Thank you, she said to the source she knew would renew her no matter what obstacles were to come.

Chapter 29

JACKSON

Catherine and Casey were baptized at St. Michael's Episcopal Church on a clear and sunny Sunday in mid-May. Lilla wasn't ready, and Jackson was not going to push her. He'd done enough pushing in his life, and the Lord was finally getting it through his thick skull that even in his zeal over something finally worth pushing for, even in his keen and righteous sense of urgency to point others to the one and only light, there was more to love than a firm shove. Jackson was beginning to realize that in order to point to the light, you had to wait until the scales were softening from someone's eyes. If you pulled too soon or too quickly, you could do more harm than good.

Patience, God had continually whispered into Jackson's soul the last two months as he'd knelt down at night and prayed about Lilla's faith, about strengthening his marriage and Mary Lynn's wounded leg, about Catherine's post–high school options. (Catherine had raised her SAT score significantly, and now the question was— Christian college or not? A place where her faith could be nurtured or challenged?) Everything shifted with a change in priorities and perspective. He didn't know the answers, but he knew they would eventually come.

Patience, the Lord said as Jackson tossed and turned in the dark of the night thinking and praying for the residents he had evacuated from the faulty apartment buildings he owned in north Charleston and Orangeburg. Mark Waters was behind the ambulance chasing lawyers who were threatening to throw a huge lawsuit his way, alleging that Jackson knew about the wiring problems and the black mold. How naïve he had been to accept Hunt's fake paperwork that showed the buildings had passed inspection and were up to code. It had all been a part of Waters's plan to do away with him when the time was right. To move in on Mary Lynn.

But even though Jackson now saw that Waters had always wanted to corner him, he had to confess that he didn't always have his eyes wide open when it came to business matters. He had gone along too easily with Waters and Hunt in order to fund his goals and his family mission statement. So many wrongs to make right, but he would not give up.

When Jackson got wind of the truth about the buildings during a nasty meeting with Waters the day after Mary Lynn's accident a few months ago, he immediately hired a contractor and a building inspector, and they had gone from door to door meticulously combing the properties and making note of any and every building problem. Any apartment that was not up to snuff, he paid the residents to move to a nearby location and promised to cover their rent for the next year until he made their homes right. He also paid for any personal damages and medical bills. One middle-aged woman had suffered a serious chest infection from the mold in an Orangeburg unit, but she was on the mend and other than that, no one seemed to be ill or hurt.

This commitment to make things right with the apartment residents wasn't going to wipe the Scovilles out, but they were going to need to drastically change their lifestyle in order to keep going. And where, exactly, did God want them to go?

Patience, was the answer over and over again when Jackson got antsy and attempted to come up with a game plan. And as for the lifestyle changes, Jackson knew they needed to put their home on the market, let Anarosa go as soon as she found other work she was happy with, and research new school options for the girls. This time last year, he would have spent endless hours fretting over this turn of events, but every time he was tempted to be discouraged or anxious, the Holy Spirit came upon him like a fiery coal someone set on top of his chest, and he knew God was with his residents and with his family. And the certainty of His presence gave Jackson the peace that passes all understanding.

The doctor had taken Mary Lynn's protective boot off the day before the girls' baptism, and she was finally able to walk on her own, but truth be told, Jackson was going to miss having her sit still and rest the way she had the last ten weeks. He had taken great pride and pleasure in caring for her—preparing her meals, helping her up and down from the sofa and the bed, dressing her (even fastening those maddening little hooks and buttons on women's clothes that seemed impossible to work without a child's small and nimble hand).

This quiet time together, the menial tasks of everyday life had refastened Mary Lynn and Jackson to one another in a stronger, more secure way, and he savored her gentle touch on his shoulder, her smile, her "thank you," the time to sit and talk and share what was truly going through their minds, what was genuinely on their hearts. This was what marriage was all about and how thankful he was that after nearly twenty years together, he was finally getting it. The next twenty would be much sweeter, much more intimate than the first. He was committed to that, and he could tell by her gentle touch on his forearm or the look in her deep brown eyes that she was too.

Now as his family walked through the St. Michael's Episcopal Church portico toward home after the church service the morning of the baptisms, the Charleston air filled Jackson's lungs with its balmy late-spring sweetness. It could have been the confederate jasmine or the wisteria or the fragrant gardenias blooming in many of the gardens along Meeting Street—whatever it was, he felt dizzy. Dizzy with joy and excitement, and he had to talk himself out of a full-blown leap in his seersucker suit and bow tie that would have mortified his daughters for life (and probably given him a pulled muscle to boot).

Then he looked back to Mary Lynn in a pale yellow linen suit going her own pace so as not to aggravate her leg, and he shook off the dizziness and walked back toward her and did the thing he knew with certainty he was made to do this side of heaven: he held out his arm to his wife.

Mary Lynn looked up at him slowly, her mahogany eyes glistening, and she took his arm.

Then with one contained smile, he knew what she was thinking: *I know you inside and out, Jackson Scoville. Don't go leaping down Meeting Street in broad daylight in your seersucker suit. That's over the top.* And he grinned back and nodded reassuringly as she leaned her weight on him and together they walked, one step at a time, down the picturesque old street as their three daughters, two in white sundresses and one in blue, raced ahead, their long hair and their satin sashes billowing out behind them like streamers.

A little baptism reception awaited the family at their South Battery house, but a grand party feast beyond their wildest imaginings was in the works at their true home in paradise, and as he walked with his wife on his arm, inhaling the thick sweetness of the May blossoms, he thanked the Lord that the majority of the Scoville clan had already RSVP'd.

Chapter 30

Mary Lynn

Now Mary Lynn stood in her beautiful, sun-drenched formal living room greeting the small collection of people who were attending the reception following Cat's and Casey's baptism. She embraced Becky Christiansen, Catherine's coach who agreed along with Father Roy

Summerall and his lovely wife, Anne, to serve as Catherine's godparents. Even her son, Bryan, had come along, and as he shook Mary Lynn's hand with a gentle firmness she noticed the same St. Christopher medallion that her eldest had worn since Christmas gleaming beneath the collar of his starched white oxford shirt. She watched as he turned and hurried over to embrace his track teammate in her white linen sundress and pearls. Mary Lynn took a deep breath and smiled. She knew her daughter liked Bryan Christiansen, and she knew this young man had a strong faith, and to watch Cat embrace him back filled Mary Lynn's heart not with fear or worry or dread but with anticipation. Catherine was becoming a young woman. And it was clear that the Lord's hand was upon her life—despite her own foibles, and despite her parents' foibles too.

Becky Christiansen seemed to admire their embrace as well, and when she finally turned back, Mary Lynn could see the hope in Becky's eyes. Mary Lynn smiled and winked, then remembered her job as hostess and pointed Becky toward the den where there were glasses of fresh iced tea with mint and lemon, and crystal flutes of champagne.

Next Mary Lynn hugged Scottie and her husband, Gil, as well as her new friend Edgar, all of whom had agreed to serve as Casey's godparents. She and Jackson were ashamed that they hadn't even thought of Edgar to serve as a godfather, but as soon as Casey said she wanted to be baptized the first thing out of her mouth was, "And I want Edgar for my godfather because he is a rescuer, which makes him very much like Jesus." Mary Lynn had been overwhelmed with joy that afternoon and she had taken Casey in her arms. "You sure are smart, love bug. You know that?"

After the small group of guests had arrived, including cousin Ticky, a few new friends from church, and Craig MacPherson and his crew, Mary Lynn helped Anarosa set out the platters of shrimp salad and biscuits and steamed asparagus and fresh cut berries, gleaming on the silver trays. She asked Roy to say a blessing, and as they all bowed their heads in a circle around the dining room Mary Lynn remembered the words from this morning as first Catherine and then Casey leaned over the marble baptismal font in the back of St. Michael's church. When the girls had stood back up from the font, Roy gently patted their wet heads with a linen towel as he said each of their names and made the sign of the cross on their forehead while proclaiming, "Anna Catherine Scoville, you are sealed by the Holy Spirit in baptism and marked as Christ's own forever! Elizabeth Casey Scoville, you are sealed with the Holy Spirit in baptism and marked as Christ's own forever."

"Amen!" The congregation had responded

333

emphatically. And "Amen!" Mary Lynn now said with vigor at the close of Roy's prayer as she noticed the shaft of the bright midday sun pouring through the dining room windows, lighting up the table where there were little white presents stacked with satin bows and illuminating the gilded frame above the mantle where they had recently replaced the grumpy old lady from England with a framed version of their newly formed family mission statement.

It was a mission statement that didn't belong in a jewelry box like a secret. And it was a statement that wasn't some personal goal of triumph resulting in a lot of human effort and money and strategizing and apple tasting. It was a statement inspired from the good book, from the whisperer who was there, from the electric heat Mary Lynn felt in church on Christmas Eve. As the sunlight hit the edge of the frame, she said, "Amen" again and made a mental picture of buckling her seat-belt for what would surely be some kind of wild ride this side of heaven as they prepared to sell their home, find new schools for the girls, take care of the apartment residents, and get to work on their true mission.

She was ready. Finally, Mary Lynn Scoville was ready. *Let's go,* she said to the Lord as she reread the words above the mantle amid the sounds of warm voices and laughter and the clang of silver on china.

Scoville Family Mission Statement:

"To love the Lord back with all of our heart, all our soul, and all our mind and to love our neighbors to the ends of the earth as we would love ourselves."

April 2010

ACKNOWLEDGMENTS

I have a lot of folks to thank. First, David Platt for writing *Radical*. Platt's book uncovered blind spots in my own life, and it helped me to fully imagine just where Jackson's uninhibited new faith might take him.

Second to my dear friend and editor, Ami McConnell, who connected with the Scovilles from the beginning and challenged me to show the story from more than one perspective. Your wisdom is a treasure, and I can't imagine writing a story without you.

Thanks also to the leader of the stellar Thomas Nelson team – my publisher, Allen Arnold, as well as the folks who work for Allen to get the books into the hands of readers: Becky Monds, Katie Bond, Ashley Schneider, Heather Cadenhead, Ruthie Harper and Jodi Hughes. You all are awesome!

I am particularly grateful for my agent, Claudia Cross, who is an enormous source of support and encouragement. It's an honor to know and work with you. And to my shrewd line editor, Rachelle Gardener. You have a gift.

Thank you to the booksellers across the southeast who hand-sell the stories day in and day out with immense care, warmth and zeal especially

Saints Alive, Blue Bicycle Books, and Walden of Charleston, Litchfield Books of Pawleys Island, the Mount Pleasant and West Ashley Barnes & Noble Booksellers, Fiction Addiction of Greenville, Hub City of Spartanburg, The Edisto Bookstore on Edisto Island, The Book Exchange in Atlanta and Park Road Books in Charlotte. You all are wonderful.

I also want to thank my fellow southern, inspirational novelists who I blog with every week at www.southernbelleview.com: Lisa Wingate, Marybeth Whalen, Rachel Hauck and Jenny B. Jones. Thanks for saving me a rocking chair on the cyber porch!

Thank you to the dear friends who read early drafts of this book—Jeannie Lyles and The Rev. Al Zadig, Jr. as well as his story-savvy wife, Elizabeth. You three are amazing, and your insights made a significant impact on the novel's subsequent drafts. Thanks also to John Sosnowski who answered my questions about tomato farming and to my parents, Betty and Joe Jelks who did quite a lot of babysitting. As always, I'm blessed by the precious gals who love and pray for me: Peggy McKinney, Libby Johnson, Amy Smith, Jenny Dickinson, Meredith Myers, Karen Larson Turner, Elisabeth Hunter, Rachel Temple, Avery Smith, Lisa Hughes, Evie Cristou, and Suzanne Livengood. It is a joy to "do life" with you and your families.

I am most grateful to my husband, Dr. Edward B. Hart, Jr. You are my rock and the love of my life. And I also want to thank my beloved children, Frances and Edward. There are many apples you can sample in this world, but I want you to choose the one that leads to eternal life. This book was written for you two.

READING GROUP GUIDE

1. In the opening of the novel, Mary Lynn thinks God is trying to get her attention. What do you make of what happened to her on her morning jog the day before Christmas?

2. Do you believe God can break through the seemingly natural order of things and heal a wounded leg? Why or why not?

3. In the beginning of the story, do you think Mary Lynn and Jackson have a strong marriage? In the Christmas day scene where Catherine receives a new car, Mary Lynn says she has become a woman "who bites her tongue." What has caused this committed relationship to begin to deteriorate?

4. Jackson feels that his father woefully short-changed him during his childhood. Why? In what ways are both Jackson and Mary Lynn still bound by (and living in reaction to) their childhood wounds?

5. Before Jackson's conversion, what kind of parent is he? Consider his original mission statement. Why is he determined to give his

children the life he never had? Is there a down-side or danger to this mission?

6. Why is it necessary for Catherine to have a point-of-view in this story? What do you gain from her perspective?

7. What kind of parent do you think Catherine will grow up to be?

8. There are several "running" scenes in this book. What does the act of running come to symbolize for Catherine and Mary Lynn?

9. Describe Jackson's conversion and Mary Lynn's reaction to it. Why does she have such a hard time once her prayer for her husband to have a faith gets answered? What does his newfound faith reveal about her faith and the idols in her own life?

10. What do you make of Jackson's zealousness? Why doesn't he have any inhibitions about sharing his faith or about reaching out to all walks of life? Do you find his zeal refreshing or do you think he's too pushy? Why?

11. How has Mary Lynn and Jackson's relationship changed by the end of the story? In what ways has their marriage been renewed?

12. The Scoville family mission statement changes dramatically over the course of the novel. By the end of the story the new mission is as follows: *To love the Lord back with all of our heart, all our soul and all our mind and to love our neighbors to the ends of the earth as we would love ourselves.* Imagine the Scovilles five years from now. What do their lives look like?

BEHIND THE STORY

With every novel I write, I start with a question that I desperately want to know the answer to. I write to the heart of that question, often revealing my own tensions, doubts and fears, and I always find that God meets me in the midst of the narrative, takes my hand (as well as the characters) and shows us the way to go.

For *Sunrise on the Battery*, here is the question I had in mind before I ever wrote the first word of the story:

What would it look like if we really loved each other? If we had no inhibitions about sharing our faith and our very lives with a hurting world? How would we really spend our time and our money? And what impact would this have on our own families, especially our children? What impact would it have on our communities, our country, and the world?

ABOUT THE AUTHOR

Beth Webb Hart, a South Carolina native, is the best-selling author of *Grace at Low Tide*, *Adelaide Piper*, *The Wedding Machine*, and *Love, Charleston*. She blogs weekly at SouthernBelleView.com, and she serves as a speaker and creative writing instructor at schools, conferences, and churches across the country. Two of her novels have been nominated for a SIBA award, and she has received two national teaching awards from Scholastic, Inc. Hart lives with her husband and their family in Charleston.

Center Point Publishing
600 Brooks Road ● PO Box 1
Thorndike ME 04986-0001 USA

(207) 568-3717

US & Canada:
1 800 929-9108
www.centerpointlargeprint.com